THAT CRAZY WITCH!

THE COFFEE COVEN'S COZY CAPERS: BOOK 2

M.Z. ANDREWS

That Crazy Witch!
The Coffee Coven's Cozy Capers: Book #2

by
M.Z. Andrews

VS. 02052018.01

ISBN-13: 978-1985122734
ISBN-10: 1985122731

Cover Character Illustration by Crissha's Art
Edited by Clio Editing Services

1

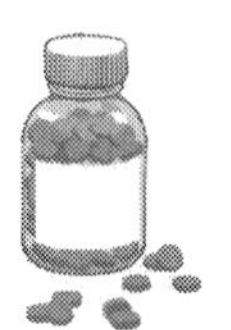

It was a bright, sunshiny spring morning when Gwyndolin Prescott stared at her slightly distorted reflection in the window. She adjusted the collar of the silk blouse she wore under her rose-pink cardigan, fluffed her shoulder-length strawberry-blond locks, and gave her cheeks a little pinch.

She cleared her throat. "Hello, Harrison." She extended a hand to her reflection, then giggled nervously and flipped a bit of hair over her shoulder. "Oh, I didn't see you there. Good morning, Sergeant Bradshaw." She giggled again. "Oh, I'm sorry. Yes, of course, *Harrison*."

Gwyn's heart rattled in her chest. She blew out a puff of air and stared at the door handle. *You can do this, Gwynnie*, she told herself. *He's just a man*.

She looked at her reflection in the window again, and her alter ego seemed to respond. "Just an incredibly gorgeous man, who got your mother's permission to take you on a date," she murmured under her breath.

Gwyn stiffened her spine, lifted her chin up, and stuck her chest out. "So what if you haven't been on a date since the Clinton administration? Men can't have changed *that much*, and neither have you."

She tried one more time to be natural. This time she gave the air a little hug and envisioned herself giving the dapper man a friendly embrace. "Good morning, Harrison. Lovely day, isn't it?" She air-kissed both of his invisible cheeks.

"What in the hell are you doing, Gwynnie?" called a voice from behind her.

Gwyn's body froze mid-kiss. She closed her eyes. When she opened them again, Phyllis Habernackle stood in front of her, her green eyes open wide and her mouth parted in a ridiculously mocking smile.

Gwyn scowled as she fidgeted with her purse. "Oh, what are you smiling about?"

Phyllis pointed at Gwyn and her reflection in the window. "Something going on between the two of you that I need to know about?" she laughed. "Maybe you ought to get a room?"

Gwyn's face screwed up into a pout. "I was just waiting for you to show up."

"Is *Harrison* also waiting for me to show up?" laughed Phyllis.

"Harrison?" Gwyn's cheeks flushed red and she put on her best I-don't-have-any-idea-what-you're-talking-about look.

"Wasn't that who you were pretending to hug and kiss just now?" Phyllis wrapped her arms around herself like she was giving herself a hug and then turned her back to Gwyn. She wiggled, pretending to be in a passionate embrace while making kissing noises. "Mwah, mwah, mwah, oh, Harrison, mwah, mwah, mwah!"

Gwyn reached out her purse and swatted Phyllis's backside with it. "You can knock it off now."

Phyllis guffawed and turned around with tears of laughter dampening the corners of her eyes.

"You know, you *look* like you're eighty years old, but you *act* like you're twelve," said Gwyn, crossing her arms over her chest and frowning.

Phyllis chucked Gwyn under the chin. "Eh, we can't all be beauty queens like you, now can we, princess?" She put a hand on the doorknob. "Come on, let's go inside. Char's already in there, and I'm *starving*."

Gwyn watched as one of her oldest and dearest friends disappeared inside Habernackle's. She glanced back at the immaculately clean two-tone brown Ford truck parked across the street and sucked in a deep breath.

Phyllis stuck her head back out the door. "You coming, or do I need to send the Sarge out here to throw you over his shoulder and drag you inside caveman style?"

Gwyn's shoulders slumped. "You're so brash, Phyllis Habernackle," she muttered, but she followed Phyllis inside, where the hearty smell of bacon, eggs, and hot coffee enveloped her.

Over half the booths and tables inside Habernackle's Bed, Breakfast, and Beyond were full. Linda Habernackle, Phyllis's daughter, stood with her back to the door, waiting on a table of college-aged girls. Reign Alexander, Phyllis's grandson, stood behind the bar, punching an order into the cash register, and a young blond waitress Gwyn had never seen before was on a mission to refill coffee cups around the restaurant.

"My goodness, this place is hopping," Phyllis said to Gwyn as they made their way across the room towards their usual table, where Charlotte Bailey already sat, flipping through the *Aspen Falls Observer.*

"That's because your daughter makes the best food in all of Aspen Falls," said Gwyn, keeping a close eye on the table full of men having coffee just two tables away from where Char sat. Harrison, who was part of that table, had his back to the door.

Phyllis cut through the crowded restaurant, making a beeline for Char. Gwyn paused, wondering if she should take a right and go over and say good morning to him or if she should just follow Phil directly to their table and let Harrison make the first move. *Ugh, why must dating be so difficult?*

Char looked up from her paper and waved the women over. It was now or never. She needed to make a decision. Gwyn's heartbeat pulsed in her ears over the steady buzz of voices around her. She smiled at Char and then glanced back at Harrison's table, full of his coffee pals. She suddenly felt too awkward to talk to him in front of all his friends. She veered left and followed Phyllis to their table.

"Good morning, ladies," said Char, closing up her newspaper and sliding it aside.

"Busy place this morning," said Phil to the puffy white-haired woman at the table.

Gwyn took the seat across from Char so that her back was to Harrison. Maybe then he wouldn't even notice she was there and they wouldn't have to have that awkward moment in front of all of their friends.

"Yes, it is," Gwyn agreed absentmindedly.

Char lowered her penciled-on eyebrows. "Where's Hazel?"

Phyllis scooted herself up to the table and nodded. "Yeah, I'm shocked you actually went somewhere without her leash attached to your wrist. What'd you do? Lace her prune juice with NyQuil and chain her to the bed?"

Char shot their friend a look. "You're terrible, Phil. Remind me not to put you down as my caretaker when I get old."

"*When* you get old?!" Phil roared. "Sweetie, newsflash. That train has come and gone and dropped you off at the iron gates of Geezerville."

Char rolled her eyes and fanned the air with three fingers. "If that's the case, then may I remind you it dropped all *three* of us off there." She turned her attention back to Gwyn. "Now, where's Hazel, Gwynnie? Is everything alright?"

Gwyn sighed. "She's under the weather, unfortunately."

Char tilted her head sideways. "Oh, the poor dear. Nothing serious, I hope?"

"Well, I had Brenda Kayton, the Village's home health care nurse, take a look at her this morning, and she says it's just a little cold. But you know me, I worry it could turn into pneumonia."

Char reached out and patted Gwyn's hand. "I've got the perfect remedy. An old witch elixir my mother passed down to me. I'll make a batch and bring some over later this afternoon, and we'll see if we can't get her feeling better."

Gwyn squeezed Char's hand. "Oh, Char. You have no idea how much we'd appreciate that. This cold has just wiped Mom out. She refused to get out of bed this morning." Gwyn sighed and slumped back in her seat. "You know how much I worry about her."

"We both know," said Phyllis. "You do a fine job of taking care of her, Gwynnie. It can't be easy. Hazel's quite the handful."

"Oh, girls, you don't know the half of it. I hate to be that overbearing daughter, but if I didn't look out for her, I just don't know what kind of trouble she'd get into." Gwyn unfolded her napkin and laid it across her lap. "Take this morning, for example. You'd think it wouldn't be that big of a deal just to let her stay at the Village and sleep while I came for breakfast. But it is a big deal! I never know if Mom's *really* sick or if she's just pretending to be sick so she gets a little time without me."

Char made a face. "Surely Hazel doesn't *pretend* to be sick?"

Gwyn let out a puff of air. "Oh, you'd be shocked to know all the little things she's tried over the years. If she wasn't sick, I might be worried that she was halfway to the moon by now."

Char and Phyllis giggled.

"I'm not even joking. She'd probably find a broomstick and see how far into outer space she could get before running out of oxygen. Just for kicks."

"So how do you know that she's not pulling the wool over your eyes today?" asked Phyllis.

"Well, like I said, I had Brenda give her a once-over."

Char's eyes widened as she splayed her hands out in front of her. "But it's only a cold. It's not like Hazel couldn't have taken off with a cold."

Gwyn leaned forward, smiling mischievously. "I know," she whispered. "That's why I paid Brenda to sit outside our room for an hour while I snuck away for breakfast."

The three of them shared a good laugh. Gwyn felt a bit of the tension in her shoulders slip away. She found herself once again thankful that she'd moved back to Aspen Falls and reconnected with her old witch-college friends.

"Good morning, ladies," said Linda Habernackle, pulling a pen out of her auburn bun. "No Hazel this morning?"

Gwyn looked up at Linda and smiled. "Good morning, Linda. No, Mom's got a touch of a cold, I'm afraid."

"Oh, yes. Something's going around," she said with a knowing nod. "Mercy said half of the girls at the Institute are sick."

"How is my granddaughter?" asked Phyllis. "I come

here every morning for breakfast, yet I never see her." She narrowed her eyes. "She's not avoiding me, is she?"

Linda grinned. "Oh, Mom, don't be silly. Mercy's not avoiding you. You three should know how it is at the Institute. Early classes, tons of labs, and never-ending homework."

"Don't we ever!" Phyllis turned to the girls. "Although I do remember us skipping many an early-morning class."

Gwyn sucked in a breath. "Speak for yourself, Phyllis! I don't remember skipping classes."

"Well, you always have been the goody-two-shoes of the group," clucked Phyllis. "But don't try and pretend you were completely innocent back then. You skipped a few." Phyllis tapped a finger against her temple. "This memory hasn't failed me."

"Things sure have changed since you went to school there," sighed Linda. "Sorceress Stone is in charge, and she's a stickler for good attendance. Mercy can't risk getting expelled for skipping a few classes."

"My, things *are* different," said Char, shaking her head. "When we went to the Institute, Sorceress Halliwell was in charge, and she was the sweetest, kindest…"

"Most lenient…" added Phyllis.

"Most lenient," echoed Char, "headmistress there was. We loved her so much."

"Whatever happened to Sorceress Halliwell?" asked Gwyn, suddenly curious about her old teacher.

Phyllis looked at Char with furrowed brows. "That's a good question. What *did* happen to Sorceress Halliwell?"

Char threw both hands up in the air. "Why are you asking me?"

"You've been in Aspen Falls the longest out of all of us," said Phyllis.

"Yeah, but I left town for a while. I honestly don't know what happened to her. Kat would've been the one to ask. But since she's gone, God rest her soul, we'll have to ask Loni. I'm sure Kat kept her informed."

"Speaking of Loni, why doesn't she ever come have breakfast with you ladies?" asked Linda, tossing a hand on her hip.

Phyllis waved a hand dismissively at her daughter. "Oh, who knows why Yolanda Hodges does the things she does? That woman is about ten slices short of a loaf."

Char leaned towards Linda. "Loni thinks the FBI is after her. She doesn't leave the house very often."

"Unless she's wearing a costume and thinks no one will recognize her," added Gwyn.

Linda quirked a brow. "The FBI, huh? Well, is there any truth to that?"

Char shrugged and handed her menu to Linda. "Who knows? Maybe someday she'll explain it to us, but for now, she's not talking. I'll have the oatmeal, Linda. And two slices of wheat toast. Don't forget my senior discount, dear."

Linda nodded and jotted Char's order down. "A roll for you this morning, Gwyn?"

Gwyn nodded. Linda Habernackle made the best sticky rolls she'd ever tasted. "Two, please. I'll take Mom's in a to-go container."

Linda looked down at Phyllis. "And you, Mom?"

"I'll have the special. Same as always."

Linda took their menus and stashed them under her arm. "I don't even know why I bother to take your order. You all choose the same things every morning."

"You take our order because maybe someday we'll surprise you," said Phyllis.

Linda grinned and walked away. "I'll have your order out in a jiffy."

"Okay, enough of the chitchat. Now we need to get down to brass taxes, literally," said Char. She leaned over and pulled a white envelope out of her purse. "Yesterday on our walk, Vic and I stopped over at Kat's just to check on the house and get the mail, and this was in there." She slapped the envelope down on the table and slid it forward.

2

Before Gwyn could even unfold her arms, Phyllis snatched the envelope up. Lifting her black cat-eye glasses that hung on a chain around her neck, Phyllis read the official-looking lettering. "Oh man, it's from the county tax office." She sucked in her breath. "Holy enchiladas! Twenty-five hundred dollars?!" She looked up at Char.

Char nodded. "Property tax time, girls. And now that Kat's gone and the house is ours, it's our responsibility to pay the tax man. Split four ways, that's six hundred and twenty-five dollars apiece."

"Can't we just send him a nice Bundt cake or something?" asked Gwyn, her heart sinking. Between their recent move to Aspen Falls, Hazel's medical bills, and the lapse between jobs, Gwyn's savings account was barely surviving on life support.

Char grinned. "Don't we all wish he'd take a cake! I'd bake him one every day for a year if that worked!"

Phyllis leaned back in her seat, shaking her head. "Oh, girls. I'm tapped. I have my Social Security, but there's not enough there to pitch in six hundred and twenty-five dollars! Maybe if I'd been saving for a year, but we just got the house!"

Gwyn nodded, letting out the breath she was holding. She was thankful she wasn't the only one feeling the pinch. "I can't swing it either, girls. The move just about did me in. I just don't understand why Kat didn't want us to sell the house."

Char grimaced. "I've wondered the same thing myself. I know Kat's main concern was about reuniting us after she pitted us against one another all those years ago, but she had to have known that wouldn't have taken long to resolve. So are we now supposed to just hang on to the house for life?"

Phyllis shook her head. "I think there's more to the story."

"There has to be," Gwyn agreed. "But until we figure out the rest of the story, what are we going to do about that tax bill?"

Char took the bill from Phyllis and shoved it back into her purse. "Well, I've been thinking about it. Kat's orders were that we aren't to sell the house. She didn't say anything about her furniture and the rest of the stuff inside the house."

"Oh, Char!" breathed Gwyn. "You want to sell Kat's things?"

"What other choice do we have?" asked Char. "I don't have the money either. Vic has a nice income from the bakery, but I'm not going to ask him to pay *our* tax bill. I just don't feel like that's right."

Phyllis nodded. "You're right, I wouldn't want him to pay it either. Isn't there some way we could use our magic to make some quick cash?"

Gwyn sighed. "Oh, Phyllis. You know better than that. Sorceress Halliwell taught us all that it's wrong to use magic for financial gain."

"But I don't think this would be considered financial gain, would it?" Phyllis looked at Char.

Char leaned back in her seat and crossed her arms over the top of her grey velour jacket. "Creating counterfeit money with magic is definitely financial gain, Phil. That was number one on Sorceress Halliwell's big no-no list."

"Well, obviously we aren't *keeping the money*. So it's not like we would be *gaining* anything. And we wouldn't have to conjure the money," explained Phyllis slowly. "We could use our magic to earn it properly."

Gwyn winkled her nose. "I already work full-time and take care of Mom the rest of the time. When am I supposed to find time to earn this *magic money*?"

Phyllis scowled at her friend. "It's not *magic* money, first of all. Second of all, fine, then you'd get an exemption."

"And you know Loni's not leaving the house to earn this not-magic money," added Gwyn.

"Fine. It would be up to Char and me to earn the money. You know, the old-fashioned way." Phyllis waggled her eye brows.

Char put her hands on her hips. "The old-fashioned way? I can't be doing any of that illegal hanky-panky, if that's what you're getting at. Vic would have a cow." She lifted a brow.

Phyllis waved a hand at Char. "Oh, for heaven's sake, Char. I wasn't talking about *that*!" She took a pause to think about it. "But do you really think we could make twenty-five hundred in a month doing that?"

"Phil!" breathed Gwyn.

Phyllis shrugged. "What? I was just asking if she thought we could. I wasn't saying I *wanted* to or anything."

"Sure you weren't," said Char, rolling her eyes. "Then what were you talking about *the old-fashioned way*?"

"I meant by *working* for it. You know. I'm psychic and a medium. You're a healer. I could do tarot card readings and you could, you know, heal people."

"Grace Adkins already does tarot card readings out of her home, and Vic's bakery heals people with his magical breads and desserts."

Phil let out an annoyed sigh. "Fine. Broomstick rides for the little ones?"

Char winced. "I don't think my homeowner's insurance would cover the liability on that." She patted Phyllis's hand. "I appreciate where you're going with this, Phil, but half of the town is a paranormal. We're not going to be able to earn the money without getting regular jobs."

Phyllis wrinkled her nose. "A job?"

Char nodded. "Yes, Phil. A job. You prepared to get one of those?"

"At *our* age?"

"I'm your age, and *I* have a job," interjected Gwyn.

"Yeah, well, your spirit animal is younger than mine," quipped Phyllis before throwing her hands in the air. "I think it's settled, ladies. We don't have a choice. We should sell off some of Kat's stuff."

Gwyn leaned forward. "Oh, no! It'll be heart-breaking to watch all of Kat's beautiful possessions go!"

Phyllis shrugged. "Well, what else is there, Gwynnie?"

"I think a yard sale would be the easiest," said Char somberly. She looked at Gwyn. "You in favor?"

Gwyn's eyes swung sadly down to the table. She hated the idea of getting rid of her recently departed friend's belongings, but she didn't know what other choice they had. "We'll have to get Loni's permission too. And you know how Loni can be."

"It'll be tough convincing her," agreed Phyllis. "Maybe we should all meet over there after you get off work at the Village, Gwyn."

Gwyn nodded, her mouth set in a straight line. "Yes, I think that's a good idea."

And then out of nowhere, a deep voice sounded behind Gwyn. "Good morning, ladies."

Gwyn's heart froze in her chest. She felt the blood drain from her face. *Harrison.*

"Mornin', Sarge," said Phyllis, giving him a little two-fingered salute.

Char tipped her head at him. "Good morning, Sergeant."

"Hi, Gwyn." A thick-fingered hand rested on her shoulder.

Gwyn smiled up at Harrison Bradshaw. His white flattop was in perfect order, and his silvery-blue eyes sparkled like the ocean as he smiled back at her. He wore a crisp blue-and-white striped button-down shirt tucked neatly into a pair of perfectly pressed chinos. She patted his hand. "Good morning, Harrison."

"I was about to pry your number out of your friends if another day passed that you didn't make it to breakfast," he said with an easy smile.

"Yes, I haven't been able to join the girls much this week. Work's been very busy," she said.

"You know, I was promised a date."

Char and Phyllis exchanged amused looks.

Gwyn nodded, grinning from ear to ear. "Yes, I recall you promising Mom a date as well."

"Does Friday night work for the two of you?"

Gwyn winced. She didn't know how that would work with Hazel being sick. "Well, Mom's not feeling well right now. I'll have to see how she's feeling by then."

"Oh, I'm sorry to hear that she's ill. Nothing serious, I hope?"

"Just a cold, I'm sure," said Gwyn. "Can I let you know Friday morning at coffee?"

He patted her shoulder. "That would be perfect. Well, I won't take up any more valuable girl time. It was lovely seeing you again, Gwyn. Please give your mother my best." He gave Gwyn's shoulder the tiniest of squeezes and nodded politely at Phil and Char. "Ladies."

"Sergeant." Char nodded.

"Have a great day, Sarge," said Phyllis loudly.

Gwyn squeezed his hand back. "Nice to see you too, Harrison."

When he was out of earshot, Phyllis leaned over and hissed to the girls at the table. "That man is a T-bone in a sea of cheap, nearly expired stew meat."

Char put a hand to her mouth and laughed. "Oh, Phil, you're insane. But I must say, Gwynnie, you may have just found yourself a keeper."

"And if you don't keep him, I have a hankering for a nice steak," said Phil with a chuckle.

Gwyn peered over her shoulder, twirling a finger in her fake ginger hair as Harrison walked back to his table. "Hands off, Phyllis Habernackle. I happen to appreciate a good steak myself."

3

Across town, Hazel Prescott's hands trembled more than usual as she dialed her cell phone. Standing on the looped white bathmat in the middle of her apartment's small bathroom, she clutched a towel around her midsection and listened to the phone ringing.

"Pick up, pick up, you old bat," she grumbled under her breath. Her eyes scanned the bathroom counter, looking for her pills. The way her heart was pounding, she wondered if she shouldn't swallow a couple.

Finally, she heard a croaky voice on the other end of the phone. "Hello?"

"Loni?"

"Yeah."

"It's Hazel."

"Hazel who?"

"Hazel Prescott, you ninny. How many Hazels do you know?"

"I don't know. One?"

"Exactly. That's me. I'm the one you know."

"Yeah. Well, whaddaya want?"

"I need you to come over here and help me."

"Me?!" Yolanda Hodges's voice elevated an entire octave.

"Yeah, you. You're the one I called, aren'tcha?"

"Well, my phone rang. That's all I know."

"It rang because I called you, you loon."

"Yeah, so? What do you want?"

"I just told you," hissed Hazel. "I need you to come over here."

"Over where?"

Hazel rolled her eyes at her wrinkled, pasty-white reflection in the mirror. "To the Village."

"Are you off your rocker? You know I don't leave my house."

Hazel sighed. She didn't know what else to do. She couldn't call Gwynnie to come help her. She'd be furious. She couldn't tell Brenda, the home health care babysitter Gwyn had hired to watch her, because she'd have to report what happened to the people at the Village. She couldn't call Char or Phyllis either because they'd report right back to Gwyn. So here she was. Calling the craziest woman in all of Aspen Falls for help. The *only* woman that might actually be able to help her. "Listen, Loni. You gonna come help me or not?"

"Nope."

Hazel heard a click and realized the line had gone dead. She stared down at her phone. "Dammit!" she muttered. She dialed the phone again. This time Loni was faster on the draw.

"Yeah?"

"I need you to come over here and help me."

"Where's Gwynnie?"

"At breakfast with the girls."

"Why aren't you there with her?" asked Loni.

"Because I stayed home."

"She let you stay home alone? How come?"

"Never mind that for now," sighed Hazel. "Can you just get off your ass and come and help me? It's sort of an emergency."

There was a pause on the other end of the phone. "What kind of emergency?"

Hazel swallowed hard. She cracked open the bathroom door and peered back into her bedroom, where a naked body lay motionless on her bed. "Let's just put it this way. You're gonna wanna bring a body bag."

Loni looked down at her phone through her thick Coke-bottle glasses. Her big eyes blinked as she stared at the smooth harvest-gold receiver in her hand. "She hung up on me."

"Who was it?" asked Edwin Almond Grant III, the marmalade-colored tabby cat seated on Loni's kitchen counter.

"Hazel Prescott."

"Hazel? What did she want?"

"She wants me to go over there! Can you believe that? Everyone knows I don't leave the house." Loni slammed the receiver back into its cradle, making the long spiral cord bounce against the wall. A grey cat with white paws and a black cat with a white mustache leapt at the cord eagerly.

Ed reached his paws out in front of himself, stretched, and in a prelude to a yawn asked, "Where's 'over there'?"

"The Village." Loni paced a three-foot square, the only spot in her kitchen that wasn't completely covered with mountains of random items and garbage.

Ed sat back up and curled his long tail around himself. "Why does she want you to go over there?"

"She didn't say. She told me to bring a body bag, though."

Ed's amber-flecked eyes widened. "A body bag! Why in the world would Hazel need a body bag?"

Loni threw her arms out on either side of herself. "I have no idea. I told you! She hung up on me!"

"So what are you going to do?"

Loni shrugged as she wrung her hands. "I don't know. She knows I don't leave the house."

"Well, where's Gwyn?"

"At breakfast with Phil and Char."

"I'm shocked Gwyn left Hazel alone," said Ed.

Ed was right. Gwyn *never* left Hazel alone. Something smelled fishy, and it wasn't Ed's breath. "You think I should go over there?"

Ed nodded. "The woman asked you to bring a body bag, Loni. Of course I think you should go over there!"

"Maybe it's just a trap. Maybe that was really the FBI trying to lure me out of my house." Loni's eyes narrowed to slits. "Tricky little bastards."

Ed pawed his forehead. "But what if it wasn't the FBI? Hazel called you for help. Don't you think maybe you should help her?"

Loni rubbed the little patch of whiskers poking out of her chin and thought about it. She couldn't leave the house. The FBI were out there just waiting for her, and on top of that, she didn't own a car, so she couldn't drive. It was too bright outside for her to ride her broomstick over. Everyone in town would see her sailing through the air, including the FBI.

"Maybe I should just call Gwynnie."

The phone rang again, frightening the two playful cats on the floor. Loni strutted over to the old rotary dial phone and picked up the receiver. "Hello?"

"You're still there?!" barked Hazel.

"I'm not coming. I'll call Gwynnie and have her come home and help you."

"You can't call Gwyn!" shouted Hazel, her voice bursting out of the phone.

Loni pulled the receiver away from her ear. "I might have bad eyesight, but jeez, Haze, I'm not deaf. You don't have to yell!"

"You just can't call Gwyn. Or the girls. If they find out, they'll tell Gwyn, and she can't find out."

"Can't find out what?"

"Listen, Loni. I don't ask for much. A little food, maybe some water once in a while. So when I ask a friend to come over and bring a body bag, I expect some action."

"But—"

"No buts. We're gonna need a car too. You have a car, right?"

"A car?! No. I don't have a car. I don't even a have a driver's license."

There was silence on the other end of the phone.

Loni shook the receiver. "Hazel?"

"I'm thinking!" she snapped. "You can't borrow a car from someone?"

"I mean, I'm sure I could figure something out, but you don't understand, Hazel. I don't leave the house."

"You don't think I know that? This is not about you right now, Yolanda Hodges. This is about me. And I have an emergency situation and I need you, a car, and a body bag pronto. Got it?"

Loni sighed. "Got it." She hung up the phone and stared at Ed. "I guess I'm going to help Hazel."

After going up to her room and putting on the best disguise she could find, a furry purple bathrobe with a hood covering her hair, a hockey mask, and cowboy boots, she looked at herself in her hall mirror. *She* couldn't even tell who she was. Pleased by the thought, and oblivious to the fact that her disguises drew everyone's attention, she headed down the stairs.

"What do you think, Ed?" she asked, her voice muffled by the mask.

"I think you look ridiculous."

"Yes, but can you tell who I am?"

Ed lifted one whiskered brow. "Since you're the only person in Aspen Falls who dresses like that, *yes*, I can tell who you are."

"But if you didn't know that I was the only person in Aspen Falls who dresses like this, *then* would you know who I was?"

Ed blew air out his nose. "No, Loni. If I didn't know that interesting tidbit about you, I would have absolutely no idea who you were."

Loni clapped her hands together and lifted the mask up to rest on top of her head. "Oh, good." She smiled, exposing her lipstick-and-caffeine-stained teeth to Ed. "Then I guess I'm ready to go."

"If you don't have a car and you can't take your broomstick, then what's your plan to get there? The Village is on the other side of town."

Loni grinned. "I know exactly how I'm going to get there!" She slid open her kitchen sliding door and stuck her head outside, looking both ways to make sure there wasn't anyone in her fenced-in backyard. "Come on, I'll show you."

The sun was shining brightly when Loni led Ed through her backyard, a maze of old appliances, broken-down lawn mowers, and tall tufts of untended grass and weeds. Several handfuls of cats played all over the backyard, climbing in and out of wooden boxes, hiding amongst the rubbish, and sunning themselves. In the corner, just behind the detached garage, sat an old teal golf cart hidden partially beneath a sun-faded tarp. She stood in front of it with her hands on her narrow hips, looking proud of herself. "Ta-da!"

"You're going to take Uncle Ben's golf cart?" asked Ed with astonishment.

"Like *he* needs it anymore?!" asked Loni. "It's been parked here ever since he…" Her voice trailed off as she glanced skittishly around the backyard. "Well, ever since his little problem."

Ed leapt up onto the once-white seat and put his paws on the steering wheel. "How do you know it even works?"

Loni shrugged. "I start it every once in a while. I always thought I might need a getaway car at some point." She gave the tarp a tug and slid it off the cart's plastic roof. "Scooch over." She slid her butt into the front seat, pushing Ed onto the passenger's side. "Here goes nothin'!"

Loni turned the key in the ignition and the golf cart sputtered to life.

"Holy mackerel! It works!" said Ed with a wide grin.

"You bet your fur it works!" Loni fist-pumped the air and let out a little cackle. "Hoo-hoo-hoooo!"

"Do you even know how to drive?"

Loni stared at the steering wheel, the pedals, and the little gadgets, levers, and knobs on the dash. She'd never learned to drive. "How hard can it be?" She pressed the lever that indicated forward, but nothing happened. "Now what?"

Ed jumped down off the seat onto the floor of the cart and pointed a paw at the pedals. "Now you press that with your foot."

Loni's foot fell heavily on the accelerator. The cart surged forward with a neck-breaking jolt. "Ahhh!" she screamed as she crashed into the back of her garage.

Ed's furry body slammed against the floor panel.

The engine revved and the tires spun in the dirt.

"Foot off the gas pedal!" screamed Ed.

With her adrenaline racing, Loni pulled her foot from the pedal, and the golf cart relaxed. "Oh my God!" screamed Loni, staring at the small amount of damage she'd inflicted on her garage and the front end of her cart. "What a rush!"

Ed jumped up onto the seat and slapped Loni's face with his paw. "What were you thinking?! You could have killed us!" he hollered.

Loni looked at him uncomfortably. "You told me to push on the gas!"

"I didn't tell you to stomp on the gas! You ease your foot onto the gas!"

"Well, you didn't tell me that. How was I supposed to know?"

"Common sense?" asked Ed, his long-whiskered brows knitted together in a panic. "Oh, wait… you don't have any of that. I forgot. My bad." He climbed down off her and jumped across her lap to the grass. "I'll just be staying here. I don't trust being in a moving vehicle with you."

Loni rolled her eyes. "Thanks for the vote of confidence."

"Someone's got to stay and watch the kids." With his tail erect, Ed gave Loni an intentional view of his puckered backside and strutted back towards the house. "A light touch on the gas ought to get you there. Keep the cart between the white and yellow lines. Stay to your right. Stop at stop signs. Use your blinker when you turn, and yield to pedestrians." He disappeared inside the house.

"Thanks for the tips," Loni called back. She turned her attention back to the cart. She pressed the lever that said reverse and put her foot on the gas, this time exerting a bit more care. The golf cart jolted backwards several feet, hitting an abandoned washing machine that had been her mother's when Loni was a little girl. "Dammit!" she cursed.

She put it in forward and pushed on the gas with an even lighter touch. The golf cart jerked forward, and this time Loni had the presence of mind to turn the steering wheel while it moved forward. Waiting too long to make that decision, though, caused her to scrape the side of the garage with the passenger side of the golf car. Her side mirror ripped off and clattered to the ground. Loni gave it a sideways glance, and narrowly avoided hitting the back of her house before plowing into an abandoned refrigerator. This time, she knew right away to take her foot off the gas and to put it in reverse.

She backed the vehicle up and put it in drive again. Little by little, Loni wove her way through her cluttered backyard to the gate that faced the alley behind her house. By the time she'd escaped through the gate, pulled her mask back over her face, and made sure her whole head was covered by her disguise, she felt exhilarated! She was driving!

The golf cart motored along the back alley at a heady twenty miles per hour. Loni's heart bounced exuberantly in her chest. She felt like she was in the Indy 500 going two hundred miles an hour. "Vrmmm, vrmmm," she muttered as she drove, hunching over the steering wheel.

Doris Apron, a woman who lived three houses down from Loni, was outside digging in her flower garden when Loni drove past. Loni gave her a bold wave, but Doris dropped her spade and screamed, running for the house.

Loni gripped the steering wheel tighter and touched the nose of her hard mask to the steering wheel. "Huh. That's not very neighborly."

4

Parking her golf cart in the parking lot behind the Aspen Falls Retirement Village, Loni covertly ducked and dodged behind a row of newly planted trees as she made her way to the back entrance. Loni had been to the Village once since Gwyn and Hazel had moved to town less than a month ago. She knew that their apartment was only a few doors down from the back entrance. She also knew that by going in the back, she could avoid having to check in as a visitor at the front desk.

Peering through the glass door, Loni held her breath as a tall balding man in a burgundy bathrobe pushed a walker. When he'd passed her completely, Loni gave a glance down the hallway in both directions. A wide-bottomed woman in a nurse's uniform sat guarding Hazel's door. She had her nose buried in a saucy-looking romance novel when Loni approached her.

"Who're you?" asked Loni, her voice muffled by the mask that covered her face.

The woman, who had been too absorbed in her smutty novel to have noticed Loni coming down the hallway, glanced over the top of her book at the sound of the gruff voice. She took one look at Loni in her boots, bathrobe, and hockey mask before her eyes widened to the size of lemons, her jaw dropped, and she let out the most horrifying and bloodcurdling scream.

Loni's shoulders slumped. "Oh for Pete's sake," she muttered before flicking her fingers towards the woman like she was shaking off droplets of water. A little zapping noise crackled the air, and the woman froze mid-scream. Loni stared at the woman with her mouth hanging wide open. Then she reached out and pushed the woman's lower jaw up, closing her mouth. "Wouldn't want any flies making a home in there," she chuckled. Then she sidestepped the woman and knocked on Hazel's door.

It took only a second before Hazel threw the door wide open. Hazel took one look at Loni before screaming, "Ahh!" and slamming the door shut in her face.

"Are you kidding me?" Loni muttered before pounding on the door again.

"Go away! I have a gun!" Hazel shouted through the door.

"Hazel, you nut! It's Loni! I drove all the way over here to help you. The least you could do is let me in!"

The door creaked open a tiny slit. Hazel peered out the crack. "Loni?"

Loni nodded.

Hazel tipped her nose up. "Why in the hell are you dressed like the guy in *Friday the 13th*?"

Loni made a face behind the mask. "*Friday the 13th*? What are you talking about?"

Hazel pointed the end of her cane out the door. "Lemme see what's under that mask!"

Loni looked both ways down the hallway and, feeling that the coast was clear, lifted the mask up and set it on top of her head.

"Ahh!" screamed Hazel. "Put the mask back on!" She followed it up with a chuckle.

"Very funny," snapped Loni. "You want my help or don't you?"

Hazel reached her arm out and pulled Loni inside her room. "Anyone see you come?"

"Are you kidding me? I'm the queen of stealth. No one follows Yolanda Hodges anywhere."

"Good. You bring a body bag?"

"No, I didn't bring a body bag! You think I just keep those things lying around for shits and giggles?"

Leaning on her cane, Hazel adjusted her glasses and looked Loni up and down. "I certainly wouldn't put it past you."

Loni hobbled back around and put her hand on the doorknob. "You must not want my help that badly."

Hazel tugged on her arm. "Okay, okay. We'll figure something else out."

"Figure something else out? What in the hell is going on, Haze? And why did Gwyn leave you home alone? And what's up with Nurse Ratchet out in the hallway?"

Hazel pointed at the door. "She's my babysitter. Gwyn paid her to keep an eye on me. She didn't believe I was sick."

"Sick? You're sick?" Loni lowered the mask over her face again. "Is that what this is about? Why didn't you just call the nurse? I don't want to catch whatever it is you've got. My immune system isn't very strong. I don't get out much."

Hazel reached out and flipped Loni's mask back up over her head. "Oh, quit it, would ya? I'm not sick. I just *told* Gwynnie I was sick so she'd leave me home."

Loni stared at her blankly. "I don't get it. Then if you're not sick, what's up with Nurse Ratchet?"

"I had to fool her into thinking I had a cold so she'd tell Gwyn I needed to stay home. Of course the plan backfired when Gwyn decided to pay her to sit outside my door until she got back. My own daughter doesn't trust me."

"Can you blame her? You're a mite ornery."

Hazel shrugged. "Better ornery than dead, that's what I always say."

"So what plan backfired?"

Hazel sighed. "If I tell you, you can't tell anyone."

Loni looked around. "Who am I gonna tell?"

"Gwyn and the girls."

"Well, yeah. I'd probably tell them," agreed Loni with a little nod.

Hazel stood up a little straighter and wrinkled her nose stubbornly. "I'm not going to tell you if you're going to tell them."

Loni thought about it for a second. She wasn't sure what in the world could possibly be such a big deal that Gwyn and the girls would care about it. "Fine," she finally sighed. "What's the big secret?"

Hazel spat in the palm of her hand and held it out to Loni. "Spit swear," she commanded.

Loni curled her lip. "Oh, come on. Witch's honor," she said, holding her flattened palm up with her fingers parted down the middle in a Vulcan salute.

"Spit swear, Loni. I mean it. This is big."

Loni groaned before spitting in her hand. Pinching her big eyes shut, she held it out to Hazel. "Fine. Spit swear. What's the big secret?"

Hazel kept hold of Loni's hand and jerked her towards her bedroom. "He's in here."

"He?"

Hazel's only response was to keep pulling on Loni's arm.

"What do you mean by *he*, Hazel?" asked Loni, quirking a brow.

Hazel stopped in the threshold to her bedroom and pointed one stubby, gnarled finger towards the bed.

Loni followed her finger and sucked in a deep breath when she saw the fleshy pile of wrinkles amidst the wadded-up sheets. "Hazel! Is that a man?"

"Was it the twig 'n' berries that gave it away?" snapped Hazel.

Loni swallowed hard. "Hazel, you have a *man* in your bedroom."

Hazel hobbled forward, leaning heavily on her cane. "Try and catch up, Loni."

Loni pointed at the bed. "Hazel, he's *naked.*"

"No kidding, Sherlock Holmes. There's a naked man in my bed. I'll give you another clue. He's dead!"

"*Dead*?!"

"Yes, dead. Why'd you think I told you to bring a body bag? To pack away my winter sweaters?"

"Hazel! Why is there a dead man in your bed?"

"How am I supposed to know? He wasn't dead when he got in my bed!"

"How'd he die?"

Hazel lifted her brow, making the bags beneath her eyes move. "I'm pretty sure he had a heart attack."

"A heart attack! How do you know?"

Hazel waddled towards the man and stared down at him uncomfortably. "He might have screamed, 'I think I'm having a heart attack.'"

"Well, what was he doing?!"

Hazel stared at Loni. "Push-ups, Loni. He was doing push-ups."

"In bed?!"

"No, you moron, we were having sex!"

Loni's eyes widened as she sucked in her breath. "Sex? Hazel, you were having *sex* while you were sick?!"

Hazel smacked her forehead. "Oh, Mylanta, I called the president of the idiot patrol. I wasn't sick. I was faking, so Gwyn would leave me home alone so I could have sex with George."

"Who's George?" asked Loni.

"Are you kidding me right now?"

Loni looked down at the man on the bed. "Oh, right. He's George. So you and George…" She glanced around furtively and then whispered, "Had sex?"

"Yes, we had sex. Or we were *having sex*. And then he had a heart attack. I killed him! I killed George! And you have to help me get him out of my room before Gwynnie gets home or I'm going to be the next victim!"

Gwyn shifted the car into reverse and edged her silver Buick out of her parking spot. Nurse Brenda's babysitting duty was about to expire, and she wanted to get back to the Village in time to grab her mother a cup of herbal tea from the dining room before heading back to the apartment they shared.

As she drove away, Gwyn eyed Harrison Bradshaw's truck in her rearview mirror. If Char's healing potion did the trick, and Hazel was feeling better, they'd be going on a date that Friday night. Her heartbeat quickened at the thought of it. It had been so long since she'd dated that she almost didn't even know how to do it.

As she drove back to the Village, Gwyn found her mind wandering. Her life had suddenly become so full. Not only did she have a new full-time job, but she also had her mother to take care of, she'd reunited with her old girlfriends, and now there was the potential of a relationship with Harrison. On top of that, they now had to clean out Kat's old house in the evenings. Gwyn suddenly felt overwhelmed. There was so much to do and so little time.

Gwyn sighed. She hated the thought of having to sell her friend's precious belongings, but they had no choice. Hard decisions had to be made. She only wished she understood Kat's reasons for not allowing the women to just sell the house. What were they supposed to do with it? Surely Gwyn couldn't afford to buy the other three shares. Char and Loni both owned their own homes and didn't want to move in together. Phyllis had just signed a lease on an apartment, and Gwyn had her mother to consider. She needed her mother to live at the Village—every day was essentially *take-your-mother-to-work-with-you* day, and Gwyn needed that. Otherwise, she'd never have been able to work. She'd have been providing 24/7 Hazel care.

Gwyn turned the car onto the main road towards the Aspen Falls Retirement Village. Working at her advanced age really wasn't as bad as the girls liked to make it out to be. She enjoyed the people she served. She loved coming up with new crafty things for them to do, organizing new field trips, and planning exciting theme night parties in the dining room. It was fun for her.

The thought of her job made her smile. She had an exciting day ahead. She was taking the residents to the local paintball field, where she'd discovered that the owner had recently purchased an array of Nerf guns. Almost all the male residents had signed up to go on the trip as well as half of the women. They were going to have so much fun, she just knew it. She only hoped Hazel was going to be ready to go too.

Gwyn put her blinker on and grinned as she turned into the parking lot in the front of the building. "Today is going to be a great day!"

5

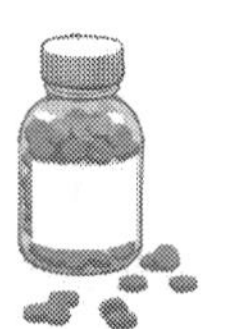

Hazel hobbled to the front room with her cane and locked the apartment door. "How long is that spell going to last on Brenda?"

"Who's Brenda?" hollered Loni from Hazel's bedroom.

"You put a spell on another nurse?"

"Oh, her. It won't last long. Five minutes tops."

Hazel ambled back to her bedroom, where Loni was wrapping the bedsheet around George's midsection. "We've got to get out of here. Gwynnie has to be on her way back here by now."

"I'm going as fast as I can. Maybe if you were to help…"

"Help! What am I supposed to do? My nerves are frazzled to a crisp!"

"Have you taken any of your heart pills?"

"I've been swallowing them like they're M&M's."

Loni nodded as she finished tying the knot in the

bedsheets. "Alright. I think I've got it."

Hazel pushed her cane against the sheet around George's hips. "It looks like a diaper."

"It *is* a diaper. He could have one last poo. I've heard dead people can do that. I'm pretty sure a trail of poo would lead Gwyn right to us."

Hazel nodded. That was actually good thinking. Maybe she *had* called the right woman after all. "Alright. So should I go get a wheelchair or something?"

Loni shook her head and pointed her stubby fingers at the body. "We don't have time for a wheelchair. That nurse is going to wake up with a scream lodged in her throat any minute. We've got to get out of here now." Loni levitated George's body off of the bed. "You're in charge of the doors," said Loni.

"Doors, got it!"

Using her magic fingers, Loni carefully maneuvered George's body out the wide bedroom door and into the living room of the small two-bedroom apartment. "Oh, for pity's sake, Hazel! You left the curtains open! Whoever's in the bedroom across the courtyard is getting a good show."

Hazel's eyes widened. She tugged on the curtains as Loni floated George to the front door.

"Door!"

"Coming, coming!" shouted Hazel. Grabbing her cane, she shuffled to the front door and slowly turned the knob. She opened it a crack and peered outside. Nurse Brenda was still seated on her chair, her eyes wide, but her mouth was shut. Hazel poked her with the end of her cane and the woman toppled forward onto the ground. "Stiff as a board," she muttered before looking both ways to find the hallway empty. "Coast is clear." Hazel opened the door a little bit wider while Loni floated George towards the hall.

Just then, a bloodcurdling scream emanated from the hallway. "Ahhh!" screamed Brenda from the ground.

The scream caused another shot of adrenaline to spike through Hazel's veins. "Ahhh!" she screamed, slamming the door shut before George crossed the threshold.

Hazel shuffled past Loni in a panic, pointing towards Gwyn's bedroom, where the window faced the back parking lot. "The window, the window!" she shouted.

There was a pounding on Hazel's door. "Hazel! Are you alright?"

"It's Brenda," hissed Hazel. "Take George to Gwyn's room and shut the door! I'll be there in a minute."

Loni nodded and magically levitated George to the back bedroom, slamming the door shut behind her.

Hazel went to the door and opened it to find Brenda *and* Gwyn staring back at her.

"Mom!" said Gwyn, looking between Brenda and Hazel, confused. "Brenda said you opened the door and screamed at her."

With one hand gripping her chest, Hazel pointed at Brenda with the other hand. "Well, that was because I heard her screaming in the hallway. She scared me half to death, Gwynnie."

Gwyn looked at Brenda. "Were you screaming, Brenda?"

The nurse looked down uncomfortably and then up at Hazel again. "Well, yes. There was this... *person* in the hallway. With a mask..." She waved a hand around her face. "And a bathrobe..."

"A mask and a bathrobe?" asked Gwyn, looking down the hall. "Maybe it was one of the residents?"

Brenda shook her head wildly. "No, no. It was a scary mask!"

"What kind of scary mask?"

"A hockey mask!"

Gwyn didn't look amused. "You screamed because someone was wearing a hockey mask?"

Brenda's face reddened. "Well, the person in the hockey mask caught me off guard."

"So you screamed and woke up Mother?"

Brenda looked at Hazel apologetically. "I guess."

Hazel rubbed her head with one hand and crossed her fingers behind her back with the other hand. "I was sleeping so soundly too!"

"Oh, you poor thing!"

Hazel nodded, casting her eyes towards the floor. "Now my head hurts something awful."

"Oh, Mom! This darn cold. Char's coming over later to bring you some medicine she's got for colds. That'll make you feel all better!"

Hazel grimaced. She needed more time alone in the apartment. "Okay, well, I'm headed back to bed. I'm beat." She tried to close the door on Gwyn and Brenda.

"Mom! I brought you one of Linda's famous rolls and a cup of hot tea to make you feel better."

As much as she wanted one of Linda's yummy rolls, there was no time to eat now. She plucked the tea out of her daughter's hands. "I'm too sick to eat, I'll just drink the tea. Thank you." She began to slam the door shut, but Gwyn stuck out a hand first.

"Mom! Wait!" She pushed the door open again. "I was just going to see if you wanted to go to the Nerf gun range with me. Lots of residents are going. It's a beautiful day outside. I think you'll have a lot of fun."

Despite Gwyn's chipper smile, Hazel could read her daughter's mind. Gwyn was worried about Hazel's cold turning into pneumonia. Hazel shook her head. "I'm much too sick to go outside, Gwynnie." She held a fist to her mouth and gave a fake cough. "I could catch pneumonia. You wouldn't want that, would you?"

The smile on Gwyn's face instantly faded. "Oh no. I certainly wouldn't want that!" Her shoulders crumpled. "I'll see if I can get Cecelia Becker to take the residents on the field trip for me so I can stay here with you."

Backfire. Hazel took a step backwards. "Oh, Gwynnie. You don't want to stay here with me and miss all the fun! I'll only be sleeping all day. In fact, I'd *still* be sleeping if it wasn't for the screaming wonder over here." She shot Brenda a dirty look.

Brenda looked down at her feet. "I'm sorry," she whispered. "But there was someone in a mask and a bathrobe…"

Gwyn tilted her head to the side. "Hmm, that *is* quite the odd combination. I wonder who would wear something like that?"

Hazel's eyes widened. She could haven't Gwyn putting the pieces together and figuring out it was Loni.

Showtime. Hazel put on her saddest-looking face, droopier-than-usual eyes, big fat pouty lip, and a little sniffle to top it all off. "Gwynnie, I'm really tuckered out. I should be getting to bed."

"But, Mom, Brenda can't stay here and babysit you anymore. She's got to get to work." Gwyn took a step into the doorway.

Hazel stood in her way, blocking the entrance to the apartment. "I don't know what you think I'm going to do, but I can promise you I'm not going anywhere except right to bed. Don't you trust me?"

Hazel concentrated on Gwyn's thoughts. *No. I don't trust you, Mom. I wish I could, but you've given me too many reasons to doubt you.*

Before Gwyn could get another word out, Hazel held up her hand. "Now, before you answer that, I know I haven't done much to earn your trust in the past, but, sweetheart, I'm truly sick. I mean, you heard Brenda earlier. I have a temperature, my throat looks like the recesses of hell, and I've already gone through an entire box of Kleenex since you left. Gwynnie, I'm sick. What kind of mischief can I get into being this sick?"

Should I list the ways you could get into mischief, Mom? Gwynnie wondered.

"How am I ever supposed to earn your trust back if you don't give me the opportunity to earn it back?" *I ought to be nominated for one of those best actress awards. This perfor-*

mance is right up there with Katharine Hepburn's in Bringing up Baby*!*

"Well, Mom, I understand that, but—"

Hazel pushed her daughter back out the door. "Now, now. No buts, Gwynnie. Be a good girl and go do your job. You just got this job, and I know how much you love being close to your old girlfriends. You can't be skipping out on your assignments right off the bat. What if they kicked us out? You wouldn't want that on your conscience, now would you?"

Gwyn was speechless.

"And I certainly don't want to be the cause of us getting kicked out. I know you blame me for us getting kicked out of a few of the last places we've lived…"

Gwyn nodded. *Try all of them*, Hazel heard Gwyn think. "Yes, there have been a few," she said aloud.

"And I just feel horrible about those," said Hazel, pushing her into the hallway.

"You do?"

"I do. So I wouldn't do anything *intentionally* to get us kicked out. You know that, right?"

Gwyn gnawed on her bottom lip. "Well, I suppose you don't intend on doing anything wrong, but that doesn't—"

Hazel swiped a hand in front of her to silence Gwyn. "Then that's that. It's settled. You're going to go see about your business, and I'm going to take a nice long nap. Maybe I'll even take a hot bath to ease these sore muscles."

Gwyn took a step forward. "Oh, Mom, I don't think

you should be getting in and out of the bathtub without me nearby. What if you fell?"

Hazel sighed inwardly. "Oh, aren't you so smart! Of course I shouldn't take a bath without you nearby. I'll wait until you get back. Okay? At lunchtime I'll take my bath. You can sit in the kitchen and have lunch while I soak my sore body."

Gwyn's brows knitted together. "So you'll wait for me?"

Hazel shoved her daughter back into the hallway. "Yes. I'll wait."

"Mom, you really seem to be trying hard to get rid of me. Are you sure you're not up to something?"

Hazel did her best to look offended. "Gwynnie! I'm sick! How could you *think* that? If you don't believe me, Brenda is perfectly welcome to continue sitting outside my room." She lifted her brows and swung her eyes away. "Of course, I'd sure appreciate it if she didn't scream every few minutes and wake me, but that's neither here nor there. I'm sure she couldn't control herself, the poor dear."

"I can control myself, it's just that—"

Hazel closed her eyes and held up a hand. "No need to explain your intrusive outbursts to this poor old woman here trying to get over a mighty bad cold."

"But..." began Brenda.

Gwyn turned and patted the nurse on the shoulder. "It's okay. You can go, Brenda. I know you've got other residents to check on."

"Are you sure? Because I could—"

"No, I'm quite sure," said Gwyn. "I appreciate you finding the time to watch Mom. I'll take it from here."

Brenda glanced at Hazel, who fought back a smile. "Alright. I'll check on her again in the morning."

"That would be lovely. Thank you, Brenda," said Gwyn.

Together, Hazel and Gwyn watched as Brenda walked down the hallway. When she was gone, Gwyn turned to Hazel. "Do you swear you'll be good if I leave you here alone?"

Hazel held up the Vulcan salute that Loni had given her earlier. "Witch's honor."

Gwyn narrowed her eyes. "You've been spending too much time with Loni, haven't you?"

Hazel grinned. "I better get to bed now, Gwynnie. My head's throbbing."

"Oh, poor Mom," sighed Gwyn. "Come on, I'll tuck you in."

Hazel held up a hand defensively. "Oh no, no. That's quite alright. I'll tuck myself in. I'm going to drink this tea and then I'll head right into my room."

"I could get you some more medicine. I just bought a new NyQuil. It's in my bedroom. I'll just go get it for you," said Gwyn, pushing her way into the apartment. *Mom, what are you hiding?* Hazel heard Gwyn thinking as she looked around.

Hazel's heart pounded fiercely in her chest. With Gwyn's hand on her bedroom doorknob, Hazel shouted, "I already found the NyQuil!" She nodded her head ferociously so Gwyn wouldn't feel the need to go in her bedroom, where Loni was hiding with George. "I had several big swigs of it. I think it's kicking in, and that's why I'm suddenly so drowsy."

"Oh," said Gwyn, her face crumpling. "Maybe I should see how much you took. I wouldn't want you to have overdosed on it. That could be dangerous too." She turned the handle on her door and pushed it open. Immediately she sucked in her breath. "Mom!"

Hazel's pulse throbbed wildly. She closed her eyes. The jig was up. Hazel put a hand up defensively. "Gwyn-nie, I can explain…"

"Mom!" said Gwyn again.

Hazel swallowed hard and opened her eyes to see Gwyn holding a half-empty NyQuil bottle. "You drank half of it! You might have overdosed!" Gwyn flipped the bottle around and adjusted her glasses to read the fine print. "I think I should call poison control now."

Hazel stared at the almost-empty bottle and then leaned sideways to look past Gwyn and stare into the empty bedroom. Where had George and Loni gone?! Hazel cleared her throat as Gwyn pulled her cell phone out of her pocket. "Oh, no need to call poison control, Gwynnie. I, uh, I didn't drink all of that."

Gwyn looked up at her mother. "What?"

Hazel shook her head. "No, I mean, I drank *some of it.*" She held up a hand to stop Gwyn from talking over her. "I drank the proper portion, no worries. I, uh, I spilled the rest."

"Spilled it?" asked Gwyn, raising her brows.

Hazel nodded. "Yes, in the bathroom."

Gwyn looked at the bathroom. "Oh, Mom!"

"Don't worry, I cleaned it up. I was taking my dose and I accidentally knocked over the bottle on the counter. Most of it went into the sink and I just wiped up the rest. No big deal."

That seemed to appease Gwyn. "Oh. Well, I guess it's a relief that you didn't drink all that."

Hazel tugged on her daughter's arm and dragged her towards the door. "See? I know how to take care of myself. I promise. Now, you need to get to work. You just go, and I'll go get myself into bed."

"Well. Alright. You'll call me if you need me? You've got your phone?"

Hazel pointed at the phone on the coffee table. "Yup."

"I'll have Arabella at the front desk check in on you from time to time." While the sweetness in Gwyn's voice didn't imply that statement was a threat, it clearly was. Hazel was to stay in her room because she was going to get checked up on.

"Yes, yes. I understand," agreed Hazel. She had no choice. If she flinched or balked over that arrangement, Hazel knew Gwyn wasn't going to leave.

That seemed to satisfy Gwyn. She nodded. "Alright, Mom. Be good. I'll see you at lunchtime. I'll bring you some french fries."

"And Twinkies," said Hazel.

"And Twinkies," agreed Gwyn.

Hazel began to shut the door as she eased Gwyn out into the hallway. "Bye, Gwynnie."

6

"She's gone!" hissed Hazel, plowing into Gwyn's bedroom, where she found the room empty. "Loni? Where'd you go?"

A noise behind her made Hazel turn around.

"We're in here!" hollered a muffled voice inside the closet.

Hazel opened the door to find George smashed up against Loni. "Oh, you got George into the closet. Good thinking!"

Loni winced. "You owe me big-time, Hazel. Do you know how freaky it was to be stuffed in a tiny closet with a dead body? I think George tried to feel me up while we were stuffed in here."

"He's dead, Loni. His days of feeling women up are over."

Loni stared at George. "He still tried to feel me up."

Hazel looked around the room.

"What are you looking for?" asked Loni.

"What did you do with the NyQuil you poured out?"

"Poured out?" asked Loni, blankly.

"Yeah, almost half the bottle was missing. That was good thinking, by the way."

"Well, I heard you talking," said Loni slowly.

"Yeah, so where'd you pour it out? We have to get rid of the evidence before we leave. Just in case Gwynnie comes back."

Loni swallowed hard. "I didn't pour it out, I drank it."

Hazel's eyes widened. "You drank half a bottle of NyQuil?! What were you thinking?"

Loni shook her head. "I don't know. Gwyn was coming. I panicked!"

Hazel palmed her forehead and wondered once again why her first instinct had been to call Yolanda Hodges. "Loni, we literally don't have time for this right now. We have to get George back into his apartment, and then we're calling poison control."

Loni stared at George's dead body hovering in the air next to her. "B-but…"

"Action first, questions later," snapped Hazel, pointing to the window. "We've got to get him out of here."

"Out the window!" Loni stared at the long, narrow rectangular window. "Hazel, it's not a very big window. You really think he's going to fit through there?"

Hazel unlocked the window and shoved it open. "Oh, he'll fit. That's how he got in here in the first place. Besides, we can't go down the hallway. Gwynnie said she's going to send the front desk girl to check up on me from time to time. Someone is bound to see us if we go through the hallway. We have to get him out of here and back to his apartment."

"Where's his apartment?"

Hazel pointed at the other wall. "On the other side of this wall."

Loni's mouth hung open. "This guy was your neighbor?"

Hazel nodded.

"How long had you two been… a thing?"

Hazel looked at Loni with confusion. "A thing? Who said we were a thing?"

"Well, you were sleeping with him."

Hazel waved a hand at Loni dismissively. "It was supposed to be a one-night stand. I've got needs, you know. Now, enough chitchat. We have to get him out this window and around to his window."

"Hazel, there are people out there. It's broad daylight. I'm pretty sure a man in nothing more than a sheet diaper is going to draw some attention."

Hazel nodded. Loni was right. "I've got it." She waddled to her bedroom and put a hand on her back as she grabbed the pile of clothes off the floor. Carrying them back into Gwyn's room, she tossed them onto the bed. "We'll have to dress him."

Loni stared at George. "Dress a dead man? Hazel, I don't think I should have come over here. M-maybe I should go now."

"Oh, quit being skittish and get over here and help me put this man's pants on," snapped Hazel.

Minutes later, the women stared at a fully dressed

George Petroski. His pants were a bit tighter than usual as they'd decided to leave his diaper on, just to be safe. Hazel's heart continued to race. While she felt horrible that George was dead of a heart attack, she was too scared of Gwyn finding out that Hazel had been the cause of the heart attack for the remorse to have kicked in yet.

"With his clothes on, he doesn't even look dead," remarked Loni. "Poor fella."

"I'll pay my respects once we've gotten him back to his bedroom!" said Hazel, wringing her hands before pointing at the window. "Okay, time to get him home now."

"Who's going to catch him once I get him outside? I can't go out the window with him, you know."

Hazel sighed. "I'll go open his bedroom window and then I'll go outside."

Minutes later, after opening George's bedroom window, Hazel went out the Village's back door and around to Gwyn's bedroom window.

Loni peered out at her. "Took you long enough. I'm getting creeped out hanging out alone with a dead guy."

"I'm sorry. In case you hadn't noticed, I don't move very fast!" Hazel leaned her cane against an iron bench beneath a tree and then gestured with her hands. "Send him out, I'm ready."

Loni wiggled her fingers and levitated George's body into the air. He floated outside smoothly.

Hazel waved him down to her. "Set him down on the bench and then you can come out here too."

Loni peered out the window as she lightly lowered his body to the bench. Hazel grabbed his legs and positioned him so he'd sit upright. "You got him?"

"Yup. He's good. Now get your fanny out here before someone sees him," hissed Hazel over her shoulder as a lawn mower sounded in the distance.

Loni released her telekinetic grip on him and George's body promptly slumped forward. Hazel pulled his shoulders back against the seat back and put his cap back on his head, covering his eyes. His head lolled to the side, falling onto Hazel's shoulder. She pushed it up again just in time to see a married couple who lived in the Village's south wing strolling by.

"Good morning. It's shaping up to be a beautiful day, isn't it?" said Ernie Von Ebsen with a nod to Hazel and George.

With her heart pounding loudly in her ears, Hazel swallowed hard. "Oh, uh, yeah, beautiful day," she answered stiffly. *Put a fork in me*, she thought. *I'm done.*

"Up for a game of poker later, George?" asked Ernie.

Hazel elbowed George's side. "Oh, uh, George stayed up too late last night playing. He can't keep his eyes open to save his life."

Mary Von Ebsen smiled. "Ernie and I had breakfast with Duke Olson this morning. He mentioned how heated the game got. But it sounded like George pulled through in the end." Then she tipped her head to the side. "Boy, George doesn't look so good. Is he alright?"

Hazel just wanted them to leave. She could feel Loni's eyes on her back, staring at her from the back door. "Oh, yeah, yeah. He's fine. Well, when George wakes up I'll make sure to tell him you're looking for a match-up."

Ernie smiled at her pleasantly. "That would be great. Oh, and tell him to make sure and sign up for the poker tournament on Friday." He took his wife's hand. "Come on, Mary, we've got to get you to your hair appointment now."

"Toodleloo," she said sweetly to Hazel.

Hazel gave her a little wave and then looked over her shoulder as Loni sprinted her way. Hazel stood up and Loni wiggled her fingers at George again, bringing him to his feet.

The sound of the lawn mower that had been steadily humming in the distance seemed to be getting closer. "Hurry. I think someone's coming," hissed Hazel.

"I'm going as fast as I can, Hazel," Loni spat back as she raised George's body into the air.

They'd just about maneuvered him to his window when a man pushing a lawn mower came around the corner of the building.

"Loni!"

"I know!" she hissed back, carefully setting George down on his feet. With her mask on, she turned to face the brick wall but was careful to keep George's body floating in the air so it looked like he was standing.

The man pushing the mower gave the three of them a one-handed salute. Hazel waved back with her right arm, holding George's left arm so they'd wave together. But that was when she realized that he wasn't just passing by.

He was intent on mowing the patch of grass that connected the back parking lot to the courtyard.

Loni gave a glance over her shoulder. "What do we do now?"

"That guy's going to be there for a while," said Hazel. "I don't think we'll be getting George in his room anytime soon. There's just too much traffic back here."

"So what are we supposed to do with him?" asked Loni. Hazel could hear the panic in her voice. "I can't get arrested, Hazel. The police are in cahoots with the FBI. This could be bad. Very bad."

Hazel put a hand to her face. Her brain hurt and she felt dizzy. "Can you just shut up for a minute? I'm trying to think!"

"Think faster. The lawn mower man is coming back."

Hazel debated taking George to the game room. To the Chapel. To the laundry room. *Ugh.* There was too much going on. She couldn't think.

Finally, Loni couldn't take it any longer. Hazel felt her moving George from her side. "Come on. We can't stay here. There are too many people around."

Hazel followed as Loni led her and George to a blue-green golf cart in the back parking lot. "What are you doing?"

"I'm putting him in the cart. We'll figure out what to do with him later. For now we just need to get out of sight."

While Hazel wasn't sure if that was the right thing to do or not, she suddenly realized she didn't have many other options. "Oh, fine," she grumbled, climbing into the front seat of the cart.

With George sandwiched between them, the cart surged into reverse. George's head lolled onto Hazel's shoulder again, and she had to set it upright. She held his hand up again to wave at a car pulling into the parking lot. "Why in tarnation are you going this way?! Take the back streets," said Hazel. "We're going to get made going this way!"

Loni gave the steering wheel a sharp turn and George flew sideways onto Hazel.

"Ahh!" hollered Hazel as she also flew sideways and nearly toppled out of the cart. "Loni!"

Loni reached a hand over and pulled the two of them back in. "Hang on!" she screamed, turning the corner sharply and following the road for several blocks before it turned into a gravel road on the outskirts of Aspen Falls.

Hazel grabbed her chest. "I should have brought my heart pills, but I had no idea this would be such a wild ride!"

Loni looked around. "I'm sorry. I've never driven before and it's been years since I've cruised the back streets of Aspen Falls, I don't even know where I'm going."

Hazel adjusted her glasses and looked up at Loni. "What do you mean, you've never driven before?"

Loni turned her head. "Just what I said. I've never driven before."

"You mean you've never driven a golf cart?"

"I've never driven a golf cart. A car. A truck. A bus. A cement mixer. Anything. I don't have a driver's license."

"Well, I knew you didn't have a license, but I assumed you'd at the very least *driven* before."

Loni shrugged as she cruised down the gravel road. "Nope. I had no reason to." She rubbed her head. "Plus, I think that NyQuil is starting to kick in. My head feels kinda fuzzy."

Hazel's eyes widened. In all the confusion, she'd almost forgotten that Loni had ingested half a bottle of Nyquil. "Oh, for crying out loud," she muttered. She rubbed her own head. She had no idea what to do now.

"Are we just gonna ride off into the sunset together with George, or are ya gonna tell me where to go?" said Loni. Her words were now coming out slightly slurred.

Hazel sighed. She didn't know her way around Aspen Falls either. She knew the route from the Village to downtown, she knew her way to Loni's and Kat's houses, and she knew where the park was because Gwyn took the residents on lots of walks on the walking paths along the river. That was about it. She hadn't lived in Aspen Falls long enough to know the backroads. But she knew she had to think of something and fast. The charges against her were stacking up like poker chips on a winning streak and now she was pretty sure poisoning Loni needed to be added to the list. "Make a right at the next intersection," she finally said.

Loni nodded and hit the gas. Minutes later they were parked next to Falls Park on the outskirts of town. The water coming down from the waterfall in the center of town emptied into this small river that wound its way through town and made its way to the park.

"Now what?" asked Loni.

"Let's get him to the bench over there." Hazel pointed towards a small wooden bench overlooking the river.

"And then what?"

"One thing at a time."

Loni drove the golf cart up onto the soft grass and pulled up to the bench. From there, she wiggled her fingers and moved George from the cart to the bench, where the three of them sat down together, side by side.

As George's head lolled backwards on his neck, Loni and Hazel stared out at the slow-moving river. The grass around the park had all started to green up and the trees were all budding. The smell of damp earth was fresh in the air, and for once Hazel was finally able to take a deep breath and assess the situation.

She'd killed a man.

That was something she'd never done before. The image of George Petroski clutching his chest was seared into her brain. What was she going to do? Gwynnie would be so disappointed in her. Hazel felt like she was always disappointing her only daughter. It was just that Hazel wanted to have a little fun from time to time. When George's head had popped in through her living room window while Gwyn was in the shower and he'd asked her if she wanted to have a little fun, Hazel had been excited to just say yes! Yes, she wanted to have a little fun! She hadn't planned on killing the poor man!

She swallowed hard. Now it wouldn't be just Gwyn

she'd have to deal with. She'd have to deal with the police. And George's family. And to top it all off, she'd dragged Loni into it and now she'd probably overdosed on NyQuil.

Hazel let out a heavy sigh. She felt the weight of the world suddenly on her shoulders.

Had she done the right thing moving George? Probably not, but what other choice had she had? Gwyn would have been there any minute, and if she'd caught Hazel with a dead man in their apartment… Hazel sighed and shook her head.

Hazel had been reading her daughter's mind since they'd come to Aspen Falls. Gwyn was finally happy. She'd reunited with her old girlfriends. She had a job that she enjoyed. Their apartment at the Village wasn't *that bad*; they'd surely lived in worse. And there was a nice man interested in her. Hazel wanted all of those nice things for her daughter. Even though she didn't show it often, she loved Gwyn more than anyone else in the world, and she appreciated everything she did for both of them. She couldn't mess that up now.

No, she'd done the right thing.

She looked over at Loni, whose head had fallen over and landed on George's shoulder. Hazel thwacked the woman's ankle with her cane. "Wake up."

"Wha-wha…" mumbled Loni as her head lifted, her eyes heavy.

"Don't you fall asleep on me now," said Hazel. "You're my ride home."

"It's just that I can't seem to keep my eyes open." Loni's words were slurred and heavy.

Hazel used her cane to heft herself to her feet. She looked down at George. She felt bad for what she was about to say. No one deserved such an unfortunate demise, but Hazel had to preserve things for her daughter. If the Village discovered that Hazel was responsible for another resident's death, they'd be kicked out on their ears. They'd be forced to leave Aspen Falls, and Gwyn would never forgive her.

She let out a deep breath. "Come on, I'll help you up."

Loni lifted an arm. "But whaddabout Gerg…?" she slurred.

"Gerg is staying here. Come on." She helped Loni get back into the golf cart, but this time in the passenger's seat. Hazel climbed into the driver's seat and turned the key in the ignition. She had to look away as they drove off; it was too difficult to look at George, and she felt horrible about what she was doing.

7

Char Bailey squatted down to adjust the miniature visor on the small tan-and-white Chihuahua's head. Then she gave him a little rub under the chin. "Feel better?"

Victor Bailey scratched at his collar with his hind leg and then stood up on all fours. "Much better, thank you. I thought it was about to fall off."

"Those sure are some snazzy sneakers," said Phyllis, pointing at the two pairs of grey-and-black miniature running shoes on Vic's paws.

Vic pranced around in circles, picking up each foot in turn and looking at his new shoes. "What a find it was when my little Love Muffin discovered the dog shoemaker online! Now I can keep up with both of you on our walks."

"Anything for my little snickerdoodle," cooed Char, shooting her husband, the Chihuahua, a wide grin.

Phyllis grinned at them both. "You two give me a bellyache, you're so sweet."

Vic stretched his hind legs and then took off like a shot on all fours. "Woohoo!" he howled into the wind.

Char put a hand to her mouth and giggled. "Now that Vic's finally used to being a dog, he's enjoying feeling youthful again."

"I can see that!"

As they power-walked up the sidewalk towards Falls Park, Char pointed to the house across the street. "Look, Ava Schmeckpepper's crocuses are blooming."

"The whole town is really greening up," agreed Phyllis as she tried to mimic Char's stiff posture and brisk pace. She sucked in a big puff of air, struggling to keep up. "Do you always walk this fast?" she finally huffed.

Without so much as a sideways glance, Char dipped her head in a nod. "My doctor says I've got to keep my heart rate up. If my heart isn't pumping, my walk isn't doing me any good."

At the mouth of the park, Phyllis finally buckled. Bending at the waist, she panted heavily while Char kept going. "I don't think I can do this."

"You need to. I can't have all my friends dropping like flies," Char shouted back at her. "You're carrying around about fifty extra pounds in that fanny alone. Come on!"

Phyllis stood up. Arching her back she kept a firm hand on it. "But my body isn't used to this… this… exercise."

Char kept walking. "Too bad. It's good for you."

"So's lying on the sofa with a box of good chocolates," Phyllis shouted back. "I think that sounds incredibly good. In fact, I think I'm going home."

Char finally stopped walking and turned around to stare at her friend. "Phyllis Habernackle. Quit your belly-achin' and catch up. We've got some planning to do."

Phyllis groaned but pushed ahead until she was beside Char again. "Planning?"

"Yes, planning."

"What planning?"

"We need to figure out how we're going to handle selling off Kat's things."

Phyllis made a face. "What's to plan? We pick out the stuff none of us want and we put a couple signs around town and then put the crap on the lawn. How hard is that?"

"I'll tell you how hard that is. Yolanda Hodges is a hoarder. She's going to want everything. I think we might have to consider going through Kat's house without her."

Phyllis sucked in a breath. "Well, Charlotte Adams Maxwell Bailey! I never thought I'd hear you scheming."

Char pushed herself harder to keep up with Vic, who was now chasing a squirrel around the playground just up from the river bed. "I wouldn't call it scheming as much as I would call it selective invitation."

"You can call it what you want, but I don't think we can exclude Loni from this process. Not only will she be offended, but it's just not right. Kat left her stuff to all of us. Not just us and Gwyn. Loni has a right to Kat's stuff just as much as we do."

Char sighed. "Yes, I know. And it's not that I don't

want Loni to get her fair share. It's just that she's not going to want us to sell *anything*, and that's going to be a problem because we have to come up with twenty-five hundred dollars' worth of stuff to sell. Have you ever had a rummage sale before? That's a lot of stuff! We're talking antiques, furniture, rugs…"

"I know. It's going to be hard. Getting rid of any of Kat's stuff will be hard, but difficult choices must be made."

From up ahead, Vic suddenly stopped running and began barking like mad. Char looked up at him sharply. Since he'd been turned into a dog, he'd only barked once, and that was when Char had accidentally caught his tail in the cabinet door. And that had come out as more of a high-pitched *yip* than the frenzied, wild barking she heard now.

She pressed on Phyllis's arm. Something was wrong. "Vic!" she shouted.

She took off in a dead sprint towards him, scanning the grassy park for a wild animal or someone trying to hurt him. As she moved closer, she saw him standing beside a wooden bench. No one appeared to be on the bench, and she couldn't see any immediate signs of danger. Char wondered if maybe the squirrel Vic had been chasing was now on the bench, but she found it odd that Vic would bark at a squirrel. Yes, he enjoyed chasing them for exercise, but he was still a man inside the dog, and he usually just talked.

"What's wrong, Vic?" asked Char as she approached him.

"It's not good, Love Muffin. You might want to stay back."

"Stay back?" asked Char, peering over the back of the bench to see something in a heap. "What is it?"

Phyllis was right behind her, huffing badly. "What"—she puffed—"is it?"

"Sugar plum, I'm not kidding. Perhaps you and Phyllis should go back that way. You might want to call the police. I'll stay here until they come."

Char furrowed her brow. Now she was really curious. "The police? Whatever for?" she asked as she walked around the bench to see a body draped lifelessly on the seat.

"Oh my God!" shrieked Char, holding a hand to her mouth. "Is he…?"

Vic nodded sadly. "I think so."

Phyllis walked around the bench too to stand next to Char. She sucked in her breath and grabbed Char's arm. "Is he dead?"

Char looked at Phyllis and then at Vic. "I don't know. Should I check for a pulse?"

Phyllis squeezed Char's arm. "No, I'll do it." She reached forward and gave the man a little poke. When he didn't move, she edged forward slowly and grabbed hold of his arm. She lifted it and then let it go quickly. It made a little thunk as it dropped onto the wooden bench. She glanced up at Char again.

"I can check," said Char, even though the thought of it made her skin crawl.

"No, it's alright. I can do it," Phyllis assured her. She

took a deep breath and reached down to grab his wrist. This time she closed her eyes and pressed two fingers down. "Nothing," she said sadly.

"Oh my goodness," sighed Char, her hand to her mouth.

"Sugar dumpling, why don't you or Phyllis call the police? You can go home then, and I'll wait here until they show up," suggested Vic, rubbing his wife's leg with a paw.

Char reached down and scooped up her husband. She needed to hold him close to her. The sight of a dead body on the park bench had rattled her.

"I'll wait with Vic," said Phyllis. "You can go, Char. Dead bodies don't really bother me."

Char looked down at the man. A grey hat covered his face. "Before I go, I want to know who it is," she whispered.

Phyllis nodded and then reached forward and moved the hat so the man's face was visible.

Vic sucked in his breath. "It's George Petroski!"

"You know him?" asked Phyllis.

Vic put a paw to his forehead. "Yes, I knew George. He used to come into the bakery quite a bit when he was younger. I haven't seen him much, especially since he moved to the Village."

"The Village?!" Char and Phyllis cried in unison.

"Yes," said Vic. "After his wife asked for a divorce a few years ago, George tried living on his own. He actually lived just down the street from the bakery, above the gift shop. That only lasted a few months. He hadn't lived alone maybe ever in his life, so when he realized his wife wasn't going to take him back, he moved to the Village. He said he needed to be around people."

"I don't blame him," said Char. "It's hard to be alone after you've spent your whole life raising a family."

"If this guy came from the Village, Gwyn's probably going out of her mind looking for him!" said Phyllis, her green eyes wide. "Maybe we should call her before we call the police. I could see Gwyn being upset with us if she's the last to find out."

Char nodded. "Very good point." She began to dig her phone out of the back pocket of her velour pants. "You want to call her, or should I?"

"Go ahead!" said Phyllis. "I don't want to be the bearer of bad news."

Char sighed and dialed Gwyn's number. Her phone rang and rang, but no one picked up. "She's not answering. She's probably elbow deep in glue and glitter."

"Sweet treat, I think you should just call Detective Whitman. Get him down here. You can tell Gwyn then."

Char shook her head at her husband. "Oh, no. You don't know Gwyn like I do. She's the most anal-retentive woman in the world."

"In the world," Phyllis echoed nodding her head.

"She has to have everything just so, and if she finds out that one of her residents died and she wasn't even here to meet the detective…"

Phyllis rubbed her forehead. "She's gonna freak. You know this, right. It's literally her first month on the job and there's a dead body to deal with."

Char clucked her tongue. "I wonder what he's even doing out here all alone." She looked around for the first time taking in her surroundings. "Did you see these tire tracks?"

Phyllis and Vic took steps back to look at them.

"They pull right up to the bench," said Phyllis.

"Almost looks like someone dumped him here," agreed Vic.

"Oh man," sighed Char. "If this is foul play…" She threw her arms up.

"Now don't go getting ahead of yourself, Cupcake," said Vic. "None of us are as young as we used to be. George likely just died of natural causes. Maybe he came out here knowing full well it was his last day and maybe he just wanted to be surrounded by Mother Nature."

"Or maybe he was whacked and the killer just dropped him off like a sack of bricks!" Phyllis said.

Vic nodded. "Well, yes, I suppose there's that possibility also."

Char couldn't stand to hear the possibilities any more. They had to get to Gwyn so they could alert Detective Whitman. "We have to tell Gwyn. Why don't you two stay here and watch Mr. Petroski? I'll run to the Village to tell her and be right back."

Vic nodded. "That sounds like a very good idea."

"Well, hurry up," snapped Phyllis. "It's not good for my reputation around town to be seen with a dead body every week."

"Oh, you just hold your britches, Phyllis. I've got to run back for the car. I'll go as fast as I can."

8

Anxious to get Gwyn notified so they could get a police officer out to the park as soon as possible, Char knocked on Gwyn and Hazel's apartment door with the enthusiasm of a next-door neighbor annoyed by the volume of a stereo. From her side of the door, Char could clearly hear people moving around inside the apartment and the distinct murmur of voices, yet no one came to the door. After thirty seconds of standing there, impatiently waiting, Char knocked again. "Gwyn. It's Char. Open up, it's an emergency."

The movement inside the apartment stopped.

"Gwynnie? Hazel? You girls in there?"

Then she heard the tapping of Hazel's cane against the floor, and the handle turned. The door creaked open a crack and Hazel stuck her nose through the narrow opening. "What?"

"Hazel, I need to speak to Gwyn. It's an emergency."

"Gwyn's not here," snapped Hazel before slamming the door shut in Char's face.

Well, that was rude! Char thought indignantly before realizing that the sounds she'd heard had indicated that there were *two* people inside the apartment. Was Gwyn hiding from her for some reason? "Then who else is inside?" Char hollered through the door.

"None of your business," Hazel hollered back.

"Is Gwyn in there?"

"No. Now go away."

Char took a step away from the door, put both hands on her hips, and stared at the door. There was something fishy going on in there. "Hazel Prescott. You open this door right now."

"Make me."

Char had had enough. If Gwyn wasn't in there, she certainly needed to know that Hazel was up to something. And whatever it was, it didn't feel like it was a surprise Gwyn would be happy to know about. "Hazel. I'm calling Gwyn."

Char heard voices through the door again. Unless Hazel had gone senile and was talking to herself, someone else was *definitely* in there. Finally, the doorknob turned again and the door creaked open a crack. This time, Yolanda Hodges poked her fat nose out. "Yes?"

"Loni!" said Char with surprise. "What are *you* doing here?!"

"I'm sorry, am I not allowed to visit my friends?" asked Loni furtively.

Char's mouth fell open. In all the years that Char and

Loni had lived in Aspen Falls, not *once* had Loni visited her. Of course, they had been feuding all those years, but still! Loni *never* visited friends. Something was definitely wrong. Not only had they just found a dead body in the park, but Gwyn was missing, Hazel was being ruder than usual, and Loni was running wild in Aspen Falls instead of in her self-imposed jail of a house.

Am I in the Twilight Zone? she wondered. Char tried to regain her composure by sputtering, "Well, of course you're allowed to visit your friends, but you *don't.* So excuse me if this is a little weird."

With expressionless eyes behind her thick glasses, Loni shook her head. "It's not weird. Hazel wasn't feeling well, so she asked me to come over."

Char tipped her head sideways. "Hazel wasn't feeling well, so she called *you* instead of Gwyn?"

Loni shrugged. "Yup." She hiccupped and then giggled.

"Oh." Char's shoulders relaxed slightly. Gwyn *had* said that Hazel wasn't feeling well. In fact, in all the chaos of finding George Petroski's dead body in the park, Char had almost forgotten that after her walk, she was going to fix Hazel an old witch elixir for her cold. "Okay, well, I suppose that's not completely ridiculous."

"Thanks," said Loni, rolling her eyes.

Char smiled. "That's not what I meant. I promised Gwyn I'd come over later to bring Hazel an old witch remedy that my mother used to clear up my colds. May I come in and see how Hazel's doing?"

Loni gave Char an expressionless stare. "Just a

moment. Let me confer with my client," she said before shutting the door in Char's face again.

My client? Char's brows lowered. Those two were acting so strangely. Char's instincts had kicked in, and now she knew she had to find out exactly what they were up to. She knocked on the door again. "Hazel. I need to speak to you."

The door opened again, this time wide enough to expose Loni and Hazel standing in the doorway. Loni leaned heavily on Hazel's shoulder and her eyes were thin slits.

"Yes?" asked Hazel.

Char tried to take a step into the apartment, but the two women didn't even so much as pretend to move. "May I come in?"

Hazel gave a little fake-sounding cough. "I might be contagious."

"Your cough doesn't sound that bad."

"That's why I called Loni. She brought me something to take for my cough. It's gotten better."

Char looked at Loni in surprise. "You did? What did you bring her?"

Loni grinned at Char and then let out a little giggle. "Ex-Lax."

"Ex-Lax! For a cough?!"

Loni nodded. "It's an old witch's remedy passed down from *my* mother."

Char lifted her brows. "Well, I've never heard of such a thing. Ex-Lax to treat a cough?"

Loni patted Hazel on the back. "Yup. I made her take

the whole box. Now she's too scared to cough very hard."

The sides of Hazel's mouth quirked up.

Char eyed them both. Hazel didn't even look remotely sick. In fact. She looked... *suspicious*. "Very funny," said Char. She reached out and put a hand on Hazel's forehead. "You don't feel warm."

"It's because I'm old. When you got one foot in the grave like I do, you always feel cold. I'll probably feel warmer when I'm dead."

Char looked over their heads into the seemingly empty apartment. Everything *looked* in order. "What are you two up to? What's going on?" As they turned their heads to follow her gaze, Char pushed her way between them and into the apartment.

The two women looked at each other.

"Nothin's goin' on," slurred Loni, nearly toppling over as Char passed her by.

"Why are you slurring? Are you drunk?" asked Char, peering at Loni closely.

"Drunk? No, I ain't drunk. I'm just a wee bit sleepy is all," she said, taking a seat on the sofa.

"Why are you sleepy?"

"Cuz Hazel made me get outta bed an' come over first thing this mornin' an' I didn't have my coffee."

Char sniffed the air in front of Loni. Then she looked at Hazel. "Where's Gwyn?"

"On a field trip," said Hazel.

Char's eyes narrowed to tiny slits. "And she left you here alone?"

Hazel nodded. "She trusts me."

Now Char *knew* Hazel was lying. "No, she doesn't. Where's the nurse that was watching you before?"

"She left. Loni came over instead."

"So Gwyn knows that Loni's here?"

Hazel pressed her lips between her dentures.

"Ahhh," said Char with a little knowing nod. "Gwyn *doesn't* know Loni's here. Does she know that your nurse left?"

Hazel lowered her brows. "Of course she knows that. I told you, Gwyn trusts me!"

Char could tell she was going to get nowhere with Hazel, so she turned to look at Loni, who looked like she was just about to pass out on the sofa. "Loni. Tell me what's going on. Why are you really here?"

Loni gave her head a shake to wake herself up. "I'm just here because Hazel needed me."

"Hazel needed you. What did she *need* you for?"

"I told ya. She was sick," said Loni, the tone of her voice rising ever so slightly.

Char could tell she was lying when Loni couldn't maintain eye contact with her. "Uh-huh. But she doesn't *look* sick. In fact, she looks just fine. You look worse than Hazel does."

"I guess she's feeling better," said Loni.

"And I think I gave Loni my cold," said Hazel.

Char shook her head. She didn't have time for this. Phil and Vic were stranded at the park, staring at a dead man. She needed to complete her task and move on. "Okay. The jig is up. What did you two do?"

"Do?" asked Hazel, wringing her hands.

"Yeah."

"How do you know we *did* something?" asked Loni.

Char smiled. "Your answer just told me you did. Now I just need to know what it is so I can go about my business."

Loni and Hazel stared at each other, each of them mashing their lips shut.

"Uh-huh. Well. I'll just get it out of Gwyn, then. I'm sure she'll be interested to hear that Loni's over here without her knowledge, as well as the other news I have to tell her. Where is she?"

Undaunted by the threat, Hazel's expression didn't change. She merely crossed both hands over the head of her cane and pursed her lips.

Loni quirked an eyebrow. "What other news do you have to tell her?"

Char rocked back on the spongy heels of her walking shoes. "Oh, I see. So you want me to tell *you* what I know and yet you two can keep a secret from me? That hardly seems fair!"

Loni shrugged and leaned back into the sofa. "Fine. Don't tell us."

Char sighed. She needed to know where Gwyn was, and they didn't seem interested in telling her. Maybe if they understood the severity of the situation they'd spill the beans. "Oh, fine. You are not going to believe this, but Phyllis, Vic, and I just found a dead body."

Loni's eyes widened. "Another one?"

Char's head swiveled to stare at Loni. "Another one?

What do you mean? Was another dead body found today?"

Hazel stared at Loni. "What Loni meant to say was, 'Oh, really, a dead body, you say?'"

Char was suspicious. "Yes. On a bench in the park."

Loni winced. "In the park, you say?"

"Yes. I do say. A dead body in the park. You starting to need hearing aids too?"

Loni's mouth swished to the side. "I'm just in shock. That's all."

Char walked towards the door. "Well, since you two are no help, I better go. I need to find Gwyn to tell her the news."

That made Hazel turn around. "Tell Gwyn? About the dead body in the park? Why do you have to tell Gwyn?"

"Well, I'm sorry to have to tell you this, Hazel, but the man that we found dead was a resident here at the Village."

"You're sure he lived at the Village?" asked Loni. "M-maybe he lived somewhere else?"

Char shook her head. "Nope. I'm sure. Vic knew him. He's a resident here. I have to let Gwyn know before we call the police."

"B-but maybe Vic was confused. Maybe George lived in the nursing home on the other side of town."

Char sucked in her breath. "Yolanda Hodges! I hadn't said George's name."

Loni clapped a hand over her mouth and instantly glanced at Hazel.

"Oh, nice going, you moron!" snapped Hazel, swatting Loni's legs with her cane. "Remind me not to call you for any more top secret assignments."

"I'm sorry! I thought she said his name! I can't help it. It's the NyQuil talking!"

Char's mind reeled. How in the world had Loni and Hazel known it was George? "Alright, spill. How did you two know it was George that's dead?"

"I don't think I like your tone," snapped Hazel.

"Too bad. I'll ask again. How did you two know it was George that died?"

"She read your mind," lied Hazel.

Char shook her head. "Nope. Not buying it. Loni doesn't read minds. You do."

"Fine," said Hazel. "I read your mind and I magically teleported my thoughts into her brain. It was easy, really. Considering her brain was already almost empty."

Char shook her puffy white head. "Nope. Not buying it now. You two knew he was dead." She strutted through the living room and took a seat in one of the armchairs. "I'm not leaving until the two of you start talking. Something's going on here, and I want to know what it is."

Loni's hand trembled slightly as she adjusted the glasses on her face. "I think we have to tell her, Haze."

"We don't have to tell her anything."

"But I think we need help sorting all this out. Char's probably better at that than I am."

Hazel pointed her gnarled finger at Loni. "Don't you dare say another word. I'm invoking my attorney-client privilege."

"Hazel. Loni's not an attorney and neither are you. Attorney-client privilege doesn't apply."

"What are you? A judge? It applies if I say it applies."

Char sighed. She had no idea how Gwyn lived with Hazel twenty-four hours a day, seven days a week. She looked at Loni and sighed. Hazel was exhausting. "Whatever's going on, Loni, I'll help you. Okay? I just want to know what's going on."

"Don't do it, Loni! It's a trap!"

Loni's oversized eyes swiveled between the two women. Char could tell she wanted to talk, but Hazel didn't want her to.

Char rolled her eyes and let out a heavy sigh. "Don't worry about Hazel. She's all shot and no powder."

Hazel held up the blunt end of her cane at Char threateningly. "Oh, I'll show you powder."

Char swatted it away. "Even if you could get that cane unjammed, you wouldn't use it on me *or* Loni, so just put that damn thing away before you hurt yourself." She turned to look at Loni. "Just tell me what she's conned the two of you into screwing up so I can help you unscrew it."

"Funny you should choose the word screw," said Loni slowly.

Char made a face. "What's that supposed to mean?"

Hazel's eyes blazed as she stared at Loni from across the room. "Loni! Don't you dare!"

But Loni couldn't hold it in anymore. She put a hand over each ear, pinched her eyes shut, and spat it out. "Hazel killed George Petroski by having sex with him!"

Hazel's eyes widened to the size of quarters as she sucked in her breath. "I'll never forgive you, Loni Hodges. As soon as I find my voodoo doll collection, you'll be the first to get her tongue chewed off by my dog."

"But you don't have a dog," said Loni, peeking at Hazel through one eye.

"I don't have a voodoo doll collection either! The point is, next chance I get, I'm cursing you!"

"I'm already confined to my house. How much more cursed can I get?"

Char held out two hands to quiet the women. "Ladies! Enough!" She looked at Hazel. "Hazel, you had *sex* with George Petroski?"

Hazel grimaced. "Well. Not that it's any of *your* business, but, yes, as a matter of fact, I did."

Char's face wrinkled. "Does Gwyn know you were fornicating with one of the residents?"

"Do you tell *your* children every time you *fornicate* with your dog?"

It was Loni's turn for her face to wrinkle. "Ewww. I didn't need *that* mental picture, thank you."

Char held a hand to her heart. "Hazel! That was *rude*! Vic's not my dog, first of all, he's my *husband*, and *obviously* that part of our relationship ended when his *body died*. It was very mean-spirited of you to say such a thing. After all, I was only trying to help you!"

That made Hazel's face soften. She shuffled over to the sofa and sat down slowly. After giving it thought for a few seconds, she looked up at Char. "I'm sorry. You're right. That was rude. I'm just…" She wiped away a tear. "I'm panicking a little, and I don't know what to do."

Char's shoulders dropped and she suddenly felt for Hazel's predicament. "That's why you and Loni need to trust me. I'll help you figure this all out. You just need to be honest with me and we'll go from there. Okay?"

Hazel and Loni both nodded.

"Okay," she sighed. "Start from the beginning."

9

"So you see! We can't tell Gwyn!" pleaded Hazel.

Char shook her head. "No, I really don't see. You didn't do anything wrong, Hazel. You just wanted to be intimate with George. You're both consenting adults. There's nothing wrong with that."

"But what if the Village doesn't think like that?"

"So what if they don't think like that? It's really none of their business."

Hazel scowled. "You don't understand. I'm always the reason that Gwyn and I get kicked out of retirement homes. Sometimes it's because I like to gamble. Sometimes it's because I say or do the wrong thing to the wrong person. Sometimes it's because I run out to have a little fun. But I never mean to do anything *wrong*, and yet we still get kicked out."

"I hardly think they can blame you for an elderly man's heart attack, Hazel."

Loni cleared her throat. "But is that a risk we're willing to take?"

"What do you mean?"

"Well, what if Hazel's right? What if the Village thinks that Hazel should bear some of the responsibility for George's heart attack? What if they decide that Hazel has to go because she's a troublemaker? Or what if they put this in her file and bring it up the *next* time she does something mischievous?"

Char slumped back in her seat. She certainly hadn't thought about it like that.

Hazel held out a hand. "My Gwynnie really likes it here," she said quietly. "And so do I. We've got friends. Gwyn's got a job she likes. There's a handsome man that wants to take us out for dinner. I don't want to have to leave Aspen Falls yet. We just got here. I'm old. I'm tired of moving. I just want to settle down."

Char reached out and rubbed Hazel's arm. "And we want you to stay. We just got Gwyn back in our lives. None of us want her or you to go."

"Then please don't tell Gwynnie. If you tell her, she'll *have* to tell the Village. If she doesn't know the truth, then she can't be held responsible in any way. But if she knows that I'm involved, she'll have to tell, and we'll be on the interstate out of town by tomorrow."

Char sighed. She certainly didn't want to lose her friends. She felt the pressure to make a decision weighing heavily on her shoulders. Finally, she sighed. "I don't know what to say. I can't think right now. I'll go back to the park and tell Vic and Phil what happened and see what they think."

Hazel pushed herself to her feet, grabbing her purse. "Then I'm going with you."

"Me too!" Loni stood up quickly and then just as quickly fell back down to the sofa. "Whoa," she groaned, holding her head. "I stood up too fast. Maybe it would be a good idea to call poison control before we go."

"Poison control?" asked Char, looking down at Loni with worry. "What happened?"

"Loni drank a half a bottle of NyQuil," said Hazel.

"Loni! Why in the world…?" began Char.

"It's a long story," Hazel assured her. "I think she's a little drunk."

Char sighed and hooked her arms under Loni's to pull her to her feet. "Oh, well, for heaven's sake! We'll stop at Bailey's Bakery and Sweets on the way. I've got just the thing to fix you up."

"Where's Gwyn?" hollered Phyllis as Char, Hazel, and Loni emerged from Char's car.

"She's not coming," Char shouted back across the park. She led the group of women across the grass to the bench where George Petroski still lay motionless.

"Not coming?" asked Vic. "You mean you couldn't find her?"

"It's a long story," Char promised. "But I think we're

just going to have to call the police without telling her after all."

"But I thought we agreed she needed to know first?" said Phil. "That was the whole reason you left Vic and me alone with a dead body in the first place!"

"I mean, yeah, that was the plan, until…" Char looked at Hazel and Loni.

Phyllis stared at Loni, in her ridiculous get-up. "Is that you, Loni Hodges?"

"Yeah, it's me," she answered, her voice once again muffled by her mask.

"What are you doing here?"

"I was at Hazel's apartment when Char came over."

"Hazel's apartment!" said Phyllis in shock. "What were you doing there?"

"That's part of the long story," said Char. "I'll give you the short version. George had a heart attack while he and Hazel were…" She glanced over at Hazel, who stood motionless and somber, before clearing her throat. "Uh-hm…were being intimate."

"Intimate?!" shouted Phyllis, her eyes bulging.

Vic's jaw dropped. "You mean…?"

"They were having sex?!" Phyllis finished Vic's sentence. She stared at Hazel.

Char nodded, her cheeks reddening. "Yes. That's what I've gathered. And after she realized he was dead, she panicked and called Loni and somehow they decided they could fix the situation by moving the body."

"So you moved him to the park?!" Phyllis spread her

arms out wide as she stared at Loni and Hazel. "Why in the world didn't you just put him back in his room?"

"There were complications," said Loni.

"Complications!" sputtered Vic. "It was more complicated to put him in his room than it was to drag him all the way to the park and leave him on a park bench?"

"Must we rehash all of this again?" asked Hazel. "We might have panicked a little."

"How'd you get him all the way here?" asked Vic.

"We drove him," said Loni.

"Drove him! Neither of you have a car!" said Phyllis.

Loni held up a finger. "I have a golf cart."

Phyllis's jaw dropped. "You drove a dead body all the way to the park *in a golf cart*?!"

Loni shrugged. "No one seemed to notice. People waved at us. They probably thought he was alive."

Char sighed and glanced up at Phyllis. "Look. What's done is done. Let's deal with the situation moving forward." Her eyes swung uncomfortably towards the body. "I do think it's time to call the police."

"But what about Gwyn? Don't you think it's doubly important to tell her what's going on now that her mother is involved in this mess?" asked Phyllis.

Char grimaced. "The girls are concerned that if the Village finds out that Hazel was involved in George's death, that might be a strike against her. Too many strikes and they could kick Hazel and Gwyn out. If they get kicked out, Gwyn won't be able to stay in Aspen Falls without a job."

Phyllis's mouth hung open.

"But, lollipop, if George had a heart attack, surely they can't count that as a strike against Hazel!" said Vic.

"We don't know that for sure. Senior living centers can be finicky about the rules. Perhaps we're better off just calling the police and letting them establish that it was a natural death. No one needs to know that Hazel was involved at all. If we tell Gwyn, she'll be duty-bound to report it."

"But—" began Vic.

"You're right," agreed Phyllis, talking over Vic's objection. "We can't tell Gwyn. She'll *have* to tell the Village. And we just got her back in our lives. I don't want her and Hazel to have to leave Aspen Falls."

"Exactly. So let's just call the cops, then," said Char, pulling out her phone. "I'm pretty sure I've got Detective Whitman's number in my contacts. I think it would be best just to call him directly."

"But if we call him, won't we be tied to George's death?" asked Vic.

Char shook her head. "Not necessarily. I mean, we just happened upon him on our walk. That's the truth."

"But aren't these Loni's tire tracks leading right to his body? Won't they see those and wonder if someone dumped him here?" asked Vic.

All of the women's mouths hung open.

"Oh my God," breathed Loni. "I—I can't be discovered…"

"I hadn't thought of that," said Char.

"Me either," agreed Phyllis.

"So now what?" asked Hazel.

Char looked up to see a car drive down the street behind them. She shook her head. "I don't know, but I don't think we can stay here for much longer. What if someone comes to the park? Or what if someone in one of the houses across the street is watching? It's too obvious that something's going on."

"Well, we've already moved the body once," said Loni. "My vote is that we move it again. Somewhere that doesn't have tire tracks that can be traced back to me."

"Ladies, ladies! I don't think you're thinking clearly right now. George is dead. You can't keep moving his body! Not only is it disrespectful to the deceased, but I'm sure you're breaking an assortment of laws by moving him."

Phyllis frowned and gestured towards Hazel and Loni. "I'm pretty sure Thelma and Louise already broke a few laws when they moved him earlier." She shook her head. "No, we have to get him out of here."

"My vote's to move the body too," agreed Hazel.

"But to where?" asked Loni.

Char shook her head. "I don't know, but I do know we can't stay here. Let's put him in the car, and we'll talk about it when we've got him properly stowed away and there aren't cars driving past."

Phyllis glanced over her shoulder. "How are we getting him to the car?"

Loni's shoulders slumped forward. "Do I have to do *everything*?" She wiggled her fingers and George's body lurched off the bench so that it hovered in the air horizontally, his arms dangling limply on either side of him.

The sudden motion caught Phyllis off guard. "Ahh!" she screamed, clutching her chest. "You could have warned me you were going to do that!"

"You can't just float his body across the grass like that. Anyone who drives by will see him!" said Char, straightening his body so he looked like he was standing upright again. "There, that's better. Now let's go."

Working together, the women managed to get George into the car. Hazel, Loni, and Vic sat in the backseat. Phyllis and Char sat in the front seat with George between them. "How did I draw the short end of the stick, that I have to sit next to the dead man?" asked Phyllis as Char pulled the car away from the curb.

"I have to sit next to him, too," said Char, giving a sideways glance at George, whose head lolled to the side, precariously close to Phyllis's shoulder, making Phyllis slide an inch closer to the passenger-side door to avoid touching him.

"Well, he wouldn't fit in the backseat with all this stuff back here," said Loni, crowded between a stack of nested cardboard boxes and the door. "What's with all these boxes anyway?"

Char's eyes widened. She didn't want to tell Loni that she and Phyllis had gotten some boxes from Linda after breakfast so they could begin to pack up some of Kat's things for the rummage sale. "Oh. Umm, I was just going to go through some stuff at the house and get rid of the junk I don't use anymore."

"I'll take whatever you don't want!" said Loni excitedly. "I love old stuff. I'm kind of a pack rat, if you didn't know."

Phyllis rolled her eyes and put her elbow out the open window. "Oh, we knew."

Char smiled at Loni in the rearview mirror. "It's just some odds and ends. Garbage, really. You wouldn't want any of it."

"Oh, you'd be surprised. One man's trash is another man's treasure," said Loni as they cruised down the road.

"Well, you just can't keep everything, Loni," snapped Phyllis. "You just don't have enough room in your house."

"Oh, I can make room, don't worry about me."

Char braked at a four-way stop sign. The sudden shift in inertia made George's head topple forward on his neck, causing his body to slump to the right and his head to fall onto Phyllis' bosom.

"George!" she gasped, staring down at the dead man's head nestled in her cleavage.

Suddenly having the feeling that someone was staring at them, Char glanced out her windshield to the car across from them. She sucked in her breath. "Oh, for heaven's sake, Phil. It's Detective Whitman! Act natural!"

Phyllis stared at George's head resting on her chest. Her brows were lifted so high they looked as if they could jump off her face at any moment and brush against the car's ceiling. "How natural am I supposed to act? There's a dead man motorboating my girls."

Char took off forward, as did Detective Whitman. She plastered a fake ear-to-ear grin on her face and gave him a little twiddling of her fingers as they passed each other. "Smile and wave, girls. Smile and wave."

All the girls in the car and Vic waved as Detective Whitman passed. His head swiveled on his neck to follow the car curiously, but he gave a little wave himself. The second he passed them by, Phyllis pulled George's head off her chest and shoved him back towards the middle of the car. "Good Lord, the first man to touch my boobs in over two decades and he's dead," snapped Phyllis. "The things I do for my girlfriends."

Char kept her eyes trained on her rearview mirror. She was just waiting for Detective Whitman to whip a U-turn, flip on his cherries, and follow them. "The look he just gave us makes me nervous. Maybe we should just take George somewhere safe until we figure this all out."

Vic put his front two paws up on the back of Char's seat. "Gummi Bear, you are not bringing a dead man into our house. I put my foot down!"

Char sighed. "Okay, okay, Vic. I agree, we won't take him to our house."

"And I'm pretty sure bringing stray bodies home is against my lease agreement," said Phyllis.

"Well, we can't take him back to the Village!" said Hazel.

Char put on her blinker. "Alright, then it's settled. We'll take him to Kat's and deal with him there. Certainly no one will object to him hanging out at her house."

10

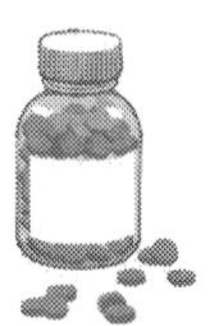

Both Kat's and Loni's houses were born of the same era when Victorian homes had been the fashion statement of their generation. Over the years, however, Loni had neglected her home, where Kat had done the complete opposite. She'd managed to keep her home an impeccable shrine to the original construction and era.

The girls pulled up into the driveway and scanned the neighborhood to ensure that the coast was clear before pulling George from the car. Loni used her magic to do the heavy lifting while Phyllis and Char maneuvered his body out of the car, up the steps, and through the door into the front room.

"Just put him down on the chair, Lon," said Char, holding Vic in her arms. The two of them plopped down onto a chair, and Char's head fell backwards. "Oh! What a morning! Who knew our little walk was going to go so very wrong!"

Phyllis took the seat next to her. "Oh, you're telling me! I am exhausted!"

"So now what?" asked Hazel, staring at George's lifeless corpse.

Char lifted her head. "I have no idea. We can't keep him here for long. We've got to figure something out, but the oatmeal I had for breakfast has worn off. I'm starving. I need to eat before my brain will start working again."

Phyllis pointed a finger at her. "Well, if you'd eat a hearty breakfast like I did, then you wouldn't be so starved!"

Char stood up. "Ha!" she cackled. "It's not like I'm moving dead bodies before lunch every day. I'd say today was a bit of a *special* occasion, wouldn't you?"

Phyllis shrugged.

Loni pointed at George's body as Char walked towards the kitchen. "You're going to go make lunch and just leave him here?"

Char frowned. "Yeah?"

Hazel shook her head. "We can't just leave him by the front door! What if Gwynnie comes looking for me and finds him here?"

Phyllis groaned. "The girls are right, Char. We can't take a break until we've got him hidden."

"Ugh," groaned Char. "Let's get it over with. We'll put him in one of the bedrooms on the second floor. Even if Gwyn does come looking for Haze, you wouldn't think she'd go looking up there."

"Do your thing, Lon," said Phyllis, wiggling her fingers at George.

Loni sighed but fluttered her fingers and moved George once again. This time, they floated him up the stairs.

Char opened the first door on the left. It was a cozy little room with a hand-stitched yellow-and-pink rosebud quilt on the bed. "Just put him on the bed," she said, tossing a hand out towards the bed.

Loni lowered him onto the center of the bed and took a step back.

"Poor George," said Vic, from Char's arms.

Char nodded. "Yes, poor, poor George."

"It sucks to grow old," said Phyllis, putting an arm around Hazel's shoulders.

Hazel just stood staring at his body quietly.

"Yes, it does," agreed Char.

Phyllis squeezed Hazel's shoulder. "You okay, Haze? This wasn't your fault. You know that, right? It's just a natural part of a person's life cycle."

Hazel nodded stiffly. "Yeah. I'm okay. I just feel bad."

Char reached a hand out to take Hazel's hand. "Don't feel bad, Hazel. Phil's right, you know. This wasn't your fault."

"I feel bad for George," said Hazel. "He seemed like a nice man."

"Had you two been seeing each other for a while?" asked Phyllis.

Hazel shook her head. "No. I'd probably only said two words to the man before he knocked on my window."

"What?!" asked Char. "You and George didn't have a relationship before you two *had sex*?!"

Hazel glared up at Char. "Hey, I don't judge you."

Char held up a hand innocently. "I'm not judging. No judging. I'm just a little surprised."

"Me too! My neighbors don't randomly crawl into my windows to have sex with me," said Phyllis. "Not that I'd be opposed to that," she mumbled under her breath.

Hazel shrugged. "I was a little surprised, but I'm always up for a good time." She turned to face the door and waved the women along. "Alright. Let's go eat."

On the way down the stairs, Phyllis fingered odds and ends, wondering which items of Kat's they'd be forced to part with. The framed needlepoint tapestry in the hall, the antique mirror at the bottom of the stairs, or the intricately carved mahogany dining set with the fluted legs and high-backed chairs. She saw Char eyeing her as she ran her finger along the matching china cabinet, and she also saw the distinct shaking of her head. She didn't want to discuss those matters now. Not with Loni present.

"I'm going to make myself a sandwich. Does anyone else want anything?" asked Char, heading for the kitchen.

Phyllis patted her stomach. "Nope. My eggs and bacon are still working in the tank."

"I'm good," said Loni.

"Hazel, I bet you're famished. You want me to make you a sandwich?" asked Char, rubbing Hazel's shoulder.

Hazel shook her head. "A man's dead. I don't know how you can think about food at a time like this."

Char shrugged. "A girl's gotta eat." She pointed towards the front parlor. "You girls sit down, Vic and I will be right in."

Phyllis nodded and led the group to the front room, where a figure obscured by shadows was seated on an antique chaise lounge. It took a moment for Phyllis's eyes to make out the familiar grey hat and realize the figure was none other than George Petroski! "Ahhhh!" she screamed, nearly jumping out of her skin.

Hazel and Loni followed Phyllis's pointing finger and then promptly joined in on the screaming.

"Ahhh!"

"Ahhh!"

"Ahhhhhh!" Phyllis continued, running from the parlor back towards the kitchen. Char and Vic met her in the hall.

"What is it?" asked Char.

Phyllis turned and pointed a trembling finger towards the parlor while Hazel and Loni hobbled behind her as fast as their legs would carry them. "George!" she screamed.

"George?" asked Char. "What about George?"

Phyllis's mouth went dry as she pointed back towards what she'd seen in the parlor. George seated on the antique chaise lounge! "In the parlor!"

"What's in the parlor?" asked Char. With her brows knitted together, she shook her head.

"George!" said Phyllis, out of breath.

"What about George?" asked Char again.

"Do you not understand English, woman?" hollered Loni. "He's in the parlor!"

"Who's in the parlor?" asked Char.

"George!" the three of them replied in unison.

With stunned, wide eyes, Char gasped, "George is in the parlor?"

"That's what we've been trying to tell you!" said Phyllis, her heart beating wildly in her chest.

"Oh, you've got to be mistaken. George is in the guest room on the second floor!" Intending to prove to the girls that they had lost their minds, Char and Vic marched into the parlor.

Phyllis followed her trepidatiously with Hazel and Loni clinging to the back of her sweater like a couple of sandburs.

"Ahhh!" screamed Char when she saw George sitting with his arm slung over the chair's ornate wooden back. "It's George!"

Phyllis peered over Char's shoulder. "That's what we've been trying to tell you!"

"How'd he get down here?!" she bellowed.

Phyllis shook her head. "I have no idea. Loni?"

Everyone turned to stare at Loni. "Me?! I was with you guys!"

"You didn't do a little accidental finger dancing on your way down the stairs?" asked Phyllis.

Loni held her hands up and stared at her fingers through her thick glasses. "Not that I'm aware of."

"You had to have done something. Dead men just

don't get up and walk down the stairs on their own," said Char.

"Unless they aren't dead," said Vic.

Slowly, all eyes turned to stare at George. Char gasped. "He has to be dead! Phyllis checked his pulse!" said Char finally, shaking her head.

"Maybe Phyllis didn't know what she was doing," suggested Loni.

"Well, did you two check his pulse?" asked Char, looking pointedly at Loni and Hazel.

Hazel shook her head. "I didn't check his pulse."

"Hazel!" sputtered Loni. "You told me he was dead. If I had known you didn't check, I certainly would have."

Hazel frowned. "You didn't let me finish. I didn't check his pulse, but I did hold a mirror up to his mouth. Trust me. I wouldn't have gone to all this trouble if all the man needed was a nap. He was dead."

Vic put a paw on Char's cheeks. "Sugar snap, maybe you should check his pulse. Just to be sure."

Char glanced around the room.

Phyllis gave her a little prodding shove. "Go on. Then you'll see I know a dead man when I touch one."

Char grimaced. "Why do I have to do it?"

Loni groaned and pushed her way through the crowded room. "Oh, for heaven's sake," she sighed. "I'll do it." She held two fingers against the vein in his neck and the whole room fell silent.

Finally, Hazel threw her arms up. "Well?"

Loni dropped her arm and looked down at him sadly. "He's dead. Deader than dead. Super dead."

"We get it," snapped Phyllis.

They all looked at George again. "I just don't understand how he got down here," said Char.

Hazel crooked her thumb over her shoulder at Loni. "It had to be spirit fingers here."

Phyllis nodded. She had no other answer than to think it had to have been Loni too. She grabbed Loni by the shoulders and pointed her at George. "Time to move him again. But once he's moved, we're holstering those weapons," she said.

"I swear it wasn't me," said Loni, pointing her fingers once again at George. She wiggled them and he lifted off the old-fashioned fainting chair.

Together the group maneuvered him up the stairs.

"Let's take him to the third floor this time," said Char, pointing up the steps even further.

Phyllis led the way, flicking the lights on in the hallway on the third floor. Suddenly, an idea hit her. "I know where to put him. Let's put him in Kat's spell room in the north turret. He should be snug as a bug in there."

"Lead the way," said Loni, still wiggling her fingers and breaking a bit of a sweat doing it. "This guy isn't holding himself up."

Weeks earlier, when the women had been searching Kat's house for their missing spell book, Phyllis had been in Kat's spell room. She led them to the door at the end of the hall, up a small rounded flight of stairs, and into a round room. On one end, a table was set up with a book holder, holding the spell book they'd recovered from the man who had stolen it not long ago. Surrounding it were an array of candles and jars of ingredients for the many spells Kat enjoyed performing.

As Loni and Char got George properly seated on a rocking chair, Phyllis ran her hand along the closed book's brown leather binding. It felt good to have the book they'd been given by Sorceress Halliwell home where it belonged.

"Okay," panted Loni. "He's settled. Now let's go get a bite to eat. All this activity has definitely worked up my appetite too."

Phyllis pointed at her. "Keep your hands where we can see them, Loni Hodges. We don't want a repeat of what happened before."

Loni nodded and put her arms out in front of her. "Stare at them all you want. You won't see a single flinch out of these puppies."

As the crew filed out of the room, Phyllis took one more look into the spell room before flicking off the lights, pulling the door shut behind her and locking it. She pulled the key from the door handle and put it in her pocket. "You aren't going anywhere this time, George!"

11

This time Phyllis kept her eyes glued to Loni's hands the entire way down the three flights of stairs. When they got to the bottom of the stairs, she took hold of Loni's wrist.

"Whew! That was a doozy! Vic and I are going to go try and make lunch again," said Char with Vic propped up on her shoulder. She linked arms with Hazel. "Come on, Hazel. I know you're not hungry, but you need to eat something too. Gwyn would be furious if we didn't make you eat."

"Loni and I will be right there. I just want to make sure George hasn't made a reappearance," said Phyllis, dragging Loni with her towards the living room and accidentally knocking her into a small decorative hall table along the way.

"Watch it," snapped Loni.

"Sorry, I just want to keep an eye on you and make sure you're not doing any hocus-pocus on George."

Loni's eyes widened. "I'm not! I didn't do any the first time either."

With her adrenaline racing, Phyllis poked her head carefully into the parlor. The chaise lounge was empty. She glanced around at the rest of the furniture and let out a sigh of relief. *No George!*

Loni noticed too. She wagged her finger in Phyllis's face. "See!"

And then a set of shrill screams ripped apart the air between them! "Ahhh!"

Phyllis's eyes widened. "Char!!" Loni and Phil raced towards the kitchen, where they found Hazel clinging to Char's back. Vic was still in her arms, but his head was buried in her chest.

Panic covered Char's face, and her finger was aimed at a chair on the other side of the kitchen, where George Petroski sat politely with his legs crossed and his head lolling to one side, the vague remnants of a grin plastered on his face.

"It's George," said Char, her voice little more than a choked whisper.

"I see that it's George," agreed Phyllis, unable to tear her eyes off of his motionless body.

"I told you it wasn't me!" said Loni, hiding behind Phyllis's plentiful backside.

"I believe you now," muttered Phyllis. "What in the world is going on? How does he keep getting down here?"

"I have no idea. Maybe the place is haunted," suggested Char.

"Haunted?" Hazel peered around Char. "I-I have to

go now. Gwynnie's going to be looking for me aaand I can't get in trouble."

Loni's head bobbled too. "I have to go too. I think I hear Ed calling me. My cats are probably hungry. I can't let them starve. Someone might call the ASPCA on me."

Char swatted at the two of them gently. "I'll take you both home when we figure out what in the world we're going to do about George. Obviously he doesn't want to be left in a bedroom."

"I hate to say I told you so, but I told you so," said Vic. "We should have called the police back at the park."

"We couldn't! Not without implicating Loni's golf cart and by association Loni!" Phyllis reminded him. "And then it wouldn't be the ASPCA she'd be dealing with. It'd be the AFPD!"

"We could have just driven him down to the police station and dropped him off then," said Vic.

Char shook her head. "Sweetheart, that wouldn't have worked. They would have just wanted to know where we found him. We would have had to say the park and then they'd go over to the park and find the tire tracks. No. We did the right thing. We just have to figure out what to do now."

There was a knock at the door.

Char and Phyllis exchanged deer-in-the-headlight stares.

"Who in the world?" asked Phyllis.

"Are any of you expecting someone?" asked Char.

Phyllis shook her head. "I'm not expecting anybody."

Loni froze. "See. It's probably the ASPCHA. They're already onto me. I need to go home."

"It's not the ASPCHA, Loni," hissed Phyllis.

Loni sucked in her breath. "Then maybe it's the FBI," she whispered. "Maybe they followed me. Oh my gosh. Maybe they found out about George!" Her hands went to her head. She pulled her mask back down over her face and then tugged her hood over the mask. Her head shook as she paced the room. "This is bad. This is very bad. Everyone be very, very quiet." She held her hands out as if to silence the group.

Phyllis slugged Loni. "It's not the FBI, you idiot. The FBI doesn't even know you're here."

Loni tugged off her mask and scowled at Phyllis. "You don't know that, Phil."

There was a knock at the door again. This time it was harder and louder. "Girls?" hollered a voice from the door. "It's Gwyn."

"Oh my God," hissed Char. "It's Gwynnie."

"Maybe if we're just quiet she'll go away," suggested Hazel.

"I know you're here. Char's car is parked in the driveway."

"Fudgesticks!" cursed Hazel.

"We can't let her in," said Loni. "She'll see George!"

Phyllis grabbed an apron from its hanging spot on the wall and tossed it on top of George. "There."

Char rolled her eyes. "Brilliant work, genius. She'll never notice the legs hanging out from under the apron."

"I'm sorry," snapped Phyllis. "Then you think of something smarty pants!"

"Simple, we've got to get him out of here."

"But he keeps popping back up again. What are we supposed to do?" asked Loni.

Char batted a hand at him. "Let's get him to the basement. Phyllis, you go entertain Gwyn while we hide him. We'll tie him to the foundation if we have to."

Loni's shoulders slumped as she stared at George. "I have to move him *again*?!"

"Yes!" hissed Char. "Now come on."

The pounding on the door continued as Phyllis weaved her way through the house to the front door. She took a deep breath. *Time to play it cool, Phil.* She plastered a big smile on her face and opened the door to see a frazzled Gwyn standing in front of her.

"There you are!" breathed Gwyn, pushing herself inside the house without an invitation. "I've been knocking!"

"Oh, I'm sorry. We were making a snack in the kitchen and didn't hear you. What's up?"

Gwyn looked frazzled. "I'm looking for Mom! She's missing from the Village. Have you seen her?"

"Hazel? Oh yeah, didn't Char call to tell you? We picked her up earlier."

Gwyn's shoulders slumped forward. "Oh, thank God!" she breathed. "Well, I did have a missed call from Char's phone, but she didn't leave a message. I was on a field trip with some Village residents and we had quite the emergency, so I wasn't able to check my phone. I tried calling her back several times, but she didn't answer."

"Oh, I see," said Phyllis, nodding her head knowingly. "Yeah, we've been running errands. Kind of busy, you know. Running here, running there. She probably just didn't hear her phone ringing."

"You could have left a note. I've been worried sick about Mom. I didn't know that you'd taken her. I thought maybe she ran off again."

Phyllis rubbed Gwyn's shoulder. "Oh. I'm sorry, Gwynnie. I assumed Char'd gotten ahold of you. Guess not, goll darn it." She snapped her fingers, hoping that Gwyn wouldn't notice her nervousness.

Gwyn frowned. "Well, why did you guys pick her up anyway? She's supposed to be home sick right now."

"Oh, right," said Phyllis. Her eyes flicked around the room, unable to make eye contact with her friend as she thought up a good reason that they'd picked Hazel up. She gulped hard.

"Did Char bring Mom that old witch remedy she was telling me about at breakfast?"

Phyllis's mouth gaped. "Remedy?" She swallowed and then slowly nodded her head. "Yesss, remedy. Exactly." Her head bobbed like a bobblehead doll on the dash of a car now. She grinned. "Yup. That's what we were doing over there, alright. We'd gone over there to bring Hazel her remedy, and it kicked in immediately." She snapped her fingers.

"It did?" Gwyn's eyes lit up. "Mom's feeling better?"

Phyllis couldn't seem to stop her head from bouncing up and down. "Mm-hmm."

Gwyn clapped her hands together. "Great! Where is she? I'd like to see her." She peered further into the house. "And where's Char? I'd like to thank her for making Mom feel better."

"Oh, Char and Haze…" Phyllis looked back into the house too, hoping like mad they'd gotten George firmly attached to something in the basement. "Yeah, they're…" She looked at Gwyn again and smiled uncomfortably.

Gwyn tipped her head sideways. "Are you sweating, Phyllis?"

Phyllis touched her forehead. Sure enough, her brow was damp. Her hand came away wet. "Hmm. Yeah," she said. "It's a warm day."

Gwyn turned around and looked at the daylight behind her. "It's pleasant, but it's not *that* warm. I hope you're not coming down with what Mom had?"

Phyllis waved away that notion. "Oh no. I'm sure I'm not."

Gwyn brushed past Phyllis, walking towards the kitchen. "Good. Now where is everybody? What are you girls doing here anyway?"

"Well, we were going to…"

"Gwynnie!" said Char, emerging from the hallway that led to the basement stairs carrying Vic in her arms. "So nice to see you."

"Oh, there you are!" said Gwyn. She gave Char a quick hug and Vic a scratch under the chin. "Hi, Vic."

"Good afternoon, Gwyndolin," said Vic with a tip of the head.

Gwyn smiled at Char. "Thank you so much for giving Mom that remedy you had. I will forever be in your debt for making her better. I was so worried it was going to turn into pneumonia."

Char smiled back at her blankly.

Phyllis elbowed Char. "I was just telling Gwyn how quickly Hazel responded to your cold potion."

Char nodded, her eyes bright. "Uh-huh. Great. Yes! The cold potion." She snapped her fingers. "Worked like a charm. Just like I thought it would! It was almost as if Hazel was never sick in the first place!"

Phyllis elbowed Char again, this time landing it in Char's gut.

"Oof," grunted Char, shooting Phyllis the evil eye.

But Gwyn didn't notice. She was too busy staring down the hallway. "Where's Mom?"

"Oh, she stopped to use the little girls' room. She'll be out in a second."

Loni appeared next, giving Gwyn a little wave.

"Loni!" said Gwyn, in surprise. "You're here too? Wow, you girls are having a party, and I wasn't even invited?"

Loni curled her lip. "Eh. No booze and no boys. It'd be a pretty lame party if that's what this was."

Gwyn giggled. "I was just kidding. Oh, boy, girls, do I feel better knowing that Mom's safe. What a day I've had!"

Phyllis nodded. "Yeah, you said something earlier about having an emergency with the residents?"

Gwyn's eyes widened. "Yes! We were supposed to have sixteen male residents on the trip today. When we departed the Village, sixteen men were counted on the bus, but lo and behold, when we went to leave the paint-ball field, we only counted *fifteen* men."

"So one of the men went missing during the event?" asked Vic.

Gwyn shook her head. "Well, that's what we thought *at first*. But then we actually did a roster check and discovered that someone had seen Duke Olson on the bus, but Duke Olson hadn't signed up to go on the excursion. So he was our sixteenth man on the way there. But at some point during the activity, Duke left without telling anyone, so when we all go back on the bus, we only had fifteen residents."

"What a pain!" said Phyllis.

Gwyn sighed. "It was not good, that's for sure. So as we were loading up the bus to go back to the Village, and we only had fifteen men, we realized that not only was Duke Olson missing, but the original sixteenth man was George Petroski. No one remembered seeing him on the way there. That was when we deduced that Duke had somehow gotten on the bus and then disappeared, but George hadn't gotten on at all like he was supposed to."

A little chortle escaped Char's throat as she glanced up at the rest of the girls. "That's crazy!"

"Tell me about it! The whole thing was a big mess, and of course I felt horrible about the whole thing because I had just done a head count instead of a roll call before we left the Village."

Phyllis patted Gwyn's back. "Oh, don't blame yourself now, Gwynnie. You had no way of knowing that all that was going to happen."

Gwyn nodded. "I know. I didn't realize that residents just got on busses they weren't supposed to!"

"So did you ever find the two missing men?" asked Char, gnawing on her lip.

Gwyn frowned. "Puh," she breathed. "We looked for them when we got back to the Village. We checked George's room, but he was nowhere to be found. Duke, though, was sound asleep in his room. We asked him how he'd gotten back from the paintball field, and he swore up and down that he'd never gone with us in the first place."

They heard a toilet flush in the hall behind them.

"So then I went to check on Mom, and lo and behold, she's nowhere to be found either. We checked the whole entire center for both George and Mom and it was like both of them had vanished. I was really starting to panic that something bad had happened."

Phyllis's stomach tipped uneasily. *Little does she know…*

They heard the tapping of a cane coming down the hall.

"Mom!" said Gwyn, the sound of relief colored her voice.

"Hi, Gwynnie. Have fun on the field trip without me?" asked Hazel.

"Unfortunately, I didn't have fun without you," said Gwyn. "It's been a heck of a day. I was worried sick about you. I wish you would have thought to leave me a note that you were going with the girls. I would have felt a lot better knowing that."

"Sorry," said Char. "That was my fault. We were in a hurry. I should have thought to leave a note. She was feeling better, and I just didn't want to leave her there without you."

Gwyn squeezed Char's hand. "Good thinking. I'm so thankful I've got such great friends that will watch out for Mom when I can't be there. You girls have no idea how much you all mean to me." She pulled them together for an impromptu group hug.

Loni wiggled her way out of the hug. "Listen, girls. This is nice and all, but I'm starving. Can we get back to our snack now?"

Gwyn let her arms drop and rubbed one hand on her slim stomach. "Yes, let's have a snack. I haven't eaten since that roll at breakfast, and after all that commotion today, I'm famished!"

Char smiled at her and turned to head to the kitchen. "Me too."

They headed for the kitchen, with Char leading the pack. But when she got there, she put on the brakes.

Gwyn crashed into her backside. "Char!"

Char turned around, in an effort to push Gwyn back towards the front room, but it was too late. Gwyn sucked in her breath as she pointed over Char's shoulder to the man in the grey hat sitting on the chair. "Oh my goodness, Char! Is that George Petroski?"

12

Gwyn couldn't believe what she saw! George was here? Why had the girls brought George Petroski to Kat's house? It didn't make any sense. Gwyn strutted over to the corner where the man sat quietly with his eyes closed. "Mr. Petroski! Everyone at the Village has been looking for you. What are you doing here?"

"Gwyn…," began Char.

Gwyn spun around and wagged a finger at Char. "No, no, no. He should know better. Residents are supposed to check out when leaving the Village. It's bad enough that Mom did it, but she's got a tendency to run off." She turned to face George again. "But Mr. Petroski doesn't."

"But, Gwynnie…," interjected Phyllis.

Gwyn waved a dismissive hand in the air. She didn't want to hear it. She wasn't going to take it easy on the man. He'd up and left and worried the whole retirement community. "He should have known better." She turned to face him again. "Even a note left in your room would have been appreciated, Mr. Petroski."

But George didn't move. His head still rested at the same forty-five-degree angle as it had when she'd first seen him sitting there.

Char let out a breath. "Gwyn, there's something—"

"Mr. Petroski, don't you have anything to say in your defense? It's been a trying day and I'd just like to get you returned to the Village to put everyone's mind at ease. If you're gone another couple of hours, they're going to call the Aspen Falls Police Department. You don't want that, do you?"

Gwyn heard her mother's cane tapping on the tile floor behind her. By the sound of it, Hazel was headed for the front door. She turned around and pointed at her mother. "Stop right there, young lady."

Hazel froze mid-escape.

"What is George Petroski doing here? Did you ask the girls to bring him with you?"

Hazel glanced up at Char with sad basset hound eyes but didn't say anything.

Char put Vic on the floor and took a step forward to take Gwyn's arm. "Gwynnie, maybe we should go sit down in the parlor?"

"Sit?" asked Gwyn, shaking her head in confusion. "I don't get it. Why isn't George or my mother talking? What's going on here?"

"Char's right," agreed Phyllis, taking Gwyn's elbow. "Let's go get you to the sofa."

Gwyn shrugged off their unwelcomed and patronizing gestures. "I don't need to sit on the sofa, girls. I need you to tell me what is going on? First the whole debacle on the field trip. Then George and Mother are missing. Now to find out they're both here? Something isn't right. Tell me what it is!"

Char glanced over at Phyllis, who glanced over at Hazel, who glanced over at Loni. Loni shrugged.

Gwyn's eyes rested on Loni. "Loni? Tell me what happened."

Loni bit her lips between her teeth and shook her head like a petulant child who refused to eat her broccoli. "Uh-uh."

"Loni. Please. Tell me what happened!"

Loni clapped her hands over her mouth and shook her head. "Uh-uh," she grunted.

Gwyn's shoulders fell. "Fine." She turned and walked back over to George. "If my best friends and my own *mother* won't tell me what's going on, then I'll have to get it out of Mr. Petroski."

"Good luck!" said Loni, uncovering her mouth to make the statement and then promptly covering it back up again.

"Ugh," groaned Gwyn. She looked down at George. Something didn't look quite right. His face looked very pale, and his head was at a very uncomfortable angle. "Is he okay? He doesn't look very good."

"He's fine," said Hazel from the other side of the kitchen.

Gwyn lowered her brows and bent over to peer more

closely at George's face. "He doesn't look fine. Mr. Petroski? Are you alright?"

"Ladies, I think you should tell her," whispered Vic. "I mean, she's going to figure it out."

"Tell me what?" asked Gwyn with her face still inches away from George's face. She poked a finger against his shoulder, but he didn't flinch. Her heart started to pound a little harder.

"She's not going to be able to handle it," Phyllis whispered back.

"Girls, I think maybe we should call an ambulance for Mr. Petroski. I don't think he's breathing," said Gwyn, cupping a hand beneath his nose. When she didn't feel any signs of life, she moved her hand from her mouth to his neck to search for a pulse.

"It's the circle of life, she'll understand. I think we have to tell her," whispered Loni.

Gwyn was starting to feel panic rising up inside of her chest like the sun coming over the horizon. "Mr. Petroski?" She put a hand on either of his shoulders now and shook him, harder than she'd intended. The panic was real. She had a sinking feeling that George wasn't breathing. She stopped shaking his shoulders and his head lolled forward, and the momentum kept him falling forward, right into Gwyn's arms. "Ahhh!" she screamed. "Mr. Petroski!"

Loni reacted promptly, reaching a hand out, she fluttered her fingers towards George. Immediately he floated off Gwyn. Loni set him back down on the chair, where his head rolled backwards on his shoulders, his mouth fell open, and his hat fell off, tumbling to the floor.

"I think we should go sit down in the living room now, okay, Gwynnie?" asked Char again as she and Phyllis lifted a stunned Gwyn back up to her feet.

Gwyn's head shook as a trembling finger pointed to one of Kat's kitchen chairs. "Chair is fine," she was able to mutter.

Hazel's cane began to tap against the floor again.

"Stop!" hissed Phyllis as they lowered Gwyn to the chair. "Get back over here, Hazel."

Hazel froze and turned. "Why don't you just tell her, and I'll just be over here?"

Phyllis shook her head. "We're telling her together."

"This is your mess. We're just helping you clean it up. Now get over here and tell Gwyn what happened." Char pointed at the ground.

"I-is h-he d-dead?" asked Gwyn, her outstretched hand still trembling as she pointed at George.

All eyes turned to Hazel.

"What?!"

"Gwyn wants to know if George is dead," said Phyllis with a hand on her hip.

"Of course he's dead!" said Hazel unapologetically. "You think a man with muscle control left in his neck would let his head fall backwards like that?"

"H-he's d-dead?" asked Gwyn.

"Yes," said Char plainly. "George is dead."

Now all eyes were on Gwyn.

Her adrenaline pulsed furiously. Had she really just

stared a dead man in the face and then *shaken him* like he just needed to wake up from a heavy sleep? She felt like she'd had the wind knocked out of her. She fought to suck in a deep breath, but she could only hear wheezing.

Was that *her* wheezing?

She could hear a faraway voice, but she didn't know whose it was. "Loni. Check Kat's pantry for a paper bag. She's hyperventilating. I'll check under the sink."

"Gwynnie? Breathe. Breathe, Gwyn."

Everything was blurry.

The voices sounded farther away.

She heard a high-pitched screeching sound.

Was that her trying to breathe?

Suddenly, someone was shoving a crumpled-up bag in her face. "Breathe in the bag, Gwynnie."

"Inhale. Exhale. You can do it."

She felt cool air raining down on her face.

"There you go, Gwynnie. Inhale. Exhale."

"Should we lay her on the floor?"

"No, I think she's going to be okay."

Her vision began to clear slightly. She could see Loni standing in front of her, fanning her face with something. The air felt good.

She closed her eyes and sucked in a deep breath.

"Gwynnie. Can you hear me? Are you alright?"

Gwyn thought she felt something close to her face. She opened her eyes again to see Loni's oversized eyes staring back at her, only inches away from her. "Ahhh!" she screamed.

13

"Ahhh!" screamed Loni, Haze, Char, and Phyllis.

"Roof, roof, roof!" barked Vic.

Gwyn's heart pounded wildly in her chest as the whole room screamed. Finally, she stopped screaming and looked around the room.

Panting heavily, everyone else stopped screaming too.

"What's going on?!" demanded Gwyn, finally snapping out of her panic attack.

"You had a panic attack and scared the living crap out of me!" said Hazel, holding her heart. "I need my pills!"

"We didn't bring your pills," said Phyllis. "You'll just have to take some deep breaths and try and relax yourself."

"I have some in my purse," said Gwyn, pointing to the spot on the floor next to George where her purse had fallen.

Phyllis walked over to the purse to retrieve a pill for Hazel while Gwyn stared at George's lifeless body.

"So George is dead?! How'd he die? Why's he here? What happened? And why haven't you called for an ambulance?" demanded Gwyn.

Char sat down in the chair across from Gwyn. "We wanted to call the ambulance, but it's not that simple unfortunately."

"Not that simple? Why not? The man is dead? Maybe if you'd called an ambulance, he'd still be alive!"

Char shook her head. "No, I don't think so, Gwynnie. George was already dead when we found him."

That caused Gwyn to take pause. She thought about it for a second and then crooked her head sideways. "You found him dead?"

They all nodded.

"In Kat's house?!"

"Oh, no, he wasn't in Kat's house when we found him, exactly," said Phyllis, wringing her hands.

"So then what's he doing here?"

"We brought him here," said Loni matter-of-factly.

"Why in the world would you have brought a dead man's body to Kat's house and not have called an ambulance or the police?"

"Well, we found him at the park, but we couldn't call the police or an ambulance because then they'd figure out how he *got* to the park," said Loni.

"Loni!" snapped Hazel, at the sink getting a drink of water. She put her glass down on the counter and then pretended to be zipping her lips shut. "Zippp."

Loni mashed her lips between her teeth.

"Don't listen to her, Loni. Tell me what happened. How did George get to the park?"

Loni shook her head.

"Hazel. We have to tell Gwyn everything," said Char, her shoulders hanging low.

"It's only going to make it worse on her if we tell her. Then she'll know and she'll be complicit."

Gwyn's blue eyes widened. "Complicit?! In moving his body?" She looked up at Phyllis and Char for answers. "Oh, come on, girls. I need to know everything. Quit beating around the bush. How did George Petroski get to the park?"

"I drove him!" said Loni, making Gwyn's head turn.

"*You* drove him? With what? You don't have a car!"

"With my Uncle Ben's golf cart. It was in my backyard. That's why we couldn't call the police, because we left tire tracks in the mud. They'd know we were the ones that dropped him off there."

Gwyn made a face. "Hello? You're witches. You guys couldn't have figured out a spell to cover up tire tracks? Instead you have to drag a dead body back to Kat's house?!"

Char, Phyllis, Loni, Vic, and Hazel all exchanged looks.

"Well, that never occurred to me," said Char, throwing her hands out on either side of her.

"Me either," said Phyllis with a smile. "I was so busy worrying about Hazel that I wasn't even thinking about that."

"Worrying about Hazel? What do you mean worrying about Hazel? How are you involved in this Mother?"

Hazel let out a heavy breath and then lifted a shoulder. "Meh. He might have died in my room."

Gwyn scampered to her feet. "In *your room*? You mean in our apartment?!"

"No, in my room at the brothel. Of course my room in our apartment!"

"What was George Petroski doing in our apartment?"

Hazel refused to speak then.

Gwyn stared at Loni.

"They were making whoopee."

"Whoopee?!"

Loni nodded seriously. "You know, playing hide the salami."

"I know what whoopee is, Loni! But I don't understand. My *mother* was having *sex* with George Petroski?"

Loni nodded. "And he had a heart attack."

Gwyn sucked in her breath. "Mother!"

Hazel's face went pale. "I'm sorry, Gwynnie. I didn't mean to kill him. I swear. I can't help it that I'm so sexy that I made his heart race so fast that he had a heart attack."

"Oh brother," said Phyllis, rolling her eyes.

Gwyn held two hands out in front of herself to steady her thoughts. "Okay, okay. So let me get this straight. You and George were having sex and he had a heart attack and died, and *you* didn't think to call Nurse Brenda, who was sitting right outside your door?"

Hazel shuffled over to her daughter. "Gwyn, you don't understand. I was trying to protect you."

Gwyn's chin jutted out. "Protect me? What in the world are you talking about, Mom? Protect me from what?"

"If I told Brenda what had happened, that I was responsible for George's death, she'd have told the bigwigs at the Village and we might have been kicked out! I know how much you like it here in Aspen Falls, and I didn't want to have to make you move."

"But, Mom! George's death wasn't your fault."

"We tried to tell her that," said Char, nodding.

Gwyn shook her head. "So she called you two instead of calling an ambulance?"

Loni thumbed her chest proudly. "Nope, she called me!"

"You! Why in the world did you call Loni, Mom?"

Loni's face crumpled. "Obviously she called me because of my problem-solving prowess."

"No, I called her because I knew the other two were on your payroll. I knew they'd tell you. I was pretty sure I could get that one to keep my secret," admitted Hazel, pointing at Loni.

They spent the next ten minutes filling Gwyn in on all the whys and hows of George's death and how he'd subsequently wound up at Kat's house.

Gwyn shook her head. "I can't believe you didn't just leave Mr. Petroski at the park. Then we wouldn't be dealing with trying to figure out what to do now!"

"We explained why," argued Phyllis. "And I'm sorry

that it didn't occur to us to cover the tire tracks. We're old. We were panicking. Cut us some slack."

"Well, we've got to call the police now. There's no other choice. We have to right all the wrongs you've made," said Gwyn.

Vic nodded agreeably. "I couldn't agree more. Sugar lips, call Detective Whitman. He'll handle this all with the utmost respect for George and our situation."

"Respect!" breathed Phyllis. "He'll throw the book at us all now! We tampered with a crime scene! We moved a dead body!"

"Lots of times!" agreed Loni, looking at her fingers.

"Yeah, speaking of moving George's body," said Char, "I wonder how he managed to get out of the basement. I tied him to a water pipe. I thought for sure he was going to stay put that time."

"What are you talking about?" asked Gwyn.

"He," Phyllis began, pointing at George, "keeps finding his way back to the first floor. We put him in a bedroom on the second floor once, and he somehow found his way into the parlor. So we put him in Kat's spell room, and he found his way to the kitchen."

"Then we put him in the basement and tied him to the water pipe with a rope we found down there, and as you can see, he made his way back to the kitchen again," said Char.

Gwyn's jaw dropped. "You're kidding?"

"Nope. Wish we were. It's creeping me out, if we're being honest," said Phyllis. "I have a bad feeling that Kat's house is haunted."

Hazel tugged on Gwyn's sweater. "Gwynnie. I think we should go. It's way past my nap time, and you know how I get if I don't nap on schedule."

"We're not going anywhere until we've dealt with the body. Now I don't know what this haunting stuff is all about, but we don't have time to think about that now. Now we need to figure out what to do with Mr. Petroski. The Village is worried sick about him. We have to do something."

"Well, now that we've all tampered with the body, I don't think we can just call the police," said Char. Then she looked at Vic. "I hate to say it, sweetheart. I know you wanted us to call Detective Whitman, but Phil's right. He could very likely manage to trump up some charges on all of us, and we're too old to do hard time. And the Village can't find out that Gwyn and Hazel are involved, or Gwyn might get fired and the two of them will get evicted."

Phyllis nodded. "Exactly. We don't want you and Hazel to have to leave town, Gwynnie. Our best bet is to hide the body somewhere that the police will find it and they can do their own deductive reasoning to figure out George had a heart attack and put it down in the books as death by natural causes and we're all in the clear."

"Deductive reasoning?" asked Gwyn.

"You know. They'll do one of those procedures where they cut him open and look at all of his innards and see what went wrong," explained Phyllis, gesturing with her hands.

"You mean an autopsy?" asked Gwyn.

Phyllis nodded. "Yeah, one of those. They'll do one of those and all will be well." She wiped her hands together. "Then case closed. We're in the clear."

"Well, how exactly are we supposed to get the body to the police without them knowing it was us?" asked Vic.

"And where are we supposed to put him? Just drop him off at their front door?" asked Char, raising an eyebrow.

"Well, if we want them to do an autopsy, then maybe we ought to just drop him off at the place that autopsies are done," suggested Phyllis with a shrug.

Char grimaced. "You want us to *sneak* George Petroski's body into the Aspen Falls Morgue? In broad daylight?! Are you *crazy*?!"

"Crazy is as crazy does," said Phyllis with a half grin. "We've already proven we're a little insane by bringing George here. I guess this will just finish the job. But first, I think we need lunch. I'm starving."

"Me too," said Char. "I brought some lunch meat over the other day. Who wants a turkey sandwich?"

14

With her nose smashed against the glass, Hazel cupped her hands around her face. "It's like they're having a white uniform convention in there."

"Yeah, it's definitely a meeting of some sort," agreed Phyllis with her own nose smashed to the glass. "This is a disaster. How are we supposed to get George in there with all these people standing around?"

"We have to create a diversion," said Char. "Get them all to leave so we can get in there with George."

"A diversion," said Loni, scratching her chin. "Hmm. I think I have an idea!" She waggled her eyebrows behind her hockey mask. "Follow me."

She led the girls around to the back of the Aspen Falls Medical Center, where the morgue was located, and then took hold of Phyllis and Hazel's hands. She nodded her head towards Char and Gwyn. "Now take their hands too," she instructed before closing her eyes. "Just follow my lead."

Phyllis, Char, and Gwyn exchanged concerned looks, but took each other's hands and closed their eyes too.

Then Loni began to chant.

"We call upon thee, Ed.
We summon you to this place.
Bring the feline relatives,
Come fast like in a race.
Don't dilly-dally or waste much time.
Your presence is implored.
Come now with all the cats,
And of your own accord."

The wind began to come up around them. Their hair all blew around their faces, except Loni's. Hers was snugly tucked up into the hood of her bathrobe. Hazel pried one eye open and looked at Gwyn with raised eyebrows. Gwyn shrugged and then they all joined in.

"We call upon thee, Ed.
We summon you to this place.
Bring the feline relatives,
Come fast like in a race.
Don't dilly-dally or waste much time.
Your presence is implored.
Come now with all the cats,
And of your own accord."

They repeated the chant three more times. Each time they repeated it, the wind came up a little bit faster and harder, until finally, the women could all hear meows riding in on the air.

Loni pried open one of her eyes when she heard it, but she still couldn't see Ed or the rest of her family of cats. She squeezed her eyes shut again and said it one last time. This time when she opened her eyes, the meowing was louder.

"Ed!" she said excitedly, seeing the familiar marmalade-colored cat staring up at her, surrounded by the other twenty-seven feline members of their family. "You got my message!"

"Well, of course we got your message. The whole town got your message. You've darn near blown the roofs off every house in Aspen Falls!" he hollered over the howling air.

Loni glanced around at the wind that stirred the air like the emergence of a tornado. She glanced at her hands, still connected to Hazel's and Phyllis's. "Oh! Sorry!" she said, dropping their hands. The minute they separated, the wind stopped as if someone had just flipped off a switch.

"Thank you," said Ed with a flourish. "Now, what's going on? You've never summoned us like this before. What do you need?"

"Uncle Ed, you know Hazel already. But have I introduced you to her daughter, Gwyn? And this is Char Bailey and Phyllis Habernackle," said Loni, pointing at each of the women in turn.

Ed stood up on his hind legs and bowed to the women. "It's a pleasure, m'ladies."

Char, Phyllis, and Gwyn's eyes widened.

"Loni. Your cat is talking," said Phyllis without taking her eyes off of Ed.

Loni grinned. "Technically he's not my cat. He's actually my second cousin twice removed, but I just consider him my uncle."

"Your uncle?" asked Char, unblinking.

Loni nodded. "It's a long story. We'll get into that another day, but for now—voilà! A diversion!" She splayed her arms out proudly, gesturing towards the wide assortment of cats roaming the ground in front of them.

Phyllis smiled. "Oh, a diversion! I get it! I can't believe I'm saying this, but good thinking, Yolanda Hodges!"

Loni grinned behind her mask.

Standing behind the morgue, Ed looked around. "What's our assignment Loni?"

Loni pointed at the building. "There's a meeting going on inside this building. We need you to bust it up."

"Bust it up?" asked Ed, lifting the long whiskers over his eyes.

Loni nodded. "Mm-hmm. Bust it up."

He shook his head. "Can anyone be a little *more* specific about what you'd like us to do?"

Char pointed at the car parked just feet away from them. "There is a man in the car that we have to get inside the Aspen Falls Morgue without anyone seeing us do it."

"But there's a meeting going on in there right now," added Gwyn.

"So you want us to..."

"Bust it up!" said Loni.

"Yeah, I got that part. But how?"

"You know, go in there and create a diversion," explained Loni.

"But how?"

Phyllis gestured towards the cats. "Twenty-eight cats is a pretty big diversion if I've ever seen one. Just go in there and scatter. But remember, we need them *out* of the office for at least five to ten minutes."

Ed looked back at his army of four-legged felines and swiped a paw through his whiskers. "Right. Okay, I think I understand now." He reared up on his hind legs and began pacing in front of the assembly of cats, twirling his whiskers with a paw as he walked. "You hear that, everyone? Loni has assembled us here today because she and her friends need a five-to-ten-minute diversion. We need to split up. Harold, you take Ginnie and the girls in through the back. Check all the rooms and get everyone out. I'll take everyone else through the front. We'll divide and conquer. Get them all out of the office as quickly as possible." Still standing on his hind legs, he gave his followers a little salute.

The army of cats all stood up on their hind legs as Ed did and saluted back before returning to all fours.

Ed turned to face Loni and the girls. "We're ready to be deployed, Captain."

Everyone stared at Loni. "Perfect. Phyllis, you open

the back doors for Harold's team. Char, you open the front doors for Ed's team. Gwyn, Hazel, and I will get George out of the car. Give a whistle when the coast is clear and we'll bring him in through the back. Are we ready?" She put her hand out.

Phyllis was the first to put her hand on top of Loni's.

One by one the rest of the girls joined in, covering one another's hands.

"Divide and conquer on three," said Loni with a serious face. "One… two…"

"Divide and conquer!" they all yelled, throwing their hands in the air.

All hell broke loose then. Cats poured down the street like water, scattering around and between all of the women's feet. Phyllis nearly took a tumble as she ran amongst them to the back door. Char waited until they'd all passed her before even attempting to find sure footing.

Loni watched with pride as her precious family streamed into the Aspen Falls Medical Center. When every last cat had disappeared, Gwyn waved her over to the car, where George Petroski sat in the middle seat, his head slumped forward, nearly touching his naval.

"Come on, Loni, we've got to get George on his feet and ready to go on their signal. We won't have much time to delay!"

Gwyn reached into the car on the passenger's side and pulled George's feet towards her. His torso fell backwards onto the driver's seat. But she kept pulling until his legs dangled out the side of the car. Then she stood up and looked around to make sure that the coast was clear. "I think we're safe. You can lift him now."

Loni nodded and wiggled her fingers, feeling the familiar tingle of kinetic energy surging through her body. She pointed them at George and his body lurched up horizontally. Slowly his body floated out, his legs first, followed quickly by his torso. It took Hazel pushing his legs towards the ground and Gwyn lifting his head to get him in a vertical position. Once he was upright, Gwyn and Hazel each put one of George's arms over their shoulders. Hazel shoved his head up to rest on her shoulder.

"His hat!" said Gwyn. "Mom, grab his hat! I've got him."

No sooner had Hazel gone back to get his hat and put it on his head then they heard a whistle coming from the front of the building. Phyllis stuck her head out the back door. "The coast is clear, hurry!"

Together they managed to get George through the back door and into the room with the stainless-steel drawers. Loni magically lifted his body onto the table and let out a heavy sigh of relief. They'd done it!

"Now what?" asked Loni. She lifted her hockey mask and let it rest on top of her head so she could stare down at the man. She felt a pang of guilt. He hadn't had a very good first day of death. Thought it had been eventful, she'd give him that.

Hazel shrugged. "Now we go. Come on."

Gwyn shook her head. "I don't know. How are they supposed to know who it is?"

"It's a small town. Don't you think everyone would know George Petroski?" said Phyllis.

"Not necessarily," said Loni. "I doubt many people would recognize me."

"Catwoman makes a point," said Hazel bobbing her head. "No one would know me either."

"That's because you're new to town," said Phyllis. "And Loni's locked herself in her house for the last half a century. Vic said George is from Aspen Falls."

"That doesn't mean some kid doing the autopsy is going to know who he is. They'll call him a John Doe and then no one will know to call the Village and tell them what happened to Mr. Petroski. We need them to call the Village so everyone there can stop freaking out," said Gwyn. "We need to leave a note."

"And say what? Tag, you're it? Here's a dead guy?" asked Hazel.

Gwyn rolled her eyes. "Mom. Mr. Petroski is dead. Can you please have a little more respect for him than that?" She sighed. "You guys stay here and make sure he doesn't go anywhere. I'm going to try and find a piece of paper. I'll just write his name on it and his address at the Village. We'll leave it on him and then we gotta go," she said and disappeared out the door.

Less than a minute later, she was back with a slip of paper that she then tucked into his jacket pocket.

"Now can we go?" asked Hazel.

"I feel like we should say something after all of that," said Loni. "It kind of feels wrong to just leave him alone here like this."

"He's not alone," said Gwyn. "There's a whole bunch of people out there chasing cats. As soon as we leave, they'll all come back inside."

"Yeah, and then hack him up!" said Loni. "He was alive this morning, and by tonight he'll be in Solo cups in the refrigerator."

"First of all, mental picture, ewww," said Phyllis, holding up a finger. She held up a second finger. "Second of all, I don't think Solo cups is how they do it. Third of all, mental picture. Eww."

Loni shrugged. "I just meant that maybe we should say something instead of just leaving him. Like a proper goodbye."

Phyllis nodded. "That sounds like an okay idea. But I didn't know George."

"Neither did I," said Loni.

"I mean, I knew Mr. Petroski in passing. He was our next-door neighbor, and he'd gone on a couple of outings with us, but he mostly liked to stay behind and play cribbage or cards with the boys. He seemed like a nice man, though. Mom, apparently you knew him the best of all of us."

All eyes turned to Hazel.

Hazel stared at the body on the table. "George was okay. He was kind of competitive. He'd do just about anything to win at cards or cribbage. I admire that in a man. It's a shame he went before we could finish our… uh-hum…" She cleared her throat. "Relations. I think he would have enjoyed the send-off."

Phyllis nodded. "So true, so true. Would you like to

say a prayer?"

Hazel was quiet for a moment, then she bowed her head slightly. "Ashes to ashes and dust to dust. It's hard to believe George ain't here with us."

Gwyn palmed her forehead.

Loni giggled.

"Okay, now we can go," said Phyllis, heading for the door.

No sooner had she opened it than Char came bursting in. "Girls! Are you done? We've got a disaster out here! Come quick!"

Together the five women rushed out into the morgue lobby to peer out the window. Cats swarmed the sidewalk. They'd cornered the whole group of white coated employees on the roof of a car parked at the curb. One of the employees had a cell phone in hand, and another jabbed a broomstick at a hissing Ed. Sirens sounded in the distance.

"Oh no!" said Phyllis. "They've called the police."

"Uncle Ed!" Loni slid her mask back over her face and rushed out the front door. "Hurry, girls, we have to get out of here, I can't let my family get arrested!"

The five women rushed out the door. The people on the car called them over right away. "Help!" screamed one of the men. "These cats are vicious! They attacked us and they won't let us back in our building!"

"Attacked you!" breathed Char, looking down at the cats, who now were just milling around the car quietly. "Why, they hardly look like attack cats to me! Look at them! They're as docile as a litter of newborn puppies."

Ed took the cue and rubbed his body up against Char's leg like a sweet, mild-mannered cat. He even let out a nice little meow to further show how sweet and innocent he was.

"B-but…," stammered one of the women, pointing at the cats. "They were hissing and clawing and chasing us just a few minutes ago!"

Phyllis squatted down and scooped one of the cats off the ground.

"Don't touch it!" warned one of the men. "It'll bite!"

Phyllis patted the grey cat's head, scratching it behind its ears. "Oh, you're not going to bite me, are you?"

The cat nuzzled Phyllis's cheek and began to purr.

Phyllis smiled. "It doesn't look like a vicious attack animal to me."

The sound of the sirens grew closer.

"Girls, we better go. We don't want to be late for our *appointment*," said Loni, walking away. "I'm sure these cats will *go home now*."

Ed took the hint. He let out one giant, chortled yowl and then turned tail and ran back in the direction he'd come from when Loni had summoned him in the first place. That was the only signal needed for the other twenty-seven cats. They all turned and ran as well.

"What in the…?" said one of the women with her mouth hanging wide open.

"What was that all about?" asked one of the men.

"They must not have liked you much," said Loni. She shrugged. "You must not be cat people. Toodle-oo."

15

Gwyn fell on Kat's antique chaise in the parlor and threw a hand back over her forehead with a sigh. "What a day!"

"You're telling us, sister," clicked Phyllis. "We've been dragging that dead body all over Aspen Falls and I'm pooped!"

Loni's head swiveled to stare at Phyllis stupendously. "*You've* been dragging the body all over Aspen Falls? I don't remember your fingers doing any hocus pocus."

"Well, that's because I wasn't born with the *gift* that you were. That doesn't mean I haven't been right next to you every step of the way!"

"You weren't there when Hazel called," said Loni. "I moved him without your help to the park."

Char grimaced. "I wouldn't go bragging about that if I were you."

Phyllis leaned forward and pointed her finger at Loni. "Yeah! If it hadn't been for that brainiac move, you could have just put George back in his room and called the cops from there."

Loni held up two hands. "Hey, I wasn't the one that killed the guy, alright? I was just the body mover. If you want a place to point a finger, point it at that one." She pointed at Hazel.

"How many times do I have to tell you it was an accident!" snapped Hazel. "I'm sure old men die all the time having sex. It's just too much for the ticker!"

Gwyn massaged her temples. "Girls, must you bicker?" she asked. "We all have our parts to play in this mess. Let's just be thankful we got him somewhere safe. The morgue will tell the Village where George is, and then they can call off the search."

"Speaking of the Village, don't you need to get back to work?" asked Char, glancing down at her watch.

Gwyn sat up, leaning her elbows on her knees. "No. With everything that happened this morning, the big bosses decided to cancel all activities for the rest of the day. Which is good. I couldn't handle going back without them knowing what had happened to George."

Phyllis punched the air with one hand. "Well, yay for you! You get the rest of the day off!"

Gwyn nodded and stood up. "Yes, and we're at Kat's and we have work to do. I think I'll spend the rest of the day here working."

"Working?" asked Loni. "Working on what?"

Gwyn glanced over at Char and Phyllis. "You didn't tell her?"

Char bit her lips between her teeth and shook

her head.

Gwyn threw both arms out in the air in frustration. "Seriously? You've been with her all day and you couldn't even find a minute to explain what's going on?"

"We've been busy!" argued Char.

"And we didn't want to tell her," said Phyllis. "We know how she's going to get."

"Well, it's her stuff too. We have to tell her," said Gwyn pointedly. She looked at Loni and sucked in a deep breath of air. She hated to be the one to have to tell her, but since Char and Phyllis hadn't done it, it fell to Gwyn. "Loni, Char got Kat's mail the other day and there was a tax bill in there."

Loni curled her lip. "A bill? For how much?"

"Twenty-five hundred dollars."

"Twenty-five hundred dollars! Where's that money coming from?" asked Loni.

Gwyn swirled her finger around the room. "From all of us. You, me, Char, and Phil."

Loni's jaw dropped. Then she pointed at Hazel. "Well, what about Hazel? How come she doesn't have to pay too?"

"Because Kat didn't leave the house to her, Loni. She left it to us, remember?" said Char. "You own a fourth of this house, just like we all do."

"So you have to come up with a fourth of the tax bill, just like we all do," said Phyllis, crossing her arms across her breasts. "You got six hundred and twenty-five dollars lying around?"

"Six hundred and twenty-five dollars?!" gasped Loni.

"Of course I don't have six hundred and twenty-five dollars lying around."

Phyllis nodded. "That's what I thought. Neither do we."

"Well, then, what are we supposed to do about the tax bill? Kat said we can't sell the house."

"Right," said Gwyn, glad that at least Loni had understood the conundrum they were in. "We're going to have to raise the funds."

"How?"

"Look around us, Loni. Look at all of Kat's stuff. Her expensive antique furniture, her knickknacks, her kitchenware, her paintings and tapestries. This house is *full* of things that could make us money," explained Gwyn.

"Make us money? How is furniture going to make us money?" asked Loni, lifting a brow.

"We're going to sell it," said Phyllis.

"Sell it?!" breathed Loni. "Sell Kat's prized possessions? She'd flip over in her grave!"

"She doesn't have a grave. Kat was cremated, remember?" said Char.

"Well, then, she'll flip over in her rose bushes!" said Loni. Her eyes scanned the room. "We can't *sell* Kat's stuff. I love all of her stuff."

"We love her stuff too," said Gwyn.

Loni folded her arms across her chest and stuck her nose up into the air defiantly. "Well, I don't want to sell any of it."

"Well, that's too bad. You don't have the cash and neither do we. So unless you want to go rob a bank and bring us twenty-five hundred dollars, we're selling Kat's stuff," huffed Phyllis.

Gwyn walked over to Loni and squeezed her shoulder. "I'm sorry, Loni, but Phil's right. We have to. None of us want to either, but we have to sell at least enough to make the tax payment. When you look at some of these antique furniture pieces, I'm sure it won't take much to earn twenty-five hundred dollars."

Char shook her head. "I've been thinking about it, and I don't think we should go for the furniture right away. I mean, yes, we could probably sell that chaise lounge for twenty-five hundred dollars, but it's such an amazing piece that it kills me to have to let it go. I'd much rather start with the small stuff and try and make enough selling Kat's books and maybe her pots and pans than her furniture. What do you think, girls?"

Gwyn ran her finger along the hard wooden back of the sofa. She didn't want to get rid of the furniture either. She nodded. "Okay, I agree. I think we start with selling enough odds and ends to pay the taxes this year, and then maybe by next year, we'll figure out a better way to pay the taxes." She looked at Loni, whose face seemed to relent slightly. "Loni, deal?"

Loni puffed air out her nose but nodded. "Oh, fine. But I get final say on everything we sell."

"We all get final say," agreed Gwyn. "Everyone good with that?"

Phyllis and Char both nodded too.

"Good. Okay, well, I've got the rest of the day off, so let's get busy."

"I've got more boxes in the car if anyone needs them," said Char as she carried down a box she'd loaded full of extra bed linens from Kat's linen closet on the second floor. They were hand cross-stitched and in mint condition. She hoped they'd bring a pretty penny at the church craft sale they were having the weekend after Easter.

Gwyn set her own box of dishes down on the counter in the kitchen. "I actually think I'm going to need them. I still need to go through Kat's pantry. She's got slow cookers in there, and a million casserole dishes. How a single woman needed that many casserole dishes is beyond me. Mom, are you done packing up Kat's salt and pepper shaker collection?"

Hazel hobbled around to look at Gwyn. "Not quite. How much salt and pepper can one woman have?" She held up a green glass pair with ball feet and a face outlined in black. The words *Dino's Lodge* were printed underneath the face. "Look at these."

Char smiled and lifted the pair of shakers out of Hazel's hands. "Oh, Dean!" she sighed. "This was one of Kat's most prized possessions. It's Dean Martin!"

Gwyn lifted a brow. "Dean Martin had his face on salt and pepper shakers?"

Char couldn't help but laugh. "Don't you remember back in the fifties, Dean opened a restaurant in LA?"

"Oh, I'm sure I knew that at one time," said Gwyn.

"Yeah, and he had this big glowing neon head out

front. It was his face. I can't believe you don't remember! It was a hot spot for a while."

Hazel nodded. "I remember. And then Jerry Lewis opened his own restaurant not far away."

Char took one of the shakers from Hazel's hands and ran her fingers along the smooth edge. "I bet this is worth something."

Gwyn pulled out her phone. "I'll look it up." She taped on her screen and seconds later she held it up to show the girls. "One just like it sold for over three hundred dollars on eBay!"

"Three hundred dollars!" breathed Char. "I had no idea a pair of salt and pepper shakers could bring so much!" She looked around the kitchen. "I wonder what other goodies Kat has in here that we could sell on eBay?"

"I think we need more boxes," said Gwyn. "She's got so much stuff in that pantry."

Char put down her box of linens on the kitchen table next to the box of salt and pepper shakers Hazel had boxed. "You want to help me carry them inside?"

Gwyn nodded. "Sure. Mom, you want to hold the door for us?"

Hazel sighed. "What, all I'm good for is being a doorstop?"

Gwyn rolled her eyes. "You're welcome to helps us carry the boxes in from the car if you'd prefer."

Hazel shook her head. "Nope. I'm alright being a doorstop."

"Good."

The three women went to the front of the house. Gwyn and Char loaded up with the cardboard boxes that Char had gotten from Linda's restaurant. They carried them back inside and directly to the kitchen. Char sat the empty boxes down on the kitchen table. But then she realized that the box she just packed wasn't there anymore. She scooted the empty boxes aside and searched the table with her eyes. Frowning, she turned and looked behind her on the floor.

"What's wrong?" asked Gwyn, putting her own boxes down on the kitchen table.

"The box I just filled up is gone. The one with the linens."

"Gone? How could it be gone?"

Hazel shoved aside the empty boxes and looked down at the table. "The box I put all the salt and pepper shakers into is gone too."

Gwyn swiveled around and searched for the boxes she'd filled with dishes. "My box is gone too. What in the world?"

Char lifted a finger in the air. "I bet Phil and Loni moved the boxes to the front room for us." She curled her finger to signal they should follow her. They passed Loni, who was seated on the floor packing up books from Kat's bookshelf. "Hey Lon, did you move our boxes from the kitchen just a minute ago?"

Loni shook her head. "Nope. I haven't moved from this spot in the last half hour. In fact"—she held her arms up—"give me a boost, will ya? I'm so stiff I feel like someone starched my joints while I sat."

Char and Gwyn helped her to her feet.

"Well, where's Phil? It must have been her that moved the boxes," said Char.

Loni shrugged. "Haven't seen her. I've just been sitting here minding my own business."

"Phil!" Char hollered up the stairs. "Come here!"

Seconds later, they heard Phyllis's heavy steps on the stairs. "What?" she barked.

"What did you do with our boxes?" asked Char.

"The ones from the car? I think they're still out there."

Char furrowed her brows. "No. The ones from the kitchen. With the linens and the salt and pepper shakers."

Phil rocked back on her heels at the top of the stairs and put her hands on her hips. "What in the hell are you talking about woman? I haven't touched any linens or salt and pepper shakers. I'm going through Kat's room. I found some old costume jewelry that might make us a few bucks."

Char's mouth gaped open. "You didn't move our boxes?"

"Do you have wax in your ears? No, I didn't move your boxes." Phyllis lowered her own brows then and then came down the stairs to stare into Char's face. "Why? What's going on?"

Char looked at Gwyn and Hazel. They exchanged worried looks. It was happening again.

"I'm going to run upstairs and see if I can find those linens again," said Char. "Gwynnie, you and Haze check the kitchen and see if you can find any of the stuff you boxed up."

Hazel clung to the back of Gwyn's sweater. "Gwyn can look. I'm not looking. I'm freaked out."

"Freaked out? What in the world is going on?" asked Loni, shaking her head in confusion.

But Char didn't want to waste time explaining. She raced up the stairs and back to the linen closet she'd pulled the cross-stitched linens from in the first place. Letting out a little breath as she stared at the closed door, she felt a surge of adrenaline. But she reached forward anyway and slowly pulled the door open to find the linen closet still completely full. The sheets and pillowcases she'd pulled earlier were there. Just as they had been. Stacked neatly as Kat had done. She put a hand to her head. "Oh my goodness," she whispered. This wasn't seriously happening.

Char closed the closet door and raced back down to the kitchen, where Gwyn and Hazel were having the same reaction. "You found the salt and pepper shakers and the dishes you'd boxed up, didn't you?"

Gwyn nodded blankly, her face white as a freshly bleached bedsheet. "They were in the cupboards." She pointed to the little display rack on the wall. "Salt and pepper shakers are all back exactly as we found them."

Char glanced over at Hazel, whose face was also white as a sheet. The poor woman looked like she might pass out at any moment. "Hazel. Are you alright?"

Her hands shook so much that even her cane rattled, making a tapping noise on the floor.

Char rushed over and pulled out a kitchen chair for her. "You need to sit down."

"Can someone please tell me what is going on?" asked Phyllis.

"It's happening again," said Char after helping Hazel sit.

"It?"

Hazel pointed at the salt and pepper shakers on the wall. "I b-boxed those up already," she stuttered.

Phyllis turned to look at the salt and pepper shakers curiously. "What?"

"I boxed up some of Kat's fancy cross-stitched linens. They hadn't even been used. I thought we could sell those at the church craft fair. I brought them down here and put them on the table. Gwyn had a load of stuff she'd boxed up from the kitchen, and Hazel had boxed up Kat's salt and pepper shaker collection."

Loni sucked in her breath. "We're *not* selling Kat's salt and pepper shaker collection!"

Char held a hand out to her to silence her. "We left them all in the kitchen and went out to the car to get more boxes, and when we came back our boxes were gone. We thought one of you must have moved them."

Loni shook her head. "I told you I didn't."

"I know. I just went upstairs and looked and the linens are all back in the linen closet. The salt and pepper shakers are back on their display shelves, and Gwyn found all the dishes she'd packed up back in the cupboards. Just like how George moved around this house —something or someone moved our stuff again."

16

"Someone? You think someone else is in the house?" asked Phyllis. Goose bumps skidded across her arms and legs.

"There has to be. This is getting ridiculous," said Char.

"Girls, a person couldn't have put away all those salt and pepper shakers, all the linens, and all the dishes in the short amount of time that we ran out to the car. It's just not possible. It took us thirty minutes each to pack all that stuff up in the first place!" said Gwyn.

"And the way that George moved around this house," agreed Char. "That wasn't humanly possible."

"Okay, so I think it's clear that we're not dealing with a human here," said Gwyn. "I think we have to face facts. Kat's house is haunted."

"Gwynnie. I wanna go home," said Hazel, pulling herself to her feet with her cane.

"I'm sorry, Mom. I know you're afraid of ghosts, but

we're all here. We won't let anything happen to you. But we do need to straighten this all out before we can leave. We have work to do, and we can't let some ghost dictate what we do with Kat's house. We have a tax bill to pay!"

Phyllis shook her head. "What I don't understand is if there's a ghost, why can't I see it? All the women in my family can see and communicate with ghosts. I've always been able to."

"Do all ghosts *want* to talk to you, though?" asked Gwyn.

Phyllis shrugged. "I mean, I'd like to think all ghosts want to talk to me. Why *wouldn't* they want to talk to me? I'm awesome, you know."

Char gave Phil a little shove. "Oh, for Pete's sake, Phil. Now's not the time for your inflated ego to rear its pointed little nose. We have a problem here and we need to figure out what's going on."

"What are you thinking, Char? A ghost summoning spell?" asked Gwyn.

Phyllis shook her head. "We don't need a ghost summoning spell if we already have a ghost present. We need to force the ghost to appear to us."

"And how exactly do we do that?" asked Char with her hand on her hip.

"We do a seance," said Phyllis matter-of-factly.

Hazel stood up again. "Uh-uh. I'm out of here. I don't do seances."

"But you're a witch, Hazel!" said Phyllis.

"A witch with a bad heart!" Hazel snapped back.

"Even if there is a ghost in the house, Haze, it's not

going to hurt you," said Char, rubbing Hazel's back. "Now, sit back down. You'll be fine, I promise." She looked up at the group. "Phil's right. We've got to get to the bottom of this, and if a seance is the only way to do it, then so mote it be."

Gwyn clapped her hands together. "Ohh girls! It's been so long since I've done a seance! I'm kind of excited."

"I found a box of candles in one of the bedrooms upstairs. I'll go get it," said Char.

Phyllis lurched forward too. "I'll get some appropriate music started."

"I saw some incense in a drawer in the parlor," said Loni. "I'll get it ready."

Gwyn nodded. "Okay, then I'll go get our spell book from Kat's spell room!"

Hazel's mouth opened. "Uh!" she exclaimed. "So you're just going to leave me here to be alone with the ghost?"

"Mom, you can come up to the third floor with me," said Gwyn.

Hazel stuck her nose up in the air. "Pass. I don't do stairs."

"I'm just going to the other room to get Kat's CD player, Hazel. You can come with me," said Phyllis.

Hazel pulled herself to her feet and followed Phyllis while the rest of the group dispersed to collect their assigned items.

"Why are you so scared of ghosts anyway?" asked Phyllis.

"Why are you crawling up my ass?" Hazel retorted.

"I'm pretty sure I couldn't crawl up a four-hundred-year-old woman's ass if I tried," Phyllis snapped right back.

Hazel grinned and held up a finger. "Four hundred and one, thank you."

Phyllis giggled. "Oh boy," she sighed, unplugging the CD player she'd found in Kat's den. "I sure hope we can make this work."

"Not me. I've learned two things in life." She held up a finger. "Never trust a ghost." She held up another finger. "And never trust a fart."

Phyllis rolled her eyes. "Hazel, you're too much. What are we going to do with you?"

"You could start by letting me go home. I've had a long day."

Phyllis stroked Hazel's arm. "You sure have. Between George and all that commotion and now this! You're going to sleep well tonight."

"Maybe I should just go sleep well now," said Hazel, gesturing towards Kat's bedroom. "You girls can do your little seance, and I'll get my beauty nap."

Phyllis swished her lips off to the side. "I don't know, Hazel. Five witches are better than four for a seance circle." She linked arms with the old woman, who was frowning now. "It won't take long. I promise. And then we'll get you right home. I'll protect you, I promise."

Minutes later, everything was in place in the parlor. Lit candles surrounded the room. The smoky, aromatic scent of incense filled everyone's nasal cavities. They'd drawn the curtains, making the room dark despite the last remnants of daylight that clung to the night sky. They'd slid the furniture around to allow them all to sit in a circle, and soft music played on the CD player in the corner.

Phyllis stood back and looked at all of the women, seated in padded chairs in a circle around the room, chatting amongst themselves. It made her smile and shake her head. There had been a time when they'd have just plopped their butts down on the hardwood floor instead of arranging cushioned chairs to sit on.

She took her seat between Loni and Gwyn. Char and Hazel sat across from her with Hazel next to Gwyn. It was just like old times. Except back then, they didn't have Hazel, but they did have two other members in their group. Kat Lynde and Auggie Stone. She could picture their youthful faces, long hair, lithe bodies. What a change from then to now!

"Oh, girls, when's the last time we did a seance?" breathed Phyllis as the feelings she was having caught up to her.

"I think the last time was back at the Institute, when Kat had a panic attack because she missed her grandmother. Sorceress Halliwell taught us to do a seance then, and it worked. Do you remember?"

Char giggled. "Do I ever. Kat's grandmother was not

happy about being summoned. She threatened to haunt Kat for the rest of her life if she did it again!"

Gwyn sucked in her breath and covered her mouth. "Girls, do you think it could be Kat's grandmother that's haunting us?"

Phyllis shook her head. "I really doubt it. My money's on it being Kat that's haunting us."

"Mine too," agreed Char. "I mean, who else could it be?"

Phyllis shrugged. "I don't know. But what I don't understand is, if it's Kat, why doesn't she just appear to me? Why all this secretive stuff?"

Gwyn reached out and took hold of her mother's hand and then took Phyllis's. "No time like the present to find out, right?"

Phyllis smiled and took Loni's hand. When they were all connected, Phyllis and the women all closed their eyes.

They all knew the drill. They'd take a few minutes of solitude to shake off any negative energy. Shake off fears and emotions. Shake off stress. It had to be a circle of light and positivity.

When Phyllis felt the energy circulating between them like a smoothly flowing river, she opened her eyes.

"Spirits around us, protect us in this sacred place. The light of our candles radiates white energy and love to all four corners of the room. All negative energies have been banished, and we ask that you utilize this room as your sanctuary for your higher purpose."

Phyllis stopped chanting and looked around, as did the rest of the women. The candles flickered in unison.

She took a cleansing breath and then began again. "Dear spirits in this house. We have bathed your sanctuary in peace and protective light. We have opened up our hearts and minds to you. We welcome and encourage your presence. We ask that you feel safe amongst our circle of friends and speak to us openly and without reservation."

Phyllis could feel an energy surrounding them. It made the hairs on the back of her neck stand up and the skin on her arms and legs ripple. She glanced up and looked at Char, giving her a little smile of excitement. Phyllis squeezed Gwyn and Loni's hands and they squeezed back. They felt it too!

"Dear spirit, we feel your presence moving amongst us. We invite you to join our circle. Present yourself to us in this sacred space. Talk to us freely."

The air around them in the parlor suddenly went from completely calm to breezy, lifting their hair up off their necks and swirling it around them.

"It's working," Gwyn whispered, squeezing Phyllis's hand again.

Phyllis smiled and nodded. It *was* working! "O spirit of the house, join us, we implore you!"

And suddenly, Phyllis felt a swoosh of air cross the bridge their arms formed. The air behind her calmed, and she looked up to see the transparent outline of a woman in their casting circle.

Hazel's jaw dropped.

Across the room, Char sucked in her breath in an audible gasp.

"Sorceress Halliwell!"

Phyllis's eyes opened wider as the apparition slowly turned around to face all of them. It *was* Sorceress Halliwell!

"Well, I'll be," sang the woman floating in front of them. Her long sunflower-blond hair looked just like it had the last day they'd seen her, not long after graduating from the Institute. "If it isn't the Coffee Coven in *my* living room!"

"Sorceress Halliwell," breathed Phyllis. "It was you? You've been the one haunting Kat's house?"

Gwyn's jaw hung open as did Loni's. They were speechless.

Sorceress Halliwell smiled. She had a beautiful smile. Her cheeks each dimpled in the corners as Phyllis remembered them doing all those years ago. She hadn't aged a day since they'd last seen her. And now they were all old women, and Sorceress Halliwell was youthful and vibrant, but also pale and transparent!

Tucking her left cheek, Sorceress Halliwell nodded. "Indeed," she sighed.

"You were the one moving George's body and all of Kat's stuff?" asked Gwyn.

Sorceress Halliwell nodded. "I moved George's body to get your attention. I'm sorry if I frightened you."

"Are you kidding?" barked Hazel. "You nearly gave me a heart attack!"

"I'm sorry about that."

"But why? How?" asked Gwyn.

Sorceress Halliwell turned to take them all in individually. "You haven't guessed by now?"

They all shook their heads in confusion.

"No, tell us. Please!" begged Char. "We're all confused about what's going on."

"It was Kat," whispered Sorceress Halliwell. "Kat did this to me."

Their voices broke out in unintentional unison. "Kat?!"

She hung her head and nodded sadly. "Yes, I'm afraid it happened years and years ago."

"Years and years ago?" asked Char. "You mean you've been stuck in this house like this for years? Since when?"

Sorceress Halliwell thought about it for a moment. "It was a few months after your graduation."

"A few months after our graduation!" Phyllis repeated, astounded at what she was hearing.

Sorceress Halliwell nodded before hanging her head. "I'm afraid so. It's quite the long story."

Phyllis couldn't believe it. Surely it had all been one big accident. "But Kat didn't do it on purpose, right?"

The ghost before them took in a deep breath before answering that. "I don't think Katherine's original intention was to harm me. She'd asked me over to help her with a spell that she was working on. But… I discovered something about Kat that day. Something I didn't approve of."

Phyllis glanced around the room. All eyes were wide and trained on Sorceress Halliwell's ghost. What could

Kat possibly have been doing that Sorceress Halliwell didn't approve of?

She continued, "As a high sorceress, I've taken certain vows. One of my most sacred vows is to uphold the ethical responsibilities of a witch and of the witches that I teach. What Kat was doing wasn't ethical, and I told her that I would have to report my findings. Kat didn't like that, and she acted in haste and without thought, I'm afraid."

Char's mouth gaped open. "So you're saying she *did* do this intentionally?!"

"Initially she did something that she later regretted with her whole being. She tried for years to reverse the spell, but she couldn't do it."

"Reverse what spell?" asked Loni.

Sorceress Halliwell swallowed hard. "She tethered my soul to the walls of this house. I haven't been able to set foot outside since."

Phyllis's eyes gaped. "Your *soul* is tethered to this house?!"

Char swallowed hard. "Oh my word! No wonder Kat didn't want us to ever sell the house. Now it makes sense!"

Sorceress Halliwell nodded sadly. "It's also why she kept the spell book from you all those years. She's been trying to undo what she did ever since. She lived with that horrible secret on her conscience until the day she died!"

"I can't believe this," gasped Char. "Why didn't Kat call us? We could have helped!"

"She was too ashamed at what she had done," said

the Sorceress. "She knew how you all felt about me, and she worried you'd all hate her for it."

"I don't understand," said Loni, shaking her head. "What could Kat have possibly been doing that was so bad that you'd have to report her and that it would have caused her to tether your soul to her house?"

Sorceress Halliwell glanced around the room. It was the question everyone wanted answered. She shook her head before hanging it. "I can't tell you that," she whispered.

"What?" breathed Gwyn in disbelief. "Kat did this horrible thing to you and you're going to keep her secret? She's dead! You can tell us now!"

"You don't understand. I have my reasons for keeping Kat's secret. It's my choice not to share the details."

"But Sorceress…" began Char.

But the woman shook her head with glossy eyes. "No. I'm sorry. I can't tell you that."

Phyllis hung her head. She felt horrible, both for Sorceress Halliwell and for the fact that her dear old friend had lived with such a gut-wrenching secret for all those years! But finally they knew the truth. And now it all made sense. Why Kat had kept the book from them, and why Kat hadn't wanted them to sell the house.

There was a long silence as each of them mulled over the information they now had.

Finally, Gwyn lifted her brows as her mouth set in a firm line. "Girls. We have to fix this. We can't let Sorceress Halliwell be tied to this house for all of eternity!"

"But how?" asked Loni. "Kat tried for years and couldn't reverse the spell."

"She didn't get *us* involved," said Char with a nod. "Five witches are better than one."

Loni shrugged her diminutive shoulders. "You really think we can do it?"

"I do," said Gwyn.

"Me too," agreed Char. "Phil?"

Phyllis's eyes widened. "Of course! I'm in, I'm in!"

"Alright, then I'm in too," agreed Loni reluctantly.

Everyone looked at Hazel then. She was sitting quietly with her lips pinched shut. When she realized everyone's eyes were on her, she looked around. "What?!"

"We're all willing to help figure out how to reverse the spell that Kat put on Sorceress Halliwell, Mom. You're the oldest witch here. Would you be willing to help us?"

Hazel didn't say a word for a long moment. Just sat staring at the apparition in front of her. Finally, she looked at Gwyn. "Does it mean this house won't be haunted anymore?"

Everyone around the circle nodded.

"Absolutely!" said Gwyn.

Hazel lifted a shoulder. "Alright. Fine, then. Count me in."

17

Gwyn held open the glass door for her mother. "What a day," she sighed as Hazel hobbled past.

Hazel stopped walking and held up a finger pointedly. "You're telling me. I haven't taken a single nap all day, and I get cranky when I don't nap."

Gwyn couldn't help but grin. "You don't say?"

Gwyn's sarcasm flew right over Hazel's head. She nodded. "You have no idea. I'm gonna sleep like the dead!"

"Good," said Gwyn, letting the door slam behind her. Her shoulders slumped and she let out a sigh, thankful to be back at the Village and only steps away from their apartment and her nice, cozy bed. She was going to crash just as hard as her mother. She'd sleep even better knowing that Hazel was going to sleep like the dead. There would be no light sleeping tonight, or listening for Hazel getting out of bed and heading for the front door. Gwyn couldn't get to their room fast enough.

They'd barely taken three steps into the hallway from the back entrance when a pair of burly men in navy-blue uniforms heaved an old sofa past them and out the door. Gwyn had noticed the moving truck in the parking lot and wondered who was moving out. She didn't have to wonder long.

Continuing the short distance to their apartment, they noticed George Petroski's apartment door wide open. People came and went freely from it with armfuls of his possessions. Gwyn and Hazel peered inside to see people milling around and found most of his furniture gone already! That was when she realized that they'd found George. Relief washed over her. It was over. She wouldn't have to pretend that she had no idea where George was or have to help people look for him. They knew.

"They're already moving him out!" said Hazel. She lifted her brows. "Jiminy Christmas! You don't wanna die around here. They can't even wait until your body's cold in the ground before they kick your ass out."

With her mouth open, Gwyn shook her head. She couldn't believe it. How *was* this all happening so fast? They couldn't have found out about George more than three hours ago—at best! A big burly moving man stepped out into the hallway, making notes on a clip-board. She tapped him on the shoulder. "Excuse me, sir. I live next door to Mr. Petroski. What's going on in there?"

The man lifted the greasy baseball cap off his head, scratched his balding scalp and then reapplied the hat. "Oh, uh, from what I understand, the fella that lived in here passed away. We have orders to empty his room."

"Orders from who?" asked Gwyn, appalled that someone wanted to dispose of George's memory so fast. She'd assumed it would take a while for the family to be notified about his passing, and then they'd want to get through the funeral at the very least before tackling his apartment. She thought it would be weeks or even months before his room was touched.

The man shrugged. "Boss man said we couldn't go home until this room was cleared."

Hazel and Gwyn looked at each other. Something felt funny.

"Mom, do you have the energy to walk to the front desk with me and see what's going on?"

Hazel slumped heavily onto her cane. "I don't know, Gwynnie. I think my get up and go has got up and went."

Gwyn gave Hazel a sympathetic smile and then grabbed the handle of a wheelchair that was in the hallway which had likely come from George's room. "George won't mind if we borrow this for a few minutes. Hop on and I'll give you a ride."

"Hehe," said Hazel with a toothy grin. "Those were George's last words to me."

Gwyn rolled her eyes but helped her mother get into the wheelchair. Hazel pointed her cane towards the lobby. "Up, up, and away!"

They made their way through the crowd of people buzzing through the hallways to find the front lobby was just as full of people as the hallway had been. "What in the world is going on?" asked Gwyn, shaking her head. "I've never seen the death of a resident in any of the retirement villages I've ever worked at cause quite the stir that George's death has." Gwyn leaned on the front counter while Arabella Struthers, the front desk clerk, spoke on the phone to someone.

"Yes, we've got people working on it now." She paused. "No, no. I assure you, it'll be done before the end of the day. Okay. Uh-huh. Bye." She hung up the phone, put her hands on either side of her face and let out a breath as she looked up at Gwyn and Hazel. "Oh my gosh! What a horrible day!"

Hazel nodded at Arabella, wrinkling her nose. "Because of that new hairdo?"

Arabella fingered her long brown hair. "My hairdo?"

"Yeah, you did something different," observed Hazel, tapping her chin as if she were trying to put her finger on what it was that was different about Arabella.

Arabella's brows knitted together. "I got it colored the other day."

"What color was it before?"

"Blond."

Hazel clicked her tongue. "Uh-huh. What's your boyfriend think of it?"

"I don't have a boyfriend."

Hazel lifted a shoulder. "You would if you were still blond."

"Mom!" snapped Gwyn. "That was rude! Apologize to Arabella!"

Hazel crossed her arms across her chest. "Being rude is how I hug." She looked at Arabella and held a flattened hand up. "No need to hug back. I'm allergic."

Thoroughly embarrassed by her mother, Gwyn spun the wheelchair around. "Arabella, I am so sorry about my mother. She hasn't napped today, and she's feeling crankier than usual."

Arabella smiled at Gwyn. "It's okay, Gwyn. I'm used to it. Most of the residents here don't have filters."

"So, what's going on? Mom and I were over at a friend's house this evening and we just got back, and they're emptying out George Petroski's room. What's going on?"

Arabella winced. "Oh, have you not heard? They found George. He's dead."

Gwyn looked down at Hazel. She knew she had to pretend to be surprised. For both of their sakes. She looked back at up at Arabella. "Dead? What?" she asked weakly.

The brunette nodded sadly. "Yeah. Strangest thing, they found him dead in the morgue."

"In the morgue?" Gwyn nibbled on the inside of her lip and hoped Arabella wouldn't be able to see the guilt painted all over her face.

"Yes, isn't that crazy? I mean, how in the world did he get to the *morgue*?!"

Gwyn lifted both hands in a slow shrug. "Mmm, I would have no clue. I mean, you'd think that would be difficult to do."

"Right?!" agreed Arabella. "It's crazy."

"How do they think he died?" asked Hazel with her back to Arabella.

"They're pretty sure it was a heart attack, but because

of the suspicious way he was discovered at the morgue, the police have ordered an autopsy just to make sure there wasn't any foul play at work."

Hazel grabbed hold of Gwyn's hand and turned herself around in the wheelchair. "Foul play?" she asked, staring up at Arabella.

Arabella nodded. She looked around to see if anyone else was listening and then leaned forward to whisper. "Uh-huh. I guess it looked very suspicious. Someone left a *note* on his body. *And* he was wearing a bedsheet like a diaper under his pants."

Gwyn's eyes widened as she looked down at Hazel. *What?!* No one had mentioned they'd *diapered* George! "You're kidding?" said Gwyn, swallowing hard.

Arabella shook her head. "No. If you ask me, Mr. Petroski did *not* die of natural causes."

"Why do you say that?" asked Hazel.

Arabella pointed at the phone. "When you two came up, I was talking to George Petroski's ex-wife on the phone. She's the one that ordered his room be emptied immediately."

Gwyn tipped her head to the side. "How can she do that if she's his *ex*-wife?"

"She still had power of attorney," said Arabella with a shrug.

"How did she even find out so soon that he was dead?"

"Noreen Petroski was the only contact George had on his emergency call list. No kids, no friends, no family. Just Noreen. So we called her, and the first thing out of her mouth was that she wanted his room cleared and his security deposit returned before the end of the day."

Gwyn's jaw dropped. "That's ridiculous! So you think she had something to do with Mr. Petroski's death?"

Arabella shook her head. "I mean, I have no idea. I just thought that was very suspicious. Even if my ex-husband and I *hated* each other, I'd have more respect for him than that! I mean, the woman couldn't have even waited twenty-four hours?"

Hazel pointed a gnarled finger at the woman. "I don't know if your mother explained to you how this works, Missy, but to get an *ex*-husband, you gotta have a husband. To get a husband, you gotta have a boyfriend, and to get a boyfriend, you need to do something about that hair."

Gwyn spun her mother back around again and gave Arabella an apologetic smile. "I better get Mom to bed. She's had a long day. Thanks for the information, Arabella."

Arabella nodded at her. "Goodnight, Hazel. Sleep tight."

"Oh, no problems there. I'm gonna sleep tighter than a camel's butt in a sandstorm."

Gwyn pushed her mother away. "Do you have to say things like that?" hissed Gwyn as they walked.

"Well, no, I don't have to, but I find it gives me great pleasure. And since you don't want me having sex, I gotta get my kicks somewhere else," said Hazel with a smirk.

Gwyn stopped pushing and covered her ears.

"Mother! I don't want to hear those things coming out of your mouth!"

Hazel snickered as she pointed to a group of seniors huddled in a corner of the lobby. "There's Ellie and the girls. Push me over there. I want to see if they've heard about George."

"I'd be shocked if they haven't," said Gwyn, pushing the wheelchair towards the group of women. "Hello, ladies."

"Hello, girls," said Alice Buerman, a white-haired woman in a mauve silk robe and house slippers. "I assume you've heard about George?"

"Yes, as a matter of fact, Arabella just told us the terrible news. It's so sad that's he's gone, isn't it?" said Gwyn sadly.

All of the women nodded. "It's stunning is what it is," said Alice. "George was in such great shape. He should have had another ten years, at least!"

"He was in better health than most of the men here," agreed Ellie Wallace, a friend of Hazel's.

"Arabella said it was a heart attack?" said Hazel.

Carol Hamburg grimaced as she leaned forward. "That's the initial consensus, but the scuttlebutt around here is that they're going to find more than they bargained for when those autopsy results come back."

Gwyn was shocked that the women were speculating also. She assumed they were referring to George's ex-wife just like Arabella had been. "Oh, really? Why do you say that?"

"Well because *everyone* knows that George and Duke

Olson got into it the other night at the poker game," said Carol.

Alice nodded. "And then Duke *mysteriously* goes on that field trip even though he wasn't signed up to go? But George *doesn't* go, and then Duke is found asleep in his room and George is found dead?"

Carol nodded, her eyes narrowed. "Yeah, we don't buy it."

Gwyn patted Hazel's hand. They both knew the real reason that George was dead, and she felt bad that she couldn't clear Duke's name by telling them. It would only make things worse for the two of them. "Well, girls. Thanks for the update. Mom and I were out with some friends, and it's worn us both out, I'm afraid."

Hazel squeezed Gwyn's hand but didn't say anything.

"Good night, Gwyn," said Ellie. "Good night, Hazel. Sleep well."

"Good night, girls," said Gwyn as she wheeled her mother away.

18

Hazel Prescott prodded the fleshy pouches of skin under her eyes with the tips of her fingers the next morning. The bags were so big, she wondered if they wouldn't just decide to pack up the rest of her face and go on a nice Tahitian vacation or something.

Usually Hazel had no problems sleeping. She could sleep sitting upright in a chair in their noisy dining hall. She could sleep in the car. She could sleep standing up in the shower. Hell, she was even convinced she could sleep while walking, if it was close to nap time. She could sleep anywhere. But last night, Hazel had hardly gotten a wink of sleep. Not only had she dreamt about George Petroski all night long, but she'd woken up in a cold sweat thinking about Duke Olson and how Ellie and the girls had suggested that *he* was responsible for George's death.

She sighed as she climbed out of bed and slipped on

her glasses before searching out something to wear. After using the bathroom, she shuffled into the kitchen, where she found a note from Gwyn waiting for her on the counter.

"I know you missed your naps yesterday, so I let you sleep in. I have to go check on a few things for today's activities, but I'll be back soon to take you to breakfast. Love, Gwynnie," she read aloud.

Hazel's eyes widened. "Wow. Gwynnie trusted me alone in the apartment. That's a first," she said. Her stomach growled at the mere mention of the word breakfast. She flipped the little piece of paper over and scribbled on the back of it, *Gwyn, I'll meet you in the dining room.*

Grabbing her cane, Hazel headed for the door. She swung it open and found a little four-wheeled red motorized scooter with a basket blocking her doorway. She pulled her head back in surprise. "What in the world?" she muttered before sticking her head out into the hall and looking both ways.

"Hello?" she called out. No one said anything. "Hello! Somebody get this stupid scooter out of my doorway!" she yelled a little bit louder this time. "I want to go to breakfast with Gwynnie!"

Still nothing, but she also noticed loads of junk lining both sides of the hallway. "Ugh," she groaned, poking at the tire with the end of her cane. Then a thought came to her. She took a step back, aimed the butt of her cane at the scooter, and tried to fire it. A tiny amount of green energy fizzled out the end in a humiliating little zapping noise. She was thankful that no one had been around to witness her lame attempt at magic.

She shook the cane several more times in an attempt at making it fire at the scooter, but it didn't work. So she padded into her kitchen and grabbed a paring knife from the drawer. She came back to the door and stuck her head out into the hallway again. "Anyone listening better come and get your wheeled goods off my front porch or I'm about to go postal!"

She waited a few seconds and then tucked the web of her skirt between her knees, bent over as far as she could, and plunged the paring knife into the front tire of the scooter. Then she hobbled over to the back of the scooter and shoved the paring knife into the back tire too. She grabbed her purse from the apartment and put it, her knife, and her cane on the seat of the scooter. Then she took a deep breath, leaned forward, and put everything she had into moving the scooter far enough away from her door that she could squeeze out into the hallway. Once she had it far enough ahead, she pulled her door shut and squeezed past the scooter into the hallway. Looking around and making sure that the coast was clear, she bent down and stabbed the front and back tires on the opposite side of the scooter for good measure.

Satisfied that she'd properly taught whoever had parked their scooter in front of her door a lesson, she put the paring knife in her purse, dusted herself off, and headed to breakfast.

Already in the dining room setting up a card table for

events later in the day, Gwyn greeted Hazel with a warm smile. "Good morning, Mom."

"Good morning, Gwynnie. I'm glad you're here already. I'm starving. Let's eat," said Hazel, sweating from her little workout in the hallway.

"Oh, I don't have to be back until ten for activities today. I was thinking we could go have coffee and breakfast with the girls at Habernackle's. Can you wait until then?"

Hazel tipped her head sideways. "Will you let me have french fries for breakfast?"

"I thought you'd moved on from fries."

Hazel shrugged and began hobbling towards the front door. "I have a hankering for fries. Must be my time of the month. Come on."

"Mom, you haven't had your time of the month in years, and fries are…"

Hazel turned around and began hobbling back towards the Village's dining room with a tight grimace on her face. "I think I'll just stay here if you're going to argue. Miss Georgia will make me fries."

Gwyn's head rolled back on her shoulders. "Ugh. Oh, fine. I'll ask Linda if she'll make you fries. Happy?"

Hazel grinned as she stopped walking and headed for the front door again. "Happier than a midget at a mini-skirt convention. Now come on. Let's go. I'm starved."

Hazel smiled as Phyllis's grandson, Reign, placed a heaping pile of french fries down on the table in front of her.

"Bon appétit, Hazel," he said with a flourish and a slight bow before taking off for the kitchen.

Gwyn's eyes widened. There was no way her mother was going to eat all of that. "That's a lot of french fries, Mom."

"Yeah, Haze. You gonna eat all those, or do you need some help?" asked Phyllis, reaching over to pull a fry from the stack.

Hazel fired a tiny amount of electrical energy from her fingertips, zapping Phyllis's hand. "Get your own! These are mine!"

Phyllis recoiled and rubbed the back of her hand. "Jeesh, after everything we did for you yesterday, you won't even let me have a single fry?"

"Phil!" hissed Char, looking around skittishly. "Think you can say that any louder?"

"What? No one's paying any attention to a table full of old biddies. And even if they were, they wouldn't know what I was referring to anyway."

Char waggled her head and sat up straighter. "I'm sure they could put two and two together and figure it out if they really tried."

"You give these people too much credit," said Hazel, stuffing a fry into her mouth.

Char shook her head and leaned forward. "Oh no.

The town's buzzing about George. Give them one more thing to talk about and it'll spread like wildfire."

Gwyn's eyes widened. "There's buzz about George here too?"

Char let her head fall. "I stopped into the bakery this morning to drop Vic off, and Sweets said it's all anyone's been talking about. Is there talk at the Village?"

Gwyn sucked in her breath and nodded. "Are you kidding? Of course! Everyone has their own idea about what happened to him."

"What kind of ideas?" asked Phyllis, cutting her eggs.

"Well, some of the ladies think Duke Olson had something to do with George's death," said Gwyn. "But I've also heard talk about his ex-wife possibly being involved."

"Yeah, I've heard the ex-wife rumors too," admitted Char. "But I hadn't heard anything about Duke Olson. What's the story there?"

Gwyn shrugged and cut off a piece of her roll. "I guess some of the ladies think it's suspicious that he's the one that took George's place on the bus yesterday and then somehow he disappeared and found his way back to the Village. I mean, if I didn't know differently, I might wonder about that myself."

Char pushed her oatmeal around in her bowl. "Well, at least we all know the truth."

"But don't you kind of feel bad that people are blaming it on Duke and Mr. Petroski's ex-wife?" asked Gwyn, rubbing her stomach. "I didn't sleep well all night thinking about it."

"I slept like a rock," announced Phyllis loudly. "Moving dead bodies around all day will do that to a girl."

"Phil!" chided Char. "For crying out loud! Has anyone ever told you that you're louder than a hoopty with no muffler?"

Phyllis sniffed the air and then shoved a piece of bacon into her mouth.

Char turned to Gwyn and Hazel. "I didn't sleep well either. It's worrisome to me that others are being blamed for George's death," she whispered. "I wonder if we shouldn't do something about that before it gets out of hand."

"What should we do?" asked Gwyn, wringing her hands. "If we tell anyone the truth, then Mom and I are as good as kicked out of the Village."

Phyllis lifted her brows. "The truth is going to come out soon enough. The medical examiner will tell everyone that George had a heart attack, and then that will be that. There's no sense in raising our own red flags if we don't need to. Now, can we discuss more important matters?"

"More important matters?" said Gwyn. "What's more important than this?!"

"Sorceress Halliwell!" said Phyllis. "We've got to figure out what we're going to do about her ghost!"

"Can you believe that Kat was able to keep that a secret for all those years?!" breathed Char.

Gwyn nodded. "She had to have been panicking. I know I would have been."

"You panic if I use too much toilet paper," said Hazel,

looking up from her pile of fries. "Panicking comes naturally to you."

"I wasn't always like this," said Gwyn with a sigh. "You bring it out of me, I'm afraid. But listen, Mom. You're the senior witch here. Don't you know some way we can undo the spell that Kat put on Sorceress Halliwell?"

Hazel stared at her. "If I can't undo that fake-from-a-bottle-red hair that you're sporting, what makes you think I can undo a spell that happened a half century ago?"

"Mom!" groaned Gwyn. "Can't you be serious just once?"

Hazel made a face. "I am serious. You look like Bozo the Clown with that hair. What's wrong with just going natural like the rest of us?"

"Oh, Hazel, leave Gwyn be. I think she looks pretty," said Char.

Gwyn let out a breath to settle her nerves, then she looked at the girls. "If Mom's not going to help us, I guess it's up to us to figure out the spell. What are we going to do?"

"I don't know," said Char. "But I thought about it a lot last night. I am so curious about what unethical thing it was that Kat could've been doing."

Gwyn clucked her tongue. "I don't know, but I wondered the exact same thing. With all these secrets coming to light, I feel like maybe Kat wasn't who we all thought she was!"

Phyllis leaned across the table. "Now let's not go lighting our torches and hauling out the pitchforks.

Everyone has secrets." She looked pointedly at Hazel. "And we've all made mistakes. I know I've made a few doozies in my time. Kat died with a big one on her heart, knowing that she wasn't able to fix it herself and that she wasn't able to tell her best friends about it and ask for help. I think now we have to focus our energies on righting her wrong, not crucifying her for it."

Char nodded. "I couldn't agree more, Phil. Should we head right over to Kat's after breakfast?"

Gwyn shook her head. "I can't. I have to work at ten. How about tonight?"

"Sure, tonight works for me," said Char.

Phyllis nodded. "We'll stop by Loni's and pick her up. Seven?"

"Better make it seven fifteen," said Gwyn. "I never know how long Mom's going to take to eat her supper."

"Good morning, ladies," said a voice from behind them.

"Oh, hello, Sergeant," said Char.

"Hey, Sarge," said Phyllis.

"Hazel, it looks like you're feeling better today!" boomed Sergeant Harrison Bradshaw.

"And it looks like the grass got freshly mowed today," said Hazel.

Harrison grinned and ran a hand through his white flattop of hair. "As a matter of fact, I did just have a trim this morning, thank you for noticing." He looked down at Gwyn. "Good morning, Gwyn. You've got quite the observant mother."

"Good morning, Harrison," said Gwyn with a

nervous smile as she swatted at her mother. "Yes, Mom's got quite the eagle eye."

Harrison squeezed Gwyn's shoulder. "So are we on for Friday, then?"

Gwyn glanced over at Hazel. "Oh, I hadn't had a chance to mention it to Mom yet. Mom, Harrison's invited us out to dinner on Friday night. Are you up for a night out?"

Hazel cocked her head to the side. "You got any cute friends?"

"Cute friends?" asked Harrison with a small smirk. He rolled his fingers. "As in for you?"

"No, Gwynnie likes 'em two at a time," said Hazel. "Of course for me!"

Gwyn palmed her forehead and stared at her mother incredulously. "Oh my gosh. Mom. You don't need a date. Maybe I should just let you stay with the girls on Friday night."

Hazel lifted her brows. "Oh, no, no. I never get to have any fun. I'll go, but just so we're clear, I'm not a cheap date."

Harrison smiled at Gwyn. "Oh, yes. I figured as much. A lady of your stature should come with a hefty price tag."

"Darn tootin'!" said Hazel, pointing her stubby finger at him.

"Very good, then I'll pick the two of you up at six. I know Hazel probably likes to eat early. Will that work for you?"

Gwyn nodded and gave him a little smile, thankful

that Harrison didn't seem to mind her mother's directness. "Six should be just fine. I'm looking forward to it."

He grinned, his blue eyes sparkling. "I'm looking forward to it as well." Then his eyes darkened a bit. "So, Gwyn, if you don't mind me asking, is the Village just a zoo today? We've all heard about George Petroski."

"Oh, you have? What have you heard?" asked Char.

Harrison shrugged. "It's probably just a rumor."

"Spill," said Phyllis.

"The guys at my table are saying that George's ex-wife murdered him and dropped his body off at the morgue on her way out of the country."

Gwyn's sucked in her breath, covering her gaping mouth with her hand.

"Is that what the scuttlebutt is?" asked Char, eyes wide.

Harrison gave a light shrug. "That's what the guys are saying. From what I hear, Noreen is going to make out in all this. George had a big insurance policy on him, and he hadn't taken Noreen off of his beneficiary list."

Gwyn lowered her brows. "I didn't know about all that, but that certainly doesn't mean that she murdered him!"

"No, of course not," agreed Harrison. "I think it's the fact that his body was snuck into the morgue with a note to call the Village that's got people talking."

"Couldn't he have simply been found somewhere, and someone dropped him off? I mean, just the fact that his body was discovered at the morgue doesn't imply murder in and of itself!" said Char, glancing towards Hazel.

Harrison smiled at the women. Gwyn thought she saw a bit of a look in his eye. He thought they were being naive about the situation. "No, but wouldn't you agree it's highly suspect? I mean, really. Who does that?"

The women all exchanged uncomfortable looks. Gwyn swallowed hard. "Yes, who does that indeed?"

19

Char unpacked the bag of groceries she'd carried in. They had a night of magic spells ahead, and she wanted to make sure that they had enough food in case someone got hungry.

Of course, she couldn't help but think about what Kat had done all those years ago. "Something unethical," she murmured. "I wonder what it could have been."

Her eyes scanned the room, bouncing over the salt and pepper shaker collection on the little wooden shelf on the wall to the blue-and-white nineteenth-century Wedgewood dinner plates they'd found in Kat's china cabinet. Char shook her head. She couldn't imagine her dear friend doing anything that wasn't aboveboard, and she certainly couldn't imagine her friend putting a spell on Sorceress Halliwell just to keep her quiet.

Char heard a noise from the front room.

"Hello!" called out Gwyn's voice.

"In the kitchen!" Char yelled back.

Seconds later, Gwyn and Hazel stood in the kitchen. "Where's Phil and Loni?"

"Oh, they went upstairs to get the spell book from Kat's spell room." Char held up a loaf of bread and some lunch meat. "I brought snacks in case we get hungry later."

Gwyn raised a brow and looked at her watch. "Uh-uh, I'm not staying that long. I haven't slept well lately with everything that's been going on. I'm exhausted. I just want to see what we can make happen, and then I want to get Mom home and get us both to bed. We need our beauty rest."

"Speak for yourself," said Hazel, fluffing her hair with one hand. "I look good."

Char chuckled. "I sure hope you're going to be willing to help us tonight, Hazel. Considering you're the oldest witch here, one would think your magic would be the most effective."

"One would also think being a witch, I could cure hemorrhoids, but that hasn't happened, so I wouldn't hold your breath."

"Hi, girls," said Gwyn as Phil and Loni entered the kitchen. Phil clutched the brown leather-bound spell book that Sorceress Halliwell had given them as a graduation gift in her arms, and Loni carried a basket of candles and other bottled ingredients.

"Hi, Gwynnie, glad you and Haze could make it," said Phyllis.

"Me too. I wasn't sure. Today was a zoo at work. News about George was all anyone could talk about. No one wanted to work on their afghans, no one wanted to do puzzles, no one wanted to play bingo either and usually that's a surefire bet." She shook her head. "You have no idea how much I just wanted to spit out that George died of a heart attack and just settle things right then and there."

Hazel pointed a finger at her daughter. "But you didn't, thank God."

"But I didn't," said Gwyn sadly, nodding her head. "I feel horrible about it. They're sullying Noreen Petroski and Duke Olson's good names."

Char grimaced. "I wouldn't worry about them sullying Noreen's good name. I don't think she had a very good name after divorcing George. I hear she was a gold digger."

Gwyn frowned. "We don't know that for sure. I just don't like people talking badly about those that aren't around to defend themselves. Especially when I know the truth and could prevent the talk. It makes me feel like a horrible person."

"Don't feel bad, Gwynnie. You didn't do anything to George," said Loni. "Hazel's the one that killed him with her amazing body."

Hazel put one hand on her hip and the other on her head and wiggled her bottom. "It is a pretty amazing body, isn't it?"

Gwyn rolled her eyes. "Can we get serious now? I don't have all night for this."

Char nodded and took the basket of supplies from Loni. "I'll just go set up these candles in the parlor."

"I need to grab a crystal bowl from the china hutch," said Loni. "I'll meet you all in the parlor too."

"Come on, Mom, let's get to the casting circle," said Gwyn, hooking an arm under her mother's elbow.

Minutes later, they were once again seated on chairs formed in a circle.

"Do we even know which spell we're doing?" asked Phyllis, looking around at the rest of the girls' faces.

Gwyn looked down at the spell book in her lap and threw her hands out on either side of herself. "I have no idea. Obviously we have no body for Sorceress Halliwell to reunite with as she's been a ghost for so many years. But at the very least, we need to figure out how to unleash her ghost so she can wander freely in the world instead of being tied to this house."

"So we do a vanquishing spell?" suggested Loni with a shrug.

Char shook her head and glanced around the circle at the rest of the women. "I don't think it would be a vanquishing spell. The way Sorceress Halliwell explained vanquishing spells to us when we went to the Institute was that they were used for the destruction of magical beings or ghosts. The poor dear has been through enough already, we don't want to destroy her!"

Gwyn flipped through the pages. "Right…so no vanquishing spells."

"What about a simple curse removal spell?" asked Loni.

Phyllis lifted her top lip. "You don't think Kat's tried one of those by now?"

Loni shrugged. "You know what they say about assuming."

"And since we don't have a body, we can't do a resurrection spell," said Gwyn, pointing at one in the book and then flipping right past it.

"Nope," agreed Char with a nod. "How about an unbinding spell?"

"I mean, we can try it," said Gwyn, flipping to the front of the book. She ran her finger down the table of contents. "There's one in here."

"I feel like Kat would have tried this by now," said Loni as she took Gwyn and Char's hands.

"I feel like she would have tried all of these," agreed Char. "But there are five of us and there was just one Kat. Combined, we've got to be more powerful than she was. Maybe that will be the difference."

"I'll call Sorceress Halliwell first, then we can try the unbinding spell," said Phyllis before sucking in a deep breath and straightening her back.

They were all quiet for several long seconds, gathering their energy and regulating their breathing before Phyllis began to recite her summoning chant.

> *"Sorceress Halliwell, we call to you,*
> *It's time to reappear.*
> *Make yourself visible,*

Show us you can hear."

After Phyllis had recited the chant once, she repeated it and this time all of the coven joined in.

"Sorceress Halliwell, we call to you,
It's time to reappear.
Make yourself visible,
Show us you can hear."

The candles around them flickered and the air began to move once again. Within two minutes of chanting, Sorceress Halliwell appeared before them as she'd done the day before.

Hovering in the air just inside their casting circle, she announced with a flourish, "You're back!"

"We've come to try and help you," said Char.

Sorceress Halliwell put a hand on either hip and leaned back, straightening. "Oh, have you? And how do you intend to help me? I've been a ghost for decades."

"Obviously we can't bring your body back to life, but we can unleash your spirit from Kat's house," said Gwyn.

"Would you like that?" asked Phyllis.

Sorceress Halliwell thought about it for a moment. Then she lifted one shoulder in a tiny shrug. "What else would I do? I've lived here for over half of my life."

"You could stay if you want, but then at least you could come and go," suggested Char. "Wouldn't that be better than being confined to this house for the rest of eternity?"

"Or my spirit might go," she whispered.

The women all looked at one another. It was something they hadn't wanted to talk about.

Gwyn looked up at her and nodded. "That's a possibility too."

The ghost gave a tight smile. "I suppose that would almost be better than being in this limbo. I'm a ghost, but I can't go anywhere. Since Kat died, it's been pretty lonely," she admitted. Finally she nodded. "Okay. I'm willing to accept your help. I'll take my chances on what happens. I think at this point, anything is better than my current situation."

Phyllis smiled at her. "Good. We're going to try an unbinding spell."

The ghost put a finger in the little divot below her bottom lip and thought about it for a second. "A spell to unbind a ghost from a house. Hmm, I can't remember if Kat tried it or not, it's been so long. You'll need hazel wort, an unbinding candle, a pair of scissors, and a fire extinguisher or a pitcher of water, just in case." Then she pointed at the rug. "And you'll need to move this rug."

Char and Phyllis stood up immediately and began to move the chairs off the rug.

"I'll go get the rest of the things we need," said Loni before disappearing through the door.

Minutes later, with all the ingredients and supplies gathered, the rug moved, and a bowl of water filled and at the ready, the women all took deep breaths. Candles flickered around the room as if anticipating what was to come.

"I think we're ready," Loni whispered.

Phyllis nodded. "Let's do this, ladies."

Before beginning, Gwyn looked up at Sorceress Halliwell. "Are you ready? This could be the first day of an entirely new life for you."

Sorceress Halliwell closed her eyes and inhaled a deep breath through her nose. Quietly, she opened them and nodded. "I think so." The women could see the smile wanting to burst forth, but she held it back, scared to hope.

Gwyn nodded and pointed to the unbinding candle in the center of the circle. "We'll start by chanting over the unbinding candle. Char, will you do the honors and light it as we chant?"

Char nodded and went to the center of the circle, where a squat white candle wrapped in twine lay on the floor.

Gwyn looked reverently down at the book and, holding her arms out on either side of her, she began to chant as Char lit the candle.

> *"Power of good, power of light,*
> *Break this binding with all your might.*
> *Allow Sorceress Halliwell to move about,*
> *She should be free there is no doubt.*
> *We cut the cord, we cut the bind,*
> *Set her free, spirit, heart, and mind."*

Gwyn looked up at the women. "Now cut the binding," she whispered to Char. "With the scissors."

Char nodded and lifted the scissors, and as the candle burned, she tipped it sideways and carefully slid one sharp edge of the scissors to slice through the twine along the candle's side.

Gwyn continued to chant as she did so.

"We call on you to set her free,
We call on you, so mote it be."

The rest of the witches all joined in. Their voices started out shaky and unsure, but eventually they were strong and firm and sounded as one.

"We call on you to set her free,
We call on you, so mote it be."

When the last snippet of twine had been cut, the air around them began to move. Sorceress Halliwell's spirit rose higher into the air. She threw her arms back, and her chest beamed towards the ceiling.

Gwyn's heart trembled as she stood and took the scissors from Char's hands. She walked to the doorway and began to cut the air with them—chopping in a smooth line parallel to the walls, windows, doors. Each cut seemed to allow a bit of the outside air in. Gwyn continued to cut until she'd severed the invisible binding that surrounded the entire outer edge of the room, the girls continuing to chant the whole time. The wind from outside was fully inside the room now. All the candles flickered wildly. The binding candle inside the casting circle moved the most, and the wind made the flame grow higher and higher, until it touched Sorceress Halliwell's feet.

As Gwyn made the last snip of air in the room, they chanted the spell one final time.

"We call on you to set her free,
We call on you, so mote it be."

Air poured into the room like water had poured into the sinking *Titanic*, spinning everyone's hair and the curtains into a wild tizzy. Sorceress Halliwell screamed! Her terror-stricken voice filled the witches' hearts with panic and fear.

The candle below her feet had tipped over and set the floor ablaze!

"Fire!" screamed Char.

"Get the water!" Phyllis hollered, pointing at the water next to Loni.

Loni leapt into action, grabbing the glass bowl and throwing the water over the flames. The minute the fire was extinguished, the wind died down as if it had never been there in the first place.

Everyone's hair dropped.

The curtains dropped.

Sorceress Halliwell's eyes bolted open. Her hand went to her chest. "Oh my goodness," she breathed. "That scared me!"

"Me too," Gwyn agreed.

They all stared at the charred, blackened spot on the

floor. "It's a good thing you thought to move the rug," said Char. "The fire would have spread a lot quicker with it down."

Sorceress Halliwell nodded. "I'm pretty sure Kat tried that spell before. The wind never got that fierce, though."

"She tried it before? Why didn't you tell us? We wouldn't have done it," said Gwyn.

Sorceress Halliwell smiled. "Five witches are always going to be more powerful than one. We had to give it a shot."

"Well, can you tell if it worked?" asked Loni.

All eyes tilted up to look at Sorceress Halliwell expectantly.

Phyllis nodded anxiously. "Yeah, do you feel any different?"

The ghost looked at her arms. "I don't feel any different."

Phyllis pointed to the exterior walls. "Try and go outside!"

Gwyn rushed to stand up. She went to the door and opened it. "Yes, try and go outside."

Sorceress Halliwell hesitated for a moment. "I haven't been outside in decades. It's kind of a scary thought."

Char clasped her hands together at her chest. "Oh, you're going to love it. It's a beautiful evening."

The sorceress stiffened her resolve and floated towards the open door. Closing her eyes, she took in one more deep breath and let it out slowly. "Here goes nothing!"

She floated forward and was immediately stopped at the doorway as if there was an invisible wall there holding her back. She backed up and tried again, this time smashing into the wall harder. Her face crumpled, as did the faces of the rest of the women in the room. "It didn't work," she whispered.

Gwyn's heart sank. She had been sure that they'd done it. "Oh, I'm so sorry," she said quietly.

"Me too," said Char.

Phyllis waggled a finger at them all. "But we're not quitters. We don't give up. We'll figure it out."

"Maybe it's just best if we drop it," suggested Sorceress Halliwell. "I—I have to go. Thanks for trying," she said, and before they could respond, she disappeared in the blink of an eye.

"Oh, girls, I feel just terrible," said Gwyn. "We can't let this be the end."

Char shook her head. "Oh, this isn't the end. It's just the beginning. We're not giving up until Sorceress Halliwell is set free!"

20

The next morning, bleary-eyed from the long night before, Hazel had no sooner slipped on some clothes and her glasses than she was out the door to meet Gwyn for breakfast. Stepping out into the hallway, she pulled the door shut behind her and started down the hall towards the dining room.

"Good morning," purred a lilting male voice behind her.

Hazel waddled around in a circle and lifted her heavy lids to look at the person standing in front of her. He wore a pink polyester polo shirt that accentuated his saggy man boobs, khaki shorts that ended just shy of his knobby white knees, and brown loafers with black socks that poked out of them, just covering his calves. In his arms he stroked an extraordinarily furry brown-and-black cat.

"Who're you?" Hazel grunted.

"My name is Martin Sinclair. I'm a new resident here," he said haughtily.

She glanced back toward George's door. Martin stood only steps away from it. "You got George's old apartment?"

The man nodded. "Indeed. I moved in yesterday."

"How'd you know about the room already? George just died a few days ago."

"I was on the waiting list for this room. It's the best one here, you know."

"Why's that?"

"Obviously because it's so close to the parking lot, and because it's an end room, it's got more square footage than the rest of the one-bedrooms."

Hazel grunted and then began to turn around to leave.

"Say, you didn't happen to have a run-in with my motorized scooter yesterday, did you?"

Hazel stopped walking. Her eyes widened. She'd almost forgotten about the scooter. Slowly she turned around again. "So you're the one that parked the thing in front of my apartment door?"

"I did no such thing. The movers did, apparently."

"Yeah, well, it didn't belong in front of my door," snapped Hazel.

"Indeed. You could have asked for me to move it instead of slashing the tires," he snapped. Even though it was clear that his temper had been piqued, he continued to pet the cat calmly. The gemstone on his thick gold-banded pinky ring caught the light as his hand moved.

"I hollered!" shouted Hazel. "Several times. No one came, and it was blocking my door."

"You could have called the front desk," he countered.

"And wait for them to take their sweet old time coming to move it?" She shook her head. "I'm a woman of action." She punctuated her statement by stabbing her cane into the floor.

Martin's bald head gleaned brightly from the fluorescent lighting in the hallway as he lifted one dark eyebrow. "I'm a man of action as well." He pulled a small envelope from his pocket and handed it to Hazel. "The repair bill. You have thirty days to pay up or I'll be pressing charges."

Hazel narrowed her eyes at him. Then she held up her cane and pointed at his head. "Hey, while you're here, I've always wanted to know. Do bald men wash their heads with soap or with shampoo?"

He stared at her emotionlessly. "You know, I'd like to see things from your perspective, but unfortunately, I just can't crouch that low."

Hazel frowned at him. No one had ever thrown a punch back at her. She suddenly felt speechless. Finally, she pointed at his cat. "Pets aren't allowed in here."

"Dexter isn't a pet," he answered plainly.

"Looks like a pet to me."

"Dexter is a *service animal.*"

Hazel's forehead creased as her eyebrows knitted together. "Cats aren't service animals. What kind of a service does he provide?"

Martin tilted his head to the side as he looked down at the cat in his arms. "He keeps me company."

She snuffed air out her nose. "Well, all I know is you better keep that rodent away from my front door or he'll meet the same fate that your tires met." With that she turned around and headed back down the hall towards the dining room.

"Thirty days, Ms. Prescott. Thirty days," he called after her.

"Oh, girls," sighed Gwyn, giving Char a hug in the lobby of the Village. "I'm so glad you could join Mom and me for breakfast here this morning."

Phyllis nodded and looked around. "I probably should have told Linda we were going somewhere else for breakfast so she wouldn't worry about us."

"Oh, phooey," said Char, waving a hand dismissively as they walked into the dining room. "Linda's not going to be worried about us. That poor girl has a million irons in the fire. She won't even notice for a minute that we didn't come for breakfast. Now, where shall we sit?"

Gwyn looked around too. The whole room seemed to be louder than usual. Everyone was buzzing about something. She pointed towards a table that had enough room for the four women. "Mom, is that table over there okay?"

Hazel followed Gwyn's pointing finger. Hazel nodded. "Why do I care where we sit? I just don't want to sit next to the glass sliders. Or the air ducts. And I don't want to sit too close to the kitchen. Or next to that guy," she added, pointing to an old man wearing a herringbone newsboy cap. "He chews with his mouth open. But I don't care where we sit. I just need some food. I'm starving."

Phyllis rolled her eyes. "But you don't care where we sit, huh?"

Hazel followed Gwyn to the table. "Exactly."

Once they were seated, Char leaned forward onto her elbows. "My goodness. Is it always this loud around here?"

"It's usually loud, but this is extraordinarily loud," admitted Gwyn.

"Are they still talking about George?" asked Phyllis.

Gwyn shrugged. "I'm not really sure what's going on."

Phyllis scooted her chair back into a table full of women. "Excuse me. There seems to be quite the commotion this morning. What's all the hubbub about?"

Alice Buerman leaned over. "You haven't heard? The preliminary autopsy results came back on George Petroski."

Phyllis glanced back at the rest of the girls.

Gwyn swallowed hard. *Good*, she thought. *Now they'll know it was a heart attack and all this ridiculous speculation will be put to rest!*

"Well, how did he die?" Phyllis asked the women.

"It was a heart attack," said Ellie Wallace with a nod. "Just like they thought."

Gwyn nodded. Her shoulders slumped forward. *What a relief!*

"Tell them all the facts, Alice," said Carol Hamburg.

Phyllis lowered her brows. "All the facts? That's not it?"

Carol shook her head. "Not only did they discover that someone had diapered George, but they also discovered a large amount of Viagra in his system."

"Viagra!" said Phyllis, her eyes wide. She looked at the girls.

Gwyn's heart sunk as her eyes flashed to her mother. *Mom!* she thought, knowing full well that Hazel was reading her mind as they sat there. *Did you feed that man Viagra?!*

Hazel looked up at Gwyn sharply. Though her lips were mashed together, Gwyn clearly read her mother's face. That was the first Hazel had heard about any Viagra.

"So what does that mean?" asked Char. "That he had Viagra in his system? Surely Viagra didn't kill him."

Carol Hamburg shrugged flippantly. "I wouldn't assume that. One of the girls told me that George was taking nitroglycerin for his angina."

Gwyn sucked in her breath. "I watched a report on ABC News that said taking Viagra while also taking nitroglycerin can cause a heart attack!"

"Exactly!" said Carol, waving her finger in the air as if she'd just announced a grand development. "George knew taking Viagra could kill him!"

Char's eyes widened. "So does everyone think that George committed suicide now?"

"Puh! George Petroski? Commit suicide? Highly doubtful," scoffed Alice Buerman. "He was so full of life. The man was just getting his life together after his divorce. Everyone loved him. There's no way he committed suicide."

"So are you trying to say that people think someone else intentionally *fed* George Viagra?" asked Gwyn, appalled at the thought.

Alice sat back in her chair and the four women at the table all exchanged knowing glances. "That's *exactly* what we're saying," said Alice. "It wasn't just a heart attack. Someone killed George."

Gwyn's mouth went dry. Her mother was the last person to have seen George alive. This couldn't be happening! She stood up and then reached down to grab her mother by the arm. "Girls. I'm suddenly not feeling well. I think Mother and I will eat in our room today. Would you mind bringing your plates to our room? I think we all have a lot of things to talk about."

Hazel looked up at her mother nervously. "We do?"

Gwyn pulled her in closely. "We do."

"Mom, please tell me you did not give George Petroski Viagra!" said Gwyn, sliding the plate of food Char and Phyllis had brought her over on the coffee table of their small shared apartment.

Hazel splayed her hands out in front of herself. "How many times do I have to tell you, Gwynnie? I didn't give him any!"

"You have to tell me a lot of times, Mom. A lot. Of. Times. Maybe enough so that I believe you."

"That's not fair! Why don't you believe me?"

"Are you kidding? You were going to keep the fact that you slept with George and he died a secret from me! Why would I believe you? You never tell me the truth about things! You're sneaky and manipulative!"

Hazel sucked in her breath. "Sneaky and manipulative? I'm not sneaky and manipulative."

"No, Hazel, you are a little sneaky," said Char, nodding her head.

"And pretty manipulative," added Phyllis.

Hazel shot them both dirty looks. "Would you two just worry about yourselves right now? This is between me and my daughter!"

Char shook her head. "Sorry, Hazel. You've got us all wrapped up in this one. We moved the body for you. Numerous times. If you actually *killed* George, then we're accomplices to murder!"

"But I didn't actually *kill* George. That's what I'm trying to tell you. Aside from giving George the best sex of his life and causing a heart attack, anyway…"

"Well, we now know it wasn't the sex that caused the heart attack," said Phyllis. "So you can just quit with that whole theory."

Hazel frowned. "Fine. But the truth of the matter is, I

didn't do anything wrong. George had Viagra in his system, but I can tell you, he didn't get it from me."

"Well, did you see him taking it?" asked Char. "Like while he was here?"

Hazel shook her head. "No, but I have a sneaking suspicion that he'd already taken it before he got here."

"Why do you think that?" asked Phyllis.

"Let's just say he was ready for action before he even came in through the window."

"He *came in through the window*?!" demanded Gwyn. "Mom! He lived next door to us! Why didn't he just come in through the front door?"

Hazel shrugged. "I don't know. He seemed like he was in a panic. I thought he was worried about you being home."

"Wait a minute," said Gwyn, looking at her mother curiously. "I was home when George came over?"

Hazel nodded. "You were in the shower."

"I was in the shower?! Mom!"

Hazel shrugged. "What?! I didn't know he was going to come over."

"Gwyn, I realize you're upset about your mother's relationship with George, but can you just let her tell her story? Maybe we can figure out what really happened to George," suggested Char lightly.

Gwyn let out the breath she'd been holding. "Fine," she said with a grimace. "Tell your story, Mom."

Hazel looked confused. "What story? That was the story! He came over here horny as the devil. You were in the shower. He was scared to come in through the front door, so he snuck in through your bedroom window. I hid him in my room until you left. We had sex. He had a heart attack. And then Loni came over. That was it. Story's over!"

"So if he came over here horny as the devil, as you so eloquently put it," said Phyllis, "he must have gotten the Viagra into his system before he came."

"Girls. I think it's time we put our detective caps on and figure out exactly who had access to George that morning and who might have wanted to hurt him," said Char. She looked at Gwyn. "What do you think, Gwynnie?"

Gwyn's mouth fell open. What other choice did they have? The police were going to start putting things together, and if they didn't figure out the murderer before the police did, they might just very well point the finger at the last person to have seen George alive—Hazel.

21

As the women were leaving Gwyn and Hazel's apartment minutes later, Nurse Brenda happened to be loitering a door down in front of George Petroski's room.

"Brenda!" called out Gwyn. "Do you have a minute?"

Brenda looked up sharply. Her brows were knitted together in a pensive sort of way. She pointed down the hallway and began to walk away. "Actually, I'm—"

"It'll just take a second, really," Gwyn promised, cutting her off before she could make any excuses.

Brenda looked behind the women down the hallway as if she were waiting for someone to show up any second. She swallowed hard. "Umm. Yeah, okay. If it's just a second."

A soft smile covered Gwyn's face. "Great. Brenda, these are friends of mine, Phyllis Habernackle and Char Bailey."

Brenda nodded at the two women, giving them a tight smile. "Hello."

Phyllis gave her a smile and nod back.

Char looked the woman up and down. Brenda looked wound tighter than a top at a spinning convention.

"First of all," Gwyn said, lowering her brows, "are you alright? You look…"

"Nervous." Char frowned.

"Nervous?" Brenda's voice caught in her throat. She looked back behind the women again. "No, I'm not nervous."

Phyllis looked over her shoulder. "Then why do you keep looking behind us? Are you expecting someone?"

Brenda took a shallow, shaky breath. "No. I, uh, I just have a lot of rounds to make today, so I'm in a bit of a hurry."

"I see," said Gwyn. "Well, we won't keep you. We were just curious if you'd heard anything about George Petroski."

Brenda's eyes flicked up quickly to meet Gwyn's. "George Petroski?" She swallowed hard again.

"Yeah," said Hazel, pointing her cane towards the room Brenda had just been standing in front of. "George. You know the old feller that lived in the apartment you were just staring at?"

"Oh, yeah, I-I know George," she said with a bit of a nervous giggle behind her words.

Char lowered her brows. *She* knows *George? Doesn't she mean, she* knew *George?* "I assume you're aware that he died?"

Brenda cleared her throat and shifted uncomfortably in her white patent leather sneakers. "Oh, yes, of course. I heard the news about George's passing. It's unfortunate. He was a nice man."

"You don't sound too upset?" said Gwyn.

Nurse Brenda grinned. "I'm a nurse in a retirement village. Unfortunately, it's part of my job to lose people on a fairly regular basis."

"But wasn't George in amazing shape?" asked Gwyn. "I mean, who would have ever thought that he would have a heart attack?"

Brenda's eyes shifted in both directions down the hallway again before settling on Gwyn. "I mean, yes, George was in good shape for his age. But you aren't considering that he might have had his own health issues he was dealing with privately. Just like everyone else here."

Char nodded knowingly and tapped her chest with her fingertips. "Oh! You must be referring to George's angina?"

Brenda's eyes widened to the size of half-dollars. "You knew about George's angina?"

"Didn't everyone?"

Brenda made a face. "Not that I was aware of. George liked to keep that to himself. Who told you he had angina?"

Suddenly Char felt bad. Perhaps that had been a secret the girls had shared with them. Char's smile faded. She cleared her throat. "Oh, ummm. We just heard it through the grapevine. I couldn't even tell you from where. I think it's all over the Village, actually."

Brenda's face flushed beet red. She pointed down the hallway, looking as if there was a force pulling her along. "I really should get moving. I have lots to do today."

"Oh, but wait," said Gwyn. "I had another question."

Brenda froze.

"Is it true that if you take nitroglycerin for angina, taking Viagra could cause a heart attack?"

"Viagra?" breathed Brenda, her voice little more than a whisper.

Phyllis looked at her curiously. "Yeah, Viagra."

"I mean…," she stuttered.

Gwyn's eyes narrowed. "You realize that the word around the Village is that George had a high dose of Viagra in his system, don't you?"

Brenda's hand fluttered to the base of her throat. Her head bobbed lightly. "I mean, yes, I…"

"Do you think George knew that he shouldn't take Viagra combined with the nitro?" asked Char.

Brenda's eyes flickered to meet Char's then and almost seemed to harden instantaneously. Even her spine seemed to stiffen. "I told George very clearly he should never take those two things together."

Char tilted her head to the side. "So he asked about taking Viagra?"

"No, he didn't. I volunteered that information as his nurse," she said. Her tone had changed to sound almost as if she'd been offended by the question. "I was very clear about that."

"So what you're saying is, George knew better?" asked Gwyn.

Brenda nodded. "He absolutely knew better. He wouldn't have taken Viagra on his own."

Something about Nurse Brenda had Char curious about her. "If George didn't ask for that information, why did you think it was necessary to tell him about that drug's interaction with Viagra?"

Brenda snuffed air out her nose. "Because I'm a nurse. And I know many men of his age that enjoy the use of Viagra. It was only a preemptive measure, I can assure you."

"And yet somehow he had it in his system," mused Phyllis.

Brenda frowned. "Yes, yes, he did."

"So either George decided to take his chances and gamble his life on a good time, or someone else managed to get George to ingest the medication without his knowledge. Would you agree?"

Brenda tipped her head sideways and scratched the crown of her head. "Those would be the two options. Yes."

"Some of the other residents here don't seem to think that George would have intentionally chosen to cause himself any harm. What do you think of that?"

Brenda's eyes widened. "You mean, do I agree that it's unlikely George was trying to kill himself? Yes, I agree. That's highly unlikely in my opinion. George was a smart man. He had lots of things going for him. I can't imagine any case where that was a scenario."

"So it's more likely that someone else must have given him the medication, either intentionally or accidentally?" asked Char.

Her face flushed. "I mean, I guess…"

"Do you have any ideas of who that person might have been?" Char asked pointedly.

Her eyes widened then. "No, I—uh, I don't know…," she stammered.

"Ms. Kayton!" called a voice from down the hallway.

Brenda looked back over the women's heads. Her shoulders slumped forward visibly. It was as if her worst fear had come true. "I have to go," she muttered and began down the hallway in the opposite direction as the voice.

"Ms. Kayton, wait!" called the voice again.

The women turned to look as broad-shouldered Detective Mark Whitman came hustling down the hallway, notepad in hand.

She froze as his long legs caught up to her.

"I need to speak to you!" he said with his eyes locked on her. "Do you have a minute?"

Slowly, she turned to face him. "Actually…," she said. "I have patients to—"

"I'm sure they can wait a few minutes. I don't think this will take long." His voice was firm and authoritative.

She swallowed hard. "Yes, I suppose they can wait."

"Great," he said, opening his notebook and clicking his pen. From the corner of his eye, he seemed to notice Gwyn, Hazel, Char, and Phyllis standing there for the first time. He gave them a little nod. "Good morning, ladies."

"Hi, Detective," said Char. "You're on the move early this morning."

"A detective's work is never done," he said with a tight smile before flipping another page on his notepad. "Ladies, perhaps you could give Ms. Kayton and me a moment or two alone?"

Hazel took off like a shot in the opposite direction. "Yeah, come on, girls. We have things to talk about anyway."

"I appreciate it," he said, giving his back to the women to focus on Brenda Kayton.

Down the hallway, Hazel pulled the women off to the side. "That was a lie."

Gwyn looked at her mother curiously. "Detective Whitman lied? About what?"

Hazel shook her head and looked back down the hallway. "No! Not the gumshoe. Nurse Ratchet! She lied! When you asked her if she knew who might have given George the Viagra intentionally or unintentionally. She said she didn't know, but that was a lie."

Phyllis's eyes widened. "You mean she knows who gave the pills to George?"

Hazel made a face as she swatted the air. "I'm not sure. That woman's mind is about as scattered as birdseed in a park. I couldn't understand exactly what was going on up in that mess, but it was clear there was something more she wasn't telling us."

"Darn it," said Phil, snapping her fingers. "If only we'd had a few more minutes with her, we might have been able to break her."

Char looked back down the hallway. She was sure that Detective Whitman was there to talk to Nurse Brenda about George as well. The realization that the police were now officially investigating his death made everything that much more real. "Girls, Detective Whitman being involved now is not good. If he finds out that Hazel was the last person who saw George alive, we could all be in some serious trouble."

Gwyn rubbed a hand over her stomach. "I was just thinking the same thing."

"We're going to have to stay two steps ahead of him at all times if we want to figure this out before he does," said Char.

Phyllis pointed towards the dining room. "Then what are we waiting for? Let's get back to the dining room and do a little snooping around before Whitman beats us to the punch."

22

Most of the tables had already been cleared of their breakfast dishes by the time the women strode back into the dining hall, and Miss Georgia Lange, the kitchen lady, was tidying up the serving line.

"Good morning, Miss Georgia," said Gwyn with a nod.

Miss Georgia merely nodded her head stoically in the women's direction and kept working.

To the women, Gwyn threw out her arms on either side of herself. "Well, girls. Where do we start?"

Char tipped her head towards a couple tables full of men playing cards. "We have to find out what people around here know about getting their hands on Viagra. Maybe we should ask some of those men here what they know."

Phyllis laughed. "You really think a bunch of men are going to admit to a group of women that they know how to get their hands on Viagra? No way, Jose. Men don't admit that kind of thing!" She shook her head resolutely and pointed towards another table—this one full of women. "Nope. We talk to the women. They'll know what's what."

Gwyn nodded. "I agree with Phyllis. Let's start with the women." Gwyn began to walk towards the group of women playing cards. It was many of the same women they'd bumped into the night before: Alice Buerman, Carol Hamburg, Ellie Wallace, and Mary Von Ebsen.

"Ladies, do you have a minute?" asked Gwyn as she approached the table.

Alice looked up after placing a ten of spades in the pile in the center of the table. "We sure do. Mary and I are just about to stick it to these girls once again."

"You wish," said Carol Hamburg, laying the queen of spades down on top of the jack. The woman bobbed her head and laughed. "Take that!"

Mary's eyes widened and she reluctantly laid a five of hearts down on top of the queen of spades.

Alice rolled her head back on her shoulders and looked at Mary. "Mary! I thought for sure you had the queen!"

Wide-eyed, Mary shook her head. "What made you think that?"

Alice's face flushed as she shrugged. "I don't know. Your facial expressions, I guess."

Carol rolled her eyes. "Don't you mean that little bit of table talk you were doing? You don't think I noticed it when you touched your head and then started yammering on and on about you and Mary digging up the flowers outside your window later with the new spade your son brought you for your birthday?"

Mary sucked in her breath. "Is *that* what that was all about? I only agreed to help Alice because I thought she'd really gotten a new spade!" She waved a hand at Alice. "I can't believe you were trying to cheat!"

Ellie let out a giggle.

Alice dropped her cards on the table and looked up at Gwyn, ready to change the subject. "What can we help you girls with?"

Gwyn smiled. "Now that we've had a little time to think on the matter, we're curious where George might have gotten ahold of Viagra if he didn't have a prescription. Do you know anyone here at the Village that might have had a prescription for it?"

Carol's eyes widened.

Alice and Ellie had to throw a hand over their mouths to keep the giggles from bursting forth.

"What?" asked Gwyn with surprise. "What's so funny?"

"It's just that… well, this is a retirement village," said Alice.

"Thank you, Captain Obvious," snapped Hazel. "I'm glad you clarified that, because I was under the impression it was a home for wayward morons."

Gwyn palmed her forehead. "Mother! Not now with the sarcasm!"

"What? They're grown women. You don't think they can handle a little sarcasm?"

Gwyn turned her back to her mother. "I'm so sorry,

Alice. So are you trying to say that no one around here uses Viagra?"

Alice giggled again. "No, that's sort of the *opposite* of what I'm saying. *Everyone* around here uses Viagra."

Phyllis's stance widened and her hands popped up onto her hips. "They do?!" she gasped. "Geesh, maybe I should've gotten an apartment here instead of downtown!"

Carol grinned. "It's kind of a *thing*, you know?"

Gwyn shook her head. "No. I don't know. I had no idea it was a *thing* here. What do you mean by a *thing*?"

"Well," began Carol before she lowered her head and kind of whispered. "There's sort of an underground market for it."

"Underground?"

Carol nodded. "You know. Not everyone can get their doctor to prescribe it, so there are a few people that *sell* their prescriptions."

Char sucked in her breath. "But that's wrong! Someone could get hurt! Someone *did* get hurt! George died!"

"Who's selling it?" asked Phyllis.

Alice made a face as she leaned back in her chair, straightening up. "Oh no. We don't get to know that," she said in a hush.

Carol nodded. "The men are *very* cautious about who gets to know that information. They don't want their supplier getting cut off at the knees."

"Well, someone has to know," said Gwyn.

Hazel clunked her cane against the legs of Mary's chair. "Your husband's still alive."

Mary looked up at Hazel curiously and then at the rest of the women. "Well, yes, of course he is. Why?"

"Has Ernie ever popped one of the little blue pills?"

Mary held a hand to the collar of her blouse primly and looked at the other women, her face turning beet red. "Hazel, I don't think that's any of your business."

Gwyn's own face flushed. "I'm so sorry, Mary!" Gwyn turned to Hazel and shot her a stern look. "Mom! That was rude! Whether or not Ernie uses Viagra is private and certainly none of our business."

Hazel frowned. "I could care less whether or not her husband can get it up. I just thought if he'd used it, she might know who was supplying it."

Mary looked indignant. "I can assure you, Hazel, I have no idea where the Viagra supply is coming from!" She cleared her throat and then looked directly at Gwyn. "But if you really want to know what happened to George, I think you should be looking at Noreen Petroski. Everyone knows that woman was all about George's money. It wouldn't surprise me in the least if she visited him and dropped a few pills into his food or drink or something."

Phyllis sighed. "You're not the only one who thinks that Noreen had something to do with George's death. That's what half the town is saying too."

Mary nodded. "When they were married, she had quite the reputation for spending all of George's money. Then they got divorced and she had to live on a budget. I don't think she liked that very much at all. George admitted to Ernie once that he still hadn't taken Noreen off of his life insurance policy. She stood to gain quite a hefty fortune when George died."

The girls all exchanged looks. They needed to get into town and question Noreen.

Gwyn gave Mary a tight smile. "Thank you, Mary. And thank you, ladies, you've been a big help."

After they said their goodbyes and headed towards the lobby, Hazel pulled them aside once again. "I think Mary was lying about Ernie taking Viagra."

Gwyn waved away her mother's suggestion. "Mom, I don't want to hear any more about it. You embarrassed that poor woman in front of her friends back there. It's none of our business if Ernie takes Viagra or if he doesn't. I certainly don't blame her one little bit if she lied about it. Some things should just stay between two people."

Hazel threw her head back and groaned. "Like I said to Mary—I could care less about whether or not Ernie's equipment is in good working order. We're trying to figure out where the Viagra supply is coming from here. I was just thinking that if she was lying, and he did have a bottle of it, and if we could get our hands on that bottle, maybe it would have someone's name on the prescription label."

Char sucked in her breath. "Hazel! You're a genius!"

Hazel grinned. "Took you long enough to figure it out."

Gwyn rolled her eyes. "Using the words *Hazel* and

genius in the same sentence might be the overstatement of the year."

"Shush," said Hazel, holding a threatening finger up to her daughter. "You just let me bask in the glory of that for a moment." Then she looked at Char. "You may continue with what you were saying."

Phyllis giggled.

Char crooked a thumb over her shoulder. "I saw Ernie Von Ebsen back there playing poker."

Gwyn wrinkled her nose. "You want to go ask Ernie about his Viagra usage in front of all of his buddies? Oh yeah, he's going to love that."

Char waved her hands. "No, no, no. Ernie's in the dining room, and Mary's in the dining room. Which mean no one is in their apartment."

"So?" asked Gwyn.

"So… Hazel thinks Mary was lying about Ernie taking the little blue pills. If we can get in there and find the bottle, maybe we'd find out who it was prescribed to!"

"Charlotte Bailey!" breathed Gwyn. "You want to break into the Von Ebsens' apartment?!"

Char groaned inwardly. "You say that like it's such a bad thing."

"It *is* such a bad thing!"

Char let out a sigh. "Think about it, Gwynnie. Detective Whitman is hot on the same trail that we are. What if someone saw Hazel and Loni taking George out of the Village? Your mother could be on the list of accused within hours. We have to be five steps ahead of that man at all times. We can't let the investigation get that far or Hazel's going to be taking the rap for George's death!"

"Well, I'm sure Mom and Loni were more careful than to let anyone see them taking George out of the Village." Gwyn looked at her mother. "Right, Mom?"

Hazel swallowed hard. "Well…"

"Mom?"

Hazel tapped her cane around on the floor and refused to make eye contact with her daughter. "Maybe a few people saw George and me together."

Gwyn's eyes bulged. "Mom! You didn't tell us anyone saw you!"

"I didn't think it mattered! I thought they'd say it was a heart attack and that was that. I didn't know all this was going to happen!"

Phyllis shook her head. "Who saw you?"

Hazel was quiet for a moment before answering. "Mary and Ernie Von Ebsen."

"The woman you just insulted?!" breathed Gwyn. She covered her forehead with her hand. "I can't believe this is happening right now."

"Relax, Gwynnie. Relax," said Char. "We'll figure this all out. But it starts with finding out who the Viagra was prescribed to. And to do that, we need to break into Mary and Ernie's apartment."

"But I could get fired for that!" hissed Gwyn, her blue eyes blazing.

Char grimaced. "You could also get fired for covering up a murder."

Gwyn's mouth gaped open. "But I didn't know it was

a murder when I helped you take the body to the morgue!"

"None of us knew it either! We all thought the poor man had just died of natural causes. But do you really think the Village is going to believe that? They'll find out you helped cover it up and then they'll *really* think Hazel's guilty. Then we're not just talking about you getting fired or kicked out of the Village. Then we're talking about murder charges and *accessory* to murder charges. We can't let this go down like this. We need to be proactive rather than reactive," said Char firmly.

Gwyn was speechless. She couldn't believe everything that was happening. She felt like she was a student at the Institute again and the girls were pulling another one of their pranks and dragging Gwyn along for the ride. "Oh, fine. We'll see if we can find that prescription bottle, but we better make it fast."

Char rubbed her hands together happily. "No worries, we'll be gone faster than a toupee in a hurricane! Let's go!"

Char looked both ways down the hallway before waving for the girls to follow her. "Coast is clear," she whispered, rushing over to apartment 176 in the south wing of the retirement home.

"Hurry up, Gwynnie," said Phyllis, tugging on Gwyn's arm.

Gwyn shoved her hand in her pocket and pulled out a

fork she'd grabbed from the dining room. She handed it to Phyllis. "Here."

"Hurry," hissed Char, keeping watch.

"Don't rush me!" Gwyn closed her eyes and tried her best to calm herself and focus her energy. She wiggled her fingers at the fork lying in Phyllis's open palm. It didn't take long before it bounced up and down in her hand and began to evolve. The tongs bent and twisted and the handle shrank down, and then, easy as pie, it dropped into Phyllis's hand—a perfectly formed key.

"Good job, Gwynnie," said Phyllis as she put the key in the lock and opened the door with it. "Works like a charm!"

Once they were inside the apartment, they looked around.

"Should we split up?" asked Char. "I'll check the kitchen. Gwyn and Hazel, you check the bathroom. Phil, you check their bedroom."

Phyllis saluted Char. "Aye, aye, Cap'n."

"Come on, Mom," said Gwyn, moving towards the bathroom while the other girls set about looking in their assigned places.

"It takes two people to look through a medicine cabinet?" asked Hazel, hobbling over to a navy-blue recliner in front of the television.

Gwyn sighed. "Yes, it does. We don't have time for you to be watching television, Mom."

Hazel let out a heavy sigh. "You've been running me around all morning. I'm exhausted. I need my nap."

"Oh, fine. You stay there. I'll go check the bathroom."

Gwyn moved the remote control out of her mother's grasp just before she had a chance to grab it. "But no TV. We don't have time for TV, and someone might hear it and know we're in here."

Hazel scowled but didn't respond.

Gwyn moved quickly into the bathroom. She opened the medicine cabinet behind the mirror and rifled through it, opening every pill bottle to make sure she wasn't missing something that was mislabeled. *Nothing*, she thought with a sigh. Then it occurred to her: if Ernie used Viagra but didn't want Mary to know, he certainly wouldn't keep it in the medicine cabinet. Where would he keep it? "Hmmm," she mused, looking around the small bathroom.

"Girls!" hollered Phyllis from the other room. "I found something!"

Gwyn rushed out of the bathroom, being careful to remember to turn the light off. "What?" she asked, meeting Phil and Char in the living room. "Where did you find them?"

"In one of the nightstands." Phyllis carried a small bottle of pills in her hand. "They're blue!" She poured the pills out and showed them to the girls.

Gwyn frowned. "I mean, I don't know what Viagra looks like. All I know is it's blue."

Picking up one of the pills, Char shrugged. "Same. But maybe there are other pills out there that are blue."

Hazel motioned them over to her chair. "Lemme see 'em," she grumped.

Char handed her the pill she'd just picked up.

Hazel let it rest in the palm of her hands. She lifted it closer to her face, peering at it carefully through her glasses. Then she held it up to the light. "It's a Viagra."

Worry crept into Gwyn's mind then. "Mom, how do you know it's a Viagra? I thought you said you hadn't given George any."

"I said I hadn't given *George* any. That doesn't mean I've never given one to anyone else."

"Hazel!" clucked Char. "You little devil!"

Hazel waggled her eyebrows and chuckled.

Gwyn shook her head and held out a hand. "I don't even want to know, Mom." She turned and looked at Phyllis. "So if these are indeed Viagra pills, where did they come from? Whose name is on the prescription label?"

Everyone stared at Phyllis.

She shook her head sadly. "The label's been ripped off."

Char strode over to her and took the bottle from her hands. "Where's the lid?"

Phyllis handed her the little white lid. "Here."

Char nodded as she screwed the lid back on the bottle. "Just as I suspected. This prescription was filled here in town. Look." She showed them the lid, which had the Aspen Falls Pharmacy logo stamped on top.

"And?" asked Gwyn. "What's that tell us?"

"It tells us where to look next!"

23

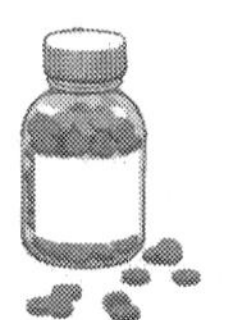

Gwyn stared up at the two-story house in an affluent part of Aspen Falls. "Char, I thought we were going to the pharmacy next? This doesn't look like a pharmacy to me."

Char scuttled out of the driver's seat of her car, slammed her door, and stood next to Gwyn with her hands on her hips. "That's because I decided to make a pit stop before we hit the pharmacy."

"Whose house is this?" asked Phyllis after helping Hazel out of the car. The four women now stood hip to hip on the curb.

"This," said Char with a broad sweeping gesture, "is Noreen Petroski's house."

"Ahhh," said Phyllis, nodding her head. "She was on our list too."

"Yes, she was. Let's just hope she's home."

As they walked up the long sidewalk, Char pointed to

a realtor's sign in the yard. "Huh. Looks like Noreen's going somewhere."

"That explains the moving truck in the driveway," said Gwyn, tapping a finger lightly against her chin. *Very interesting.*

Char was the first up the sidewalk. She and knocked on the door first.

They could hear people moving around inside, but no one readily came to the door. Phyllis knocked again.

Finally, the door opened, but it wasn't Noreen Petroski that answered. It was a man in a mover's uniform, single-handedly hefting an armchair out the door. His whole face glistened with sweat, and his biceps were swollen and his veins bulging.

"Hello, we're looking for Noreen. Is she in?" asked Char, holding the door for him.

"She's packing in the den," said the man. Breathing heavily, he cocked his head backwards. "I think you can go on in."

The rest of the women moved out of the way for the mover to carry the chair down the steps towards the moving van.

"Thanks," he said while passing them.

Char led the troops into the house. "Come on, girls."

Inside, movers were everywhere. Most of the furniture was already gone, and now they were packing up the smaller items.

"Excuse me," said Gwyn to one of the men. "Which way is the den? We're here to speak to Noreen."

Without speaking, the man just pointed towards the back of the house.

Gwyn nodded curtly. "Thank you."

They followed the trail of people and wove their way through the house until they came to an office, where they found a curvaceous woman in a short leopard-print skirt packing up a box of papers, the press-on jewels on her long, meticulously manicured fingernails sparkling under the office lights. The woman had a two-story white beehive piled on top of her head and wore several strands of gold around her neck, as well as gold hoop earrings.

"Noreen?" asked Char without hesitation.

Noreen stopped what she was doing and looked up. "Yes?" she asked and then smiled, clasping her hands together. "Oh, you four must be the cleaning ladies I hired." Her smile wavered for just a moment. "I see they sent their senior crew." She shrugged. "Oh, well, I suppose you'll do. Well, I'll tell you what. The movers are almost done in the kitchen, so you can probably start there. The cleaning company said you would be bringing your own supplies, correct?"

"No, we're not from the cleaning company." Char extended a hand to Noreen. "My name is Char Bailey. I think we've met before, but it's been years."

"Char Bailey, hmm, doesn't ring a bell," said Noreen, giving her hand a light shake. She frowned slightly, which deepened the furrows around her eyes and mouth. Even the heavy makeup she wore couldn't hide her wrinkles.

"It was actually Char Maxwell-Bailey. I've recently been married."

Noreen smiled and tipped her head sideways. "Well, isn't that something? I've recently been divorced."

"Yes, divorced from George Petroski, correct?" asked Phyllis. "That's what we were here to talk to you about."

Noreen's smile disappeared. "You came to talk about George?" She put the papers down and put her hands on her hips. "I'm sorry, who are you again?"

"I'm Char. This is Phyllis Habernackle." She pointed at Phyllis. "And that's Gwyn and Hazel Prescott. Gwyn and Hazel live in the Village."

"We were next-door neighbors to George," explained Gwyn.

Noreen's eyes widened. "Next-door neighbors to George," she breathed. Her eyes widened. "And he said something bad about me, didn't he? Oh, I just knew he was bad-mouthing me over there."

Gwyn shook her head. "Oh, no. Not at all! Not that I'm aware of anyway."

Noreen frowned. "You probably just weren't aware of it." She sighed. "Now, what are you doing here again?"

"Well, we just thought we should come and offer our condolences for your loss," said Gwyn.

"Condolences?" asked Noreen. "Is that the socially acceptable thing to do? Offer condolences to the ex-spouse of the deceased?"

Char shot her a cool smile and shook a finger. "You know, we hadn't had a chance to consult with Emily Post on that one. We just thought we'd take our chances and swing by."

Gwyn put on her best sympathetic face. "Yes, we

thought maybe you might need help with arrangements, or perhaps just someone to talk to? Is there anything we can do to make this difficult time a little easier?"

Noreen's eyes widened as she looked around the room. "Difficult time? I have no idea what you're talking about. This isn't a difficult time. The only difficulty I'm having right now is that I don't have a buyer for this house because apparently people in town think I'm a murderer. And because George's life insurance check isn't here yet, I can't book my flight to leave town. Not until I get some of his finances settled, anyway."

"So you *are* the beneficiary of George's life insurance policy?" asked Phyllis, skimming over the fact that Noreen seemed so cold about George's death.

Noreen nodded. "I was also the beneficiary of his entire estate. Who else would he have left everything to? He never remarried. We didn't have any children, and he didn't have any siblings that were still alive. I was it."

Char nodded. "Well, then I guess that makes sense that he left you on as beneficiary."

"Ms. Petroski, may I ask why the two of you divorced?" asked Gwyn.

Noreen laughed. "You mean you don't know? I assumed the whole Village knew!"

Gwyn shook her head.

"George cheated on me. Bastard. After forty-five years of marriage, he cheated on me. And now he got what was coming to him!"

"He cheated on you? That's terrible!" Gwyn's blue eyes latched onto Hazel.

Hazel's brows lifted, widening her eyes as if to say, *Don't look at me, George was single when I found him.*

"Tell me about it," Noreen sighed. "It was devastating. For a while. Eventually I got over it."

"Noreen," began Char slowly. Gwyn could tell she didn't know how to say whatever it was that was on her mind. "That you're aware of…did George ever…"

"Take Viagra?" asked Noreen, filling in the blank easily for her.

"You heard about that?" asked Char, eyes wide.

"Of course I heard about that. Like I said, I'm still his next of kin. The cops have already been here to speak to me. I'll tell you what I told them, if that'll help squash the rumors. George wouldn't have taken that Viagra. Period. He just wouldn't have. He knew what the repercussions would be if he took it. He also wouldn't have taken it to intentionally harm himself either. George wasn't like that." She shook her head. "Besides, last I knew, everything in"—she moved her hand in circles in front of her pelvis and lowered her voice an octave—"that department… was in fine working order. He didn't need it."

"So you're convinced that George didn't take it on his own?" asked Phyllis.

Noreen nodded. "I'd lay money on it."

"If George didn't take it on his own, do you have a theory for how it got into his system?" asked Gwyn.

"Isn't it obvious? Someone fed it to him."

Gwyn sighed. They'd deduced that much. What they needed to know was *who* might have wanted George dead. "But do you have any ideas about who might have done that?"

She shook her head resolutely. "Not a single inkling."

"None?" asked Char.

"None. And you can squash any other rumors that might imply that I had anything to do with his death. I will freely admit that I benefited from his death, but I didn't *want* him dead, and I certainly didn't kill him. I can't spend his money from prison, you know."

"If you don't mind me asking, where were you the day that he was killed?" asked Phyllis.

Noreen lifted a shoulder as if to say that question didn't offend her at all. "I had a long day that day. It started with an early breakfast with my sister. We ate at the Aspen Falls Eatery at seven thirty. We went straight from breakfast to get our nails done. Our appointments were at nine. We drove into the city to do some shopping right after that and didn't get back to Aspen Falls until after I'd gotten the call that George had been found dead in the morgue. Then I rushed right back to tend to his affairs, and that was that."

Gwyn leaned up against a bookshelf. One of the things the police didn't know was the exact time frame behind George's death. George had died while Gwyn had been at Habernackle's having breakfast with the girls. Hazel had said that he'd died almost right away, which put his death around eight o'clock or a few minutes after, but he'd snuck into the apartment while Gwyn had been in the shower. That would have been closer to seven thirty. If he'd taken the pills prior to seven thirty, then it was possible that Noreen had gone to the Village before she'd gone to breakfast with her sister.

"Ms. Petroski, did you visit the Village at all that morning?" asked Gwyn.

"Sweetheart, I can honestly say that I've never been to the Village. Not even after George moved in. I literally don't even know where his room would have been."

Hazel, who had been sitting quietly in a plush armchair during their whole conversation, finally piped up. "Why'd you have George's room cleared out in such an almighty hurry?"

Noreen poked one of her long fingernails into her beehive to scratch her scalp. "I was asked to."

"Asked to what?" asked Hazel.

She mashed her bright red lips together. "I really shouldn't say any more."

"Someone asked you to move George's things out? Who?" asked Char.

Noreen looked down at her wrist even though there was no watch on it. "Oh, look at the time! I have things to do. I think I'll have to walk you ladies to the door. I sure appreciate you stopping by to extend your condolences."

She held her arms out as if to usher the women towards the door, but Hazel didn't budge. "I know who asked her to speed things along."

All eyes turned to Hazel.

"Who?" asked Gwyn.

Hazel's eyes narrowed into slits as she stared Noreen down. "It was Martin Sinclair."

"Martin Sinclair?" asked Phyllis, jerking her head back. "Who in the world is Martin Sinclair?"

Noreen shook her head. "I don't know what you're talking about. No, no. It was the Village. They wanted George out post haste. So I sent my movers over there immediately."

Gwyn knew better. She shook her head. "I work at the Village. They said that *you* were the one anxious to get George moved out right away. They seemed to think it might have something to do with the security deposit, considering you demanded that it be refunded immediately."

Noreen sighed. "Ms....?"

"Prescott," said Gwyn.

"Right. Ms. Prescott, you realize that I'm going to be a multimillionaire by the time all of George's estate gets settled and I get the house sold and his life insurance policy comes through. Why in the world would I care about a measly three-hundred-dollar security deposit?"

"Why indeed?" asked Char.

Gwyn nodded. This was getting more and more interesting the more they heard from Noreen. "So if it was so insignificant to you, why did you demand getting it back so quickly?"

Noreen picked imaginary lint off the sleeves of her furry sweater. "The Village wouldn't officially consider George moved out until they refunded the security deposit. That's all I know."

Hazel nodded knowingly. "And Martin Sinclair couldn't move in until George was officially moved out."

"And Martin Sinclair is the man who moved into George's apartment?" asked Phyllis. "Ohhhh! Now it's making sense."

"It is?" asked Gwyn.

Phyllis nodded. "Martin must have asked Noreen to move things along. Is that it?"

Hazel nodded but kept her lips firmly mashed together.

Char's eyes widened. "Well, isn't *that* interesting."

Noreen frowned. "Listen, ladies. I don't know what you *think* you know, but you really have no idea about anything. Now really, I'm going to have to ask you to leave. I have cleaning ladies coming over any minute now and I've got to provide them with instructions."

Gwyn gave her a curt nod. "Very well. Thank you for speaking with us."

Char nodded too. "We're all sorry for your loss. We'll show ourselves out."

Once they were back in Char's car, Gwyn was the first to let out the breath she'd been holding. "Can you believe that woman?"

"What they say about her is right! What a money-grubbing hussy!" spat Phyllis. "I bet she did it!"

"You think she was the one that killed George?" asked Gwyn.

Char looked in her rearview mirror at Gwyn. "Don't you? She seemed guiltier than sin!"

Gwyn leaned back in her seat and folded her arms across her chest. Looking out the window, she watched the scenery fly by. "I don't know. She had a point. Her motive would have been George's money, but she can't spend it in jail."

"She wouldn't have to if she didn't get caught," said Phyllis.

Gwyn nodded. "She had to have thought she'd be caught, though. She's the most obvious killer! It's always the spouse. Or the ex-spouse. Or the jilted lover."

Everyone looked at Hazel.

Hazel lifted her hands defensively. "I didn't do it, I swear!"

"I think there's more to this story," said Char, turning a corner. "That woman was hiding something."

"I told you," said Hazel, "this is all about her getting George moved out of that room so that Martin Sinclair could move in."

"Well, then, maybe we need to have a talk with Mr. Martin Sinclair next," said Phyllis.

Char nodded before pulling the car over. "That'll be our next stop. But first… ladies, we have an assignment."

24

Gwyn peered through the pharmacy window from the sidewalk. The sun shone brightly, casting a glare across the glass, making everyone squint to look through it. "So you really think if we just go up to the counter and ask who has a prescription for Viagra at the Village, they're just going to tell us?"

Char swatted at Gwyn's arm. "Of course not. Pharmacies have strict confidentiality rules."

"Well, then, why in the hell are we here when I could be napping?" asked Hazel, leaning heavily on her cane. "I feel like I got run over by a dump truck!"

Gwyn wrung her hands. "Oh no. Maybe your cold is coming back."

Hazel's brows lifted. "My cold?"

Phyllis put a hand on her hip. "Gwynnie. You realize Hazel never had a cold, right? She was faking."

"Faking?" Gwyn's face filled with shock as she looked at her mother. "But Nurse Brenda said…"

Hazel rolled her eyes dramatically. "Oh for pity's sake, Gwynnie. I'm an old witch, not an old moron. I know how to turn the temperature up and fake a fever."

Gwyn shook her head. "See? And you wonder why I can't trust you."

"Can we focus on the matter at hand?" asked Char, peering into the window. "See that man behind the counter?"

The girls all mashed their noses against the glass. Gwyn's eyes swung over to the man behind the counter. He was an older gentleman with salt-and-pepper hair and a thick nose. "The pharmacist?" asked Gwyn.

"Yes. That's Sal Oberman. His wife died over five years ago, and he's just finally starting to date again. One of the girls at church said his daughter recently signed him for an online dating app."

Phyllis smoothed the stray hairs poking out of the bun on top of her head and stared at Char expectantly. "Ohhh? And why am I just now hearing about this man?"

Char frowned at her. "I didn't realize you were dating."

Phyllis frowned and cocked a hand on her hip. "I'm not dating, that's the problem! But I might be if you'd have told me about this guy." She swiveled slightly and looked back at her bottom. "Does he like women with big butts?"

"I honestly have no idea what lifts that man's shorts. I only mentioned it because I thought maybe Gwyn could go in there and create a little diversion. You know, flash some leg, maybe get the man away from his computer for a few minutes while the rest of us go do a little cyber sleuthing."

"Gwyn!" barked Phyllis, wide-eyed. "Gwyn's got Mr. Army Man. What about me? I could go in there and charm that man like nobody's business."

"That's the problem," said Hazel. "Nobody wants your business. Let Gwyn do it. She plays damsel in distress better than anybody."

Gwyn frowned. "Thanks?"

Hazel patted her daughter's arm. "You're welcome, dear. Now get in there and flash what your momma gave you."

"Oh, you'd like me to flash the bags under my eyes and these bird legs?" said Gwyn with a giggle. "I think I'll pass."

Char groaned. "Oh, come on, Gwynnie. We need you right now."

Gwyn pointed at the two women that were working behind Sal Oberman. "Let's just say I'm Sal's type and I can lure him away from the counter—how are you getting around those other two women?"

Char lowered her brows and peered in the window again. "Oh. Where did they come from? They weren't there a second ago."

Hazel shoved Char aside to smash her nose against the glass again. "Oh, for heaven's sake. Now I understand why they say never send children to do a woman's job. Get out of my way." Before they could stop her and devise a plan, Hazel tugged the glass door open and hobbled inside the pharmacy.

"Mom!" hissed Gwyn, poking her head in the doorway.

But Hazel kept going.

Gwyn looked back at her friends. She waved a hand at them, beckoning them to follow her into the pharmacy. "Come on, girls, let's split up. I'll follow Mom and see what she's up to. You girls get ready to spring into action."

Char nodded, and she and Phyllis veered right, taking cover between the first set of shelving units they found.

Gwyn turned around and realized Hazel was already nowhere to be seen. She took a deep breath and began to search. "Mom," she whispered, peering down every aisle. Finally, she peered down the medical supply aisle and found Hazel inspecting the canes and push walkers. "Oh, there you are. What are you doing?"

"Shhh," hissed Hazel, casting a sideways glance over at the pharmacist, who was only a few yards away, in plain view from where they now stood. "Watch a master at work. Hold my cane."

Gwyn took the cane her mother handed her and watched as Hazel hobbled unaided to the open area just in front of the pharmacy station. Hazel had one finger out in front of her. "Say, sonny, can you help a sweet old woman?"

Sal Oberman looked up from his computer. "Sure thing, ma'am. What do you need?"

"I need help with the canes," said Hazel, taking

another step forward. Then suddenly, her knees buckled and her feet seemed to slide out from underneath her.

Gwyn's eyes widened. "Mom!" she screamed, rushing to be by her side to catch her before she fell.

But Hazel was going down too fast. "Ahhh!" she screamed as she fell to the floor. Her arms went up over her head with a flourish, and then just like that, she was lying flat on her back, moaning.

"Oh no!" hollered Sal. "Betty, SueAnn, help!" He raced around the tall counter. Betty and SueAnn followed closely on his heels.

"Ohhhhhh!" moaned Hazel, rocking from side to side.

Gwyn squatted low over Hazel, her eyes filled with worry. "Oh, Mom, where does it hurt?"

Hazel quieted down for a moment as she eyed the pharmacy workers rushing towards her. Once they were upon her, she began to moan again. "Oh, it hurts *everywhere*!"

"Ma'am, are you alright? Is anything broken?" asked Sal, kneeling down to assess Hazel's condition.

Hazel rolled from side to side in a dramatic display of agony. "Ohhhh, my butt!!! I think I can feel a crack in it!"

Gwyn quirked a grin. That was when she knew Hazel had just turned the temperature up on her once again.

"Hurry, let's go, let's go," hissed Char, squatting low as she and Phyllis rushed behind the pharmacy counter once Sal, SueAnn, and Betty had all gone to assist Hazel. "We don't have much time."

"I'm going as fast as I can!" Phyllis hissed back.

On the other side of the counter, Char peered over the top of it to find all three of the pharmacy workers and Gwyn leaning over Hazel, who continued to howl like a mating wolf during a full moon.

With her heart hammering in her chest, Char stood up and wiggled the mouse on the counter. Phyllis stood up next to her, and together they stared at the computer.

"What are we looking at?" whispered Phyllis, tilting her head sideways.

The words on the screen could have been written in a foreign language for all Char understood. She clicked around on different things and brought up different screens, but suddenly realized this wasn't going to be as simple as she'd once thought. She didn't know the first thing about pharmacy software. She had no idea how to search based on the prescription. "I have no idea."

"You don't know what you're doing?" Phyllis sounded surprised.

"I've never worked for a pharmacy, Phil. Of course I don't know what I'm doing."

"Well, then, why in the hell did you suggest we do this?"

Char looked at Phyllis. "I don't know. It sounded like a good idea at the time."

"I think we should call an ambulance," came Sal Oberman's voice floating over the counter.

"I'll call, Sal," said one of the female pharmacy workers.

Char and Phyllis looked out at the group. SueAnn was standing up.

"Get down!" hissed Phyllis, tugging on Char's arm. Together the two of them fell to the ground. "We gotta get out of here!"

But the only way out was past SueAnn.

"Hurry, back here," hissed Char, instead crawling through the racks of medicines.

Phyllis followed her, scooting away just in time as SueAnn came bursting through the door to call for an ambulance.

The two women sat up with their backs against the rack, panting heavily from their near-capture. "I'm too old to be doing this," whispered Phyllis. "My granddaughter would have a field day if she knew I was crawling around on the floor like a toddler."

"Shhh," whispered Char, pointing at SueAnn, who'd just picked up the phone to dial it. And then something caught her eye. It was just across the floor. A big white paper bag, stapled shut, with the words Aspen Falls Retirement Village scrawled across the front of it. She poked Phyllis's shoulder and pointed at it. "Phil, look!"

Phyllis's eyes swung towards the bag. "What is it?"

Char shook her head. She didn't know, but she darn

sure was going to find out. She was just about to crawl out from her hiding place to grab the bag when SueAnn turned slightly. Char pulled back. "She's going to see me if I go out there."

"Hold my hand," whispered Phyllis.

Char winkled her nose. "What?"

Phyllis held out her hand for Char to take. "Trust me. Hold my hand and close your eyes."

Char made a face but did as Phyllis had suggested. She closed her eyes and took her friend's hand. Soon she could hear Phyllis chanting.

"Shadows, shadows, come to me,
Cloak me with anonymity.
I cannot be heard, I cannot be seen.
I am but a shadow, silent and lean."

Char squeezed her eyes shut and began to chant with Phyllis. She remembered this spell from their days as students at the Institute. They'd used it many times to play practical jokes on their classmates or teachers. It had been so long since she'd heard the words that she'd almost forgotten the spell.

"Shadows, shadows, come to me,
Cloak me with anonymity.
I cannot be heard, I cannot be seen.
I am but a shadow, silent and lean."

Char imagined her body going from an opaque figure

to a transparent one. She visualized shadows covering her and Phyllis as she continued to chant the spell.

Finally, Phyllis stopped chanting and let go of Char's hand. "Did it work?"

"I can see you," said Char.

"That's because we were holding hands. Don't you remember how the spell works?"

Char swished her lips to the side. "Barely. How are we supposed to know if it works on her?" She pointed to SueAnn.

"Only one way to find out." Phyllis held her breath and then darted past the woman. SueAnn didn't even flinch.

Char clasped her hands together and held her own breath while she watched Phyllis retrieve the bag that had been labeled Aspen Falls Retirement Village. Phyllis returned a second later with an ear-to-ear grin on her face and handed Char the bag with a little bow. "M'lady."

Char beamed before tearing into the bag. "Brilliant work, Phil."

"What is it? What's in the bag?" Phil clamored.

Char's eyes widened as she pulled out one of the many bottles in the bag. She unscrewed the lid and looked down inside. They were little blue pills in the same diamond shape as the ones they'd found in Mary and Ernie Von Ebsen's room. "It's Viagra," whispered Char, thoroughly surprised to have actually found the bag.

Just then, they heard a woman's voice at the counter.

"Prescription to pick up for the Aspen Falls Retirement Village."

SueAnn, who had just hung up the phone, turned to face the woman at the counter at the exact same time that Char and Phyllis turned to look at her. It was Nurse Brenda! And she was there to pick up the very bag that Char was holding in her hands.

Char's adrenaline raced. She stuffed the pill bottle back in the bag and folded it shut and then shoved it into Phil's waiting arms. "Hurry, put it back!"

Phyllis put the bag under her shirt so it would be invisible too and raced it back over to the box that they'd grabbed it from.

"Your name, please?" said SueAnn.

"Brenda Kayton."

Phyllis slid the paper bag out from under her shirt and dropped it into the box before hightailing it back towards Char just as they both heard SueAnn say, "Just a moment."

"That was too close," hissed Phyllis, breathing heavily.

Char could tell Phil's heartbeat was going just as fast as hers when they heard the sirens in the distance. "We have to get Hazel and Gwyn up before the ambulance gets here. Come on."

Still invisible, the girls passed behind SueAnn just as she was handing Nurse Brenda the bag of pills. They went back around the counter to stand over Gwyn and Hazel. "Come on, girls, the heat's breathing down our necks," hissed Phyllis, looking anxiously towards the front door. "We gotta get outta here!"

But Gwyn and Hazel didn't look up. Hazel still rolled around on the floor moaning and cussing up a storm while Gwyn nervously gnawed at her fingernails while throwing occasional glances over her shoulder towards the pharmacy.

Sal wiped his brow, which was glistening under the pharmacy's fluorescent lighting, and glanced up towards the window anxiously. "The ambulance should be here any minute."

"Mom, are you sure you really need an ambulance?" begged Gwyn.

"I'm gonna sue this place so bad the owners are gonna have to dig into their grandchildren's piggy banks!" muttered Hazel, rubbing her hip. "The floor was soaking wet!"

"Ma'am, I can assure you, the floor wasn't wet," said Sal.

"It was wet, I tell you!" hissed Hazel.

"Girls, come on!" said Char. "Time to go."

Gwyn didn't look up.

"The spell, it's still on us," whispered Phyllis. "That's why Gwynnie and Haze can't see or hear us." She tugged Char to a corner behind a tall rack and took Char's hand. "We have to reverse it."

Char pinched her eyes shut when Phyllis did. "I don't remember how to do undo it, do you?"

Phyllis nodded.

"Shadows, shadows, leave me,
Uncloak my anonymity.

I must be heard, I must be seen.
I must be visible, loud and mean."

Char joined in next and they chanted together.

"Shadows, shadows, leave me,
Uncloak my anonymity.
I must be heard, I must be seen.
I must be visible, loud, and mean."

Char visualized herself becoming visible again. Though she didn't feel her body change at all, she had a sense that all had been righted. The two women rushed back to Gwyn and Hazel.

"Gwynnie, is Hazel alright? Did she take a tumble?" asked Char innocently.

Gwyn sighed when she saw the two women. "Oh, thank goodness you're here, Char. Mom thinks she hurt herself. Char, you're a healer. Isn't there something you can do?"

Char threw her arms out on either side of herself. "Step aside, everyone. I'm a healer witch. I've got this!" She laid her hands on Hazel's hips and pretended to chant silently to herself. Even though she knew there was nothing wrong with Hazel, she made a big production over healing her. After muttering to herself for several long seconds, she removed her hands with gusto. "And, you're healed! Let's go!"

Everyone stared at Char and then stared at Hazel. Char stood up and held a hand out to Hazel. Hazel took hold of it, and Phyllis and Gwyn rushed around to the other side to hook their hands under Hazel's armpits, and together the three women got Hazel back onto her feet.

"Ma'am, are you alright?" asked Sal with shock apparent in his face.

Hazel dusted herself off, and Gwyn handed her her cane. "I feel better than the day I was born." She began to hobble away as if nothing had happened. "Let's go, girls. That made me hungry! I have a hankering for some french fries!"

25

Char glanced into her rearview mirror as the ambulance pulled up to the curb behind them. She pressed on the gas and turned the steering wheel, sending them peeling around the corner practically on two wheels. Her heart pounded wildly in her chest as they made their quick getaway. "Oh, girls! Did you see who that was?!"

Gwyn shook her head and swiveled in her seat to look out the back window. "No, I was too busy worrying about Mom getting us caught! That was far too close for comfort, Mom."

Hazel didn't turn around, but instead crossed her arms over her breasts in the front seat. "Hey, it worked, didn't it?"

"A little too well. You worry me with how much of an actress you are. How am I ever supposed to trust you?"

Hazel lifted her shoulders. "You know what they say.

You can trust anyone you want, but you should always cut the cards."

Gwyn groaned and rolled her eyes. "So after all that, did you find anything out?"

Char grinned from ear to ear. "We found a big bag of medication headed to the Village."

Phyllis grabbed the back of Hazel's headrest and nodded emphatically. "And there was Viagra in the bag!"

"You're kidding!" breathed Gwyn. "Whose name was on the label?"

"Well, we didn't exactly get a chance to look at the label, but I think what we got was better!" said Char as she turned the corner, heading back to the Village. "Someone actually picked up the pills while we were there!"

"What?!"

Phyllis nodded. "It was none other than our very own Nurse Brenda!"

Hazel turned to stare wide-eyed at Char. "Nurse Ratchet is the Village's Viagra kingpin?"

"She had a whole bag of pills!" said Char, nodding. "We didn't get a chance to inspect it all because she showed up before we could, but there was definitely a pill bottle full of Viagra."

"I just don't understand," said Gwyn, shaking her head. "Why would Nurse Brenda want to give George Viagra if she knew it was going to hurt him? I don't understand what her motive might have been."

"Maybe they didn't get along or something," suggested Phyllis with a shrug.

Gwyn shook her head. "It just doesn't add up. There's got to be more to the story."

"Oh, I'm sure there is! Between Nurse Brenda and Noreen Petroski, I'm not sure who seems guiltier," said Phyllis.

"As soon as we get back to the Village, I think we need to lean on Nurse Brenda a little more," said Char.

Hazel, whose head was already starting to loll to the side, said, "The only thing I want to lean on is my pillow. I need a nap."

After tucking Hazel in for her long overdue nap, Gwyn met the girls back in the living room of her small apartment. They had a lot of things to discuss. Gwyn flopped down on the worn sofa. The last few days had been a rollercoaster of emotions and she was ready for a little nap herself. "Okay, now what?"

Phyllis's face was smashed against the peephole in Gwyn's apartment door. She swatted blindly backwards. "Shhhh!" she hissed.

Gwyn bolted upright. "What? What is it?"

Char pointed at the door and whispered. "Phil said Nurse Brenda and Martin Sinclair are in the hallway together."

Gwyn lifted a brow. "What? I thought Phil didn't know who Martin Sinclair was. How does she know that's who it is?"

"Phyllis heard someone knocking on the room next

door, so she peeked through the peephole and that's who came out. We have to assume it's him."

Without peeling her eye off the tiny hole, Phyllis waved Gwyn over. "Get over here and have a look for yourself!"

The women quickly exchanged places and Gwyn pressed her eye up to the peephole. Sure enough, Nurse Brenda was standing in the hallway, but she couldn't see Martin Sinclair. "I can't see him."

"He went back into his apartment," said Phyllis. "Like he was going to go get something."

"Maybe we should go out in the hallway," Gwyn suggested, still peering through the little viewer.

Phyllis shook her head. "No, they'll hear us, and then whatever nefarious thing they're doing will be halted. Can't you see what he's doing?"

Gwyn shook her head. "Nope. She's just standing there right now. Waiting for something, I guess."

Char groaned and rubbed her hands on her face. "Ugh, what I wouldn't give to be able to see what's going on in that apartment right now."

That sparked something in Gwyn's mind. She had the perfect idea. She pointed at the doorway. "Phil, take over watch. I've got it!" With Phyllis watching the door, Gwyn rushed to the bathroom, where she found a round cosmetic mirror about the diameter of a coffee can. She rushed it back to the living room. "Get over here, Char. Hold this!"

Gwyn placed the mirror in Char's hand and concentrated on its physical attributes, wiggling her fingers in front of her. The mirror bounced up and down and then began to grow corners. The glass began to change from a reflective surface to a translucent surface. And then, just like that, Char was holding a square piece of see-through glass in her hands.

Char looked down at it curiously. "Your big idea is to change a mirror into glass. Sweetie, I think you've got it backwards. People pay money to turn glass into mirrors. What's this supposed to do for us?"

Gwyn smiled at her. "You'll see. Hold on. I need one more thing." She rushed back into the bathroom and grabbed an eyeliner pencil from her makeup case. She rushed back, and on the wall that separated the two apartments, Gwyn drew a four-foot-by-four-foot square.

"Gwynnie!" breathed Char. "You're writing on the wall? Won't the Village get upset?"

Gwyn didn't have time to think about that if her plan was going to work in time. "Hold the glass up in the middle of the square, Char. Hurry!" Then she looked at Phyllis. "Is Nurse Brenda still in the hallway?"

Phyllis nodded. "Yup. She's still… oh, wait! She's moving. I think she's going inside his apartment."

Gwyn's heart raced. "We've got to hurry, then. Char, don't move. Keep that glass held tight up against the wall." She closed her eyes and focused her energy, despite her racing adrenaline, and began to chant.

"Pane of glass, let us see,

What's on the other side.
Window, window, let us see,
What they're trying to hide.
Pane of glass, let us see,
What's on the other side.
Window, window, let us see,
What they're trying to hide."

Char sucked in her breath as the area inside the square that Gwyn had drawn on the wall absorbed the glass pane. The whole square morphed into a sheet of transparent glass. "It worked, Gwynnie!"

Gwyn smiled and nodded her head. Her heart was buoyed by the fact that she'd actually remembered a spell that her mother had taught her when she'd been trying to spy on her own children over three decades ago. She clasped her hands together. "It worked!" she breathed. "Phyllis! Get over here! We can see them!"

"But can they see us?" asked Phyllis, now standing hip to hip with Char and Gwyn.

Gwyn shook her head. "Nope. It's one-way."

Char clapped her heads together. "Well, now I wish I had some popcorn!"

Gwyn giggled. "I'm sorry there's no volume, though."

"It's alright. I think we can figure out what's going on, don't you?" asked Char.

Phyllis nodded and pointed at Nurse Brenda, who was now standing in Martin Sinclair's living room. Martin was nowhere to be seen at the moment. "We sure can. Look at her. She's got the bag of pills she picked up from the pharmacy."

Sure enough, Nurse Brenda was sorting through the bag she'd picked up. Then Martin appeared, holding a wallet in his hand. The women watched as he unfolded the wallet and deftly removed several greenbacks, handing them to her. In return she handed him a bottle of pills.

Gwyn sucked in her breath as a hand fluttered to her gaping mouth. "So it *is* Brenda that's providing the residents with Viagra! I can't believe it!"

"Oh, she's leaving!" hissed Phyllis, pointing at the window. They watched as Brenda pocketed the money and then turned and walked out the door, pulling it shut behind her.

"Oh, that just makes me so mad I could spit!" said Char.

Gwyn's eyes turned to Martin. She was curious what he might do with the pills. But instead of taking them to the bathroom or his bedroom, he didn't move. He stayed firmly rooted to the ground.

"What's he doing?" asked Phyllis. "Why's he just standing there like that?"

Gwyn shook her head. She didn't know either. They all stared at him.

And then, almost as if he could sense their eyes on him, he turned to face the wall! Gwyn's heart raced.

"He can't see us, right, Gwynnie?" asked Phyllis.

Gwyn nodded slowly. She was *sure* that the spell worked so that the person on the other side of the wall couldn't see the person casting the window spell. "Yeah, I'm sure…" The words spilled out of her mouth like molasses.

"Because it sure looks like he can see us…"

"It kind of does, doesn't it?" said Char.

They watched as Martin's head tipped sideways. Then, step by step, he shuffled closer to the wall, reaching a hand out.

"Oh, my God, Gwynnie! I think he can see us!" hissed Char.

Gwyn's heart raced as her eyes widened. She threw up two flattened palms towards the wall.

"Window, window, disappear.
No more views today.
Pane of glass, disappear.
Make them go away.
Window, window, disappear.
No more views today.
Pane of glass, disappear.
Make them go away."

With that, the glass began to pull away from the wall, leaving only studs and then painted sheetrock in its place. The glass that Gwyn had formed emerged, and as soon as it was free, it promptly fell to the ground and shattered into tiny pieces.

The crashing noise made Gwyn's heart stop beating for a second as she wondered if Martin had heard it.

With a hand on her heart, Char looked up at Gwyn. "He didn't see us, did he?"

Gwyn's head quaked. "I don't think so," she whispered. *But did he?* she wondered. It sure looked like he had.

Phyllis waved a hand dismissively. "Eh, he probably didn't. He probably saw a spider on the wall or something."

Suddenly, there was a knock at the door. The impromptu burst of noise frightened the three women. Each of them practically jumped out of their skin.

"Ahh!" screamed Gwyn, holding her chest.

Char grasped Gwyn's hand. "You don't think it's—"

"Open up!" called a codgerly voice from the hallway.

Phyllis's eyes widened.

"Oh dear Lord," breathed Char, hugging Gwyn's hand up to her chest. "He did see us!"

The man pounded on the door.

"Are you gonna answer it?" asked Phyllis.

Gwyn shook her head. "I don't think so. Phil, you answer it."

"Yeah, Phil. You're the butch one of the group. You answer it."

"Butch one?!" gasped Phyllis. "I'm not the butch one."

"Well, Gwyn's the girly one. I'm the grandmotherly one. Loni's the crazy one. Hazel's the old one. What are you?"

Phyllis shrugged as if she'd never given it any thought. "I don't know. The wise one?"

Char shook her head. "Wisecracking maybe. But certainly not the wise one. Butch isn't that bad. You can be like our bodyguard."

Phyllis lowered her brows. "Charlotte Adams Maxwell Bailey! You most certainly did not just tell me I could be your bodyguard!"

Gwyn shushed her. "Phil! He can hear you out there! Now just go answer the door and see what he wants."

Phyllis let out an annoyed breath and then strutted over to the door, straightened her spine, and then yanked it open. "Yes?" By now her tone conveyed annoyance, not fear. Gwyn could see what Char had done there, and it was working.

"What's going on in there?" said the voice in the doorway.

Gwyn and Char shuffled forward, cuddling together and peering around Phyllis's shoulder.

Phyllis put a hand on her hip and cocked it out sideways. "What's it to you?"

The man, who was holding an extremely furry cat in his arms, frowned. "I heard a crash."

Phyllis didn't miss a beat. "And?"

Phyllis's tough front seemed to put the man in his place as he was quiet for a long moment. Gwyn was secretly thankful that Char had assigned her the task of answering the door. There's no way Gwyn could have held it together as well as Phyllis was.

"And, I was being neighborly and checking on things," he finally said.

"I think you were being neighborly and snooping on things is what you meant to say," said Phyllis.

The man hoisted the cat up onto a shoulder. "Where's the old lady that lives here?"

"You'll have to be more specific. There are several old ladies that live here."

His brows lifted. "The short one with criminal tendencies. She owes me four new scooter tires."

"Oh, Hazel? She's unavailable at the moment. Leave a message at the tone." With that, Phyllis slammed the door in the Martin Sinclair's face.

"I can't believe you just did that, Phil," said Char, her eyes wide.

Phil shrugged. "I didn't like his attitude."

Gwyn wrung her hands in front of her. "Oh girls. Now what? I'm more confused than ever! Did Martin Sinclair give those pills to George so that he'd die and Martin could have his apartment?"

"My money's still on Noreen. I don't think we can count her out. She probably offed her ex so she could inherit all his money," said Phyllis.

Char rubbed her temples. "Oh, don't forget, Nurse Brenda is the one that we saw picking up the pills. It could be Nurse Brenda. Though I'm not really sure *why* she'd want to kill George."

"Well, there's only one way to find out," shrugged Gwyn. "I think we need to go confront her."

"You really think she's going to tell the truth?" asked Phyllis.

Gwyn shook her head. "No. But we've got the best lie detector test in all of Aspen Falls."

Phyllis lifted her brows. "We do?"

"Yes, and unfortunately, she's sleeping right now and isn't going to do us any good until she's properly rested. How about this, girls? Let's all get some food in our bellies, let Mom rest, and we'll meet back up after lunch. What do you say?"

"Deal!"

26

"Time to turn the temperature up, Mom," said Gwyn, tucking her mother in tight on the small sofa in their living room. Hazel's small frame fit perfectly with her head and shoulders propped up neatly by bed pillows. "Now, you just moan and carry on and pretend to be sick, alright?"

Hazel rolled her eyes. "You don't have to explain to me how to pretend to be sick. I invented pretending to be sick."

"Now. We're going to ask Nurse Brenda some questions," explained Char patiently. "All you need to do is lie there and read her mind. Got it?"

Hazel looked up at Phyllis incredulously. "Why are these two talking to me like I'm a child? Do they not see the wrinkles? Hello? Adult here." Hazel pointed at herself.

"I know, Mom. Just, sometimes your mind wanders, and we do one of these interviews where you're supposed to be reading minds and you get bored and forget what you're doing. We just wanted to make sure we're all clear about your role in this operation."

"Operation? You guys are performing an operation on the nurse? Without a license?" Hazel began to sit up. "Whoa whoa whoa, I'm outta here. I never signed up for any operation…"

Gwyn pushed her back down and rolled her eyes as there was a knock at the door. "Very funny, Mom. Just lay down, look sick, and pay attention. That's all we ask," she whispered as Char led Nurse Brenda Kayton into the apartment.

"Well, well, well, Hazel! You're sick again, huh? That darn bug just won't let go, will it?" said the nurse chipperly as she carried in a little caddy of medical supplies and set it down on the coffee table.

"Ohhh, my head," moaned Hazel, touching her temples lightly for effect.

Nurse Brenda looked down at her with big sad eyes. "Oh, you poor thing!" She looked at Gwyn then. "Have you given her anything?"

Gwyn shook her head. "Not yet. I wanted you to take her temperature before I did."

Brenda nodded and moved around some of the assorted pill bottles in her little handled tray. "Hmm. Let's see. Where's my thermometer?"

Phyllis pointed at it, buried beneath a couple bottles. "Right there. Beneath those pill bottles. Boy, that's a lot of pills you've got there!"

Brenda smiled up at Phyllis. "Sure are. I have a lot of patients I see throughout the day."

"How do you keep all that straight?" asked Char. "You know, to be sure you aren't giving the wrong medications to the wrong person?"

Brenda lifted a bottle. "Well, they all have patient names on them, for starters. But I also keep a notepad." She patted the pocket of her navy-blue scrubs. "That way I know when I dosed each person."

"People are still writing things down on paper?" asked Gwyn. "I thought everything was on the computer these days."

Brenda leaned forward as if she were sharing a secret. "I'm old school. I write it all down, and then at the end of the day I transfer it to the computer. I prefer to keep handwritten notes just for myself. The computer ones are the Village's requirement."

Gwyn smoothed the invisible wrinkles on her pants. She wasn't quite sure how to broach the subject, but ultimately, she knew she had to. Otherwise at some point, she and Hazel might be out on their butts if they got accused of George's murder. No, Gwyn had to be proactive. She swallowed hard.

"I know we've spoken about this before, Brenda, but I guess I didn't realize how much contact you actually have with the residents' pharmaceuticals," Gwyn began gingerly. "I'm not trying to point fingers or anything. I'm just purely curious if there's any possible way that you may have accidentally mixed up George's medicine with someone else's Viagra?"

Brenda's spine stiffened. She shook her head resolutely. "There is *absolutely* no way. I handle each and every one of my patients' pills with complete discretion and accountability. Viagra is a little blue pill. It's obvious what it is. I *know* I didn't accidentally give any of those pills to George. And besides, I don't dose out Viagra." She looked down at her caddy. "I don't even have any on me!"

Gwyn reached a hand out and touched Brenda's arm. "I'm sorry, Brenda. Please don't take that like I was accusing you. I'm sure you're very good at your job. I'm just trying to make sense of George's death."

Phyllis looked at Brenda curiously. "Do you have any idea how the Viagra gets inside the Village in the first place?"

Brenda looked down almost immediately and fiddled with the thermometer, taking off the cap and then pressing a button with her thumb. "I'm sure I don't have any idea about all the ways that Viagra can get in here. This isn't a jail and I'm not a prison warden."

"But you think there are multiple ways for it to enter the Village?" asked Gwyn.

Brenda shrugged. "Possibly."

"What about the patients that don't drive?" said Char. "How do they get their medicine?"

Brenda shrugged. "Some have family members bring it in."

"But for those that don't have family around, how do they get their medicine?" she pressed.

Brenda was having a hard time making eye contact with any of the women by then. She swallowed hard and put the thermometer in Hazel's ear. "Some people might get it through the mail. I also run to the Aspen Falls Pharmacy and pick up prescriptions from time to time."

Char's eyes widened dramatically. "Oh, do you?"

Brenda nodded.

"Do you ever pick up Viagra prescriptions?"

"I suppose on occasion I do."

"So you probably know exactly who's getting it? Don't you?" asked Phyllis, her head tilted.

Brenda eyes widened as she looked at Phyllis. "I mean, I…"

"Nurse Brenda, someone at the Village is the kingpin of a Viagra operation," said Char. "We need to know who it is."

"But I…" she mumbled.

Phyllis looked at her sharply. "Is it you?"

Brenda's head shook wildly. The thermometer beeped and she pulled it from Hazel's ear. "Me?! No, it's not me! I just pick prescriptions up from the pharmacy and deliver them to the residents. That's it. What happens to it after that isn't my responsibility! A few patients ask me to help them keep track of their medications daily, but many don't. This isn't a nursing home, it's a retirement village!"

Phyllis lifted a brow. "But you know who's getting the Viagra. You know who's distributing it to the rest of the residents that don't have prescriptions. Tell us. Who do you deliver it to?"

Brenda stood up then. "I—I can't tell you that! That's

against HIPAA. Just like I told Detective Whitman. That's classified information—protected by law!"

"Is it Martin Sinclair?" asked Gwyn.

Brenda's eyes widened. "Mr. Sinclair? He just moved in!"

"Yes, and we saw you giving him some pills earlier," explained Char.

"I bring pills in for lots of people. That doesn't mean that he's getting Viagra," she huffed. She looked down at the thermometer and read it. "Ninety-nine degrees. I think you're going to be just fine Hazel." She dropped the thermometer into the caddy in a huff. "Now if you'll excuse me, I have *real* patients to see!"

When she was gone, all eyes turned to Hazel.

"Well?" they asked in unison.

Hazel sighed. "She's innocent. All she kept wondering was how she got mixed up into this, she's innocent, why won't anyone believe her, blah blah blah."

"You didn't get a read on who's the one getting the Viagra?"

Hazel shook her head. "Nope. Apparently even her thoughts are protected by HIPAA."

Phyllis threw her arms up before falling back onto an armchair. "Great. Now what?"

Gwyn shrugged. "I don't know, but at least we can rule her out as a suspect. That makes me feel a lot better since I have to trust her to treat my mother."

Hazel frowned. "Yeah, a lot of good that does me. That woman's never stepping foot back into this apartment again, I can tell you that. Not after the way the three of you leaned on her!"

Gwyn's head lolled back and she groaned. "Mom's right. Great. Now we don't have a single lead *and* I'm out a home health care nurse. Oh, girls. I need to clear my head. This is all getting to be too much."

Char nodded. "Me too. Listen, as much as it's inconvenient to deal with right now, we have some other pressing issues, like how we're going to help Sorceress Halliwell, and we still need to rustle up twenty-five hundred dollars for the tax man. How about we all meet over at Kat's tonight for dinner to talk about it? I'll cook."

Hazel sat upright. "You got any french fries on the menu?"

"Sure thing. How about I make you my famous dirty fries?" said Char with a grin.

Hazel's brows lifted, widening her watery blue eyes. "Ooh, I like the sound of that. Maybe we ought to rename them Hazel fries."

The girls giggled.

"Hazel fries it is!"

27

"These Hazel fries are amazing," said Hazel, smacking her lips.

"Not bad," agreed Phyllis.

Loni held her plate out for another serving. "I haven't had food this good since… since… well, I haven't had food this good."

"That's because you never leave the house. If you left the house once in a while, you'd be able to go eat breakfast with us at Linda's. Her food is delicious," said Char, serving her another scoop of fries.

Loni shook her head. "Nope. Not gonna happen. Not as long as the FBI is still waiting outside my door."

Phyllis rolled her eyes before taking a bite of the cheeseburger Char had made for them in Kat's kitchen. "The FBI is not waiting outside your door. I've been to your house."

"You ever gonna tell us what that's all about?" asked Char.

Loni pressed her lips against her teeth and stared at the women like a deer caught in the headlights. She shook her head.

"Never?" Char asked incredulously.

Loni lifted a shoulder. "Doubtful. I don't like to talk about it."

"We gathered that," said Phyllis.

Char sighed and fell down into one of Kat's kitchen chairs. "Oh, girls. Does anyone else feel like the room is spinning, and as much as you try, you just can't get off the ride?"

Gwyn nodded. "That's exactly how I feel. I just feel like I can't catch my breath. It seems like the minute Mom and I got to Aspen Falls, all hell broke loose."

"Oh, watch out everybody, Gwynnie said a curse word," said Hazel, holding her arms out as if to steady the room.

Gwyn dropped her gaze to her mother. "This is your fault, you know."

Hazel's old eyes widened. "*My fault?!* How is this my fault?"

"If you hadn't slept with George, none of this would have happened!"

"Now wait just a darn tootin' minute," said Hazel, holding her finger out to her daughter. "Someone poisoned that man, and it wasn't me. He was gonna die whether I slept with him or not! I just helped ease his way to the other side. All men should be so lucky to go out like that."

"Hazel's right, Gwynnie," said Char.

A look of shock crossed Gwyn's face. "Tell me you're kidding."

Char swatted her hand as she stood up and began clearing the table. "Not about the 'all men should be so lucky' part. I just don't think you can blame this on Hazel."

"I'm not blaming George's death on Mom. I'm saying we wouldn't be playing amateur sleuth again if it hadn't been for Mom. He would have died peacefully in his room. Brenda would have found him and that would have been that. He'd probably be dead and buried by now."

"Yes, exactly! And it's very likely they wouldn't have done an autopsy, and a murderer would have gotten away with killing George!" said Char.

"So because Hazel's loose, it actually might have worked out for the best," suggested Phyllis.

Hazel backhanded Phyllis. "Hey! Watch it!"

Phyllis smiled. "No offense, Haze."

Gwyn let her head fall into her hands. "But why does it have to be *us* solving this murder? Why can't we just let Detective Whitman and the rest of the Aspen Falls PD handle it?"

"Because you know sooner or later they're going to find out that Hazel was the last person to see George Petroski alive. Then it's curtains for the two of you, and at this point, for all of us. We all had a hand in hiding the body," said Char. "I realize this is stressful, but we have to keep pushing."

"We're just running out of leads," sighed Gwyn. "Where do we go next?"

"Well, I think we can definitely rule Nurse Brenda out, don't you?" asked Char.

Hazel nodded. "It's definitely not the nurse. But I've got this really bad feeling about Martin Sinclair."

"You think he's the one? But like Nurse Brenda pointed out, he just moved in! He wasn't even living at the Village the day that George was killed," said Phyllis.

Hazel shook her head. "No, but that doesn't mean he wasn't here. He could have been lurking in the shadows, just waiting to pounce."

Phyllis rolled her eyes. "Yeah, I met Mr. Grouchy Pants. The only thing pouncy about that guy was his cat, and even the cat looked like he hadn't pounced in a cat decade."

Hazel narrowed her eyes into tiny slits. "Don't let him fool you. I know evil when I see evil, and that man is evil."

"Takes one to know one," said Loni with a crooked half smile.

Hazel wiggled her fingers at Loni menacingly. "Don't make me finger you."

Phyllis nearly lost her drink. "Well, there's something you don't hear every day."

"Mom, put your hand down before you hurt yourself," sighed Gwyn. "Okay, so let's consider for a moment the possibility that Mom's intuitions are right and Martin Sinclair actually did play a role in George's death. I think we need to see what we can dig up on the man."

Char slammed her palm down on the kitchen counter. "Exactly what I was thinking. And, I have just the way!"

She pulled her phone out of her pocket and clicked the screen, swiping this way and that until she produced a picture. She set it on the table and pushed it forward.

"What's this?" asked Phyllis, putting on the glasses that hung around her neck. She lifted the phone to her face and stared down at the picture. "Aspen Falls Charity Poker Tournament?"

"Yup. There's a poker tournament tomorrow in the auditorium, a fundraiser for the Meals on Wheels program. I saw it on the bulletin board at the grocery store when I ran to get food for supper. Guess whose name was at the top of the list?" Char paused for dramatic effect. "Martin Sinclair. So I signed Hazel up."

A smile of excitement poured across Hazel's face. "I knew you were my favorite. You hear that, Gwynnie? This one's my new favorite. Is your mother still alive, dear?" She scooted her chair closer to where Char stood.

Gwyn shook her head. "Really, Char? Without even asking me? You know how I feel about Mom gambling."

Char waved a hand at Gwyn. "Oh, what's the big deal? We need the intel, and Hazel's a mind reader. What better time to sit her down and let her read his mind than at a poker competition? Everyone's all quiet and focused anyway. It's perfect!"

"Oh, fine," snapped Gwyn.

"And if she happens to win using her mind reading skills and makes a little money in the process that we can use to pay the tax bill, then so mote it be." Phyllis shrugged, pulling the last few dirty fries off her plate and shoving them into her mouth.

The air in the room began to move, and out of nowhere, Sorceress Halliwell's ghost appeared in front of them. Her usually pale face was flushed. "Ladies!" She seemed out of breath as she made her entrance.

"Sorceress Halliwell! You're here," said Gwyn with a smile.

"And we didn't even have to summon you!" added Char.

"Ladies, I can't let you do it," she said, her face completely serious.

Loni's eyebrows furrowed together as she looked around the room at the faces of the other women in confusion. "Do what?"

"Gamble for money, using the powers of magic to win," she said sternly. "I thought I'd taught all of you that in school."

"Sorceress Halliwell!" breathed Char. "Were you *spying* on us?!"

Phyllis ignored Char's outrage and talked over her. "Sorceress Halliwell, Char didn't sign Hazel up with the intent to make money. She signed her up because there was a murder at the Aspen Falls Retirement Village and we need to get some clues to figure out who did it before Hazel is falsely accused of murder!"

Sorceress Halliwell shook her head sternly. "I clearly heard you say that if she wins money, you'll use it to pay a tax bill."

Phyllis held her hands out on either side of herself. "I mean, I just meant if she *happens* to win, she could use the money to get us out of the pickle we're in."

"The intent in this case doesn't matter. If real money is won with the use of magical powers, it needs to be donated to charity. It cannot be used for a witch's personal gains. It's unethical!"

"But Sorceress Halliwell!" said Phyllis. "If we don't pay this tax bill within the next month, we risk losing this house!"

Sorceress Halliwell shook her head. "I'm sorry, but that doesn't matter. If the house has to be sold, it has to be sold."

"But what would we do about you? We haven't untethered your soul yet!" argued Phyllis.

"Obviously, I'll have no choice but to stay with the house."

Gwyn hung her head. "It's okay, girls," she whispered. "We'll just sell off some of Kat's stuff like we'd originally planned. Between the collectible salt and pepper shakers I'm going to sell on eBay, some of Kat's knickknacks, and some of her antique furniture pieces, there's enough stuff here to make the tax payments for the next ten years at least!"

Sorceress Halliwell smiled sweetly at Gwyn. "I wish it were that easy, dear." She looked out the stunned faces in the room. "But, ladies, I can't let you sell Kat's possessions."

Char's face fell. "What?! Why not?"

Sorceress Halliwell rubbed her forehead with the pads of her fingers. "Oh," she sighed. "I really didn't want to have to tell you this."

"Are you kidding?" demanded Char. "First Kat tells

us we're stuck with this house that we aren't allowed to sell. Then we get hit with a twenty-five hundred dollar tax bill, and now you're telling us that we can't even sell Kat's belongings. You two aren't making this very easy for us. What in the world are we supposed to do to be able to hang on to this house? You want us to sell our bodies? Is that it?"

"At our age, that doesn't even work." Loni nodded with a serious expression. "Hazel tried *giving away* her body and she killed a man. Men can't pay up if they're dead."

Sorceress Halliwell sighed. "Of course I don't want you selling your bodies. You just don't understand. All of this, right now—the predicament you're in, the predicament I've been in for years—is a result of Kat's poor choices. I can't let the cycle continue!"

"What cycle?!" asked Char. "We don't even know what you're talking about!"

Sorceress Halliwell grimaced. The look on her face told the women that she was torn. Torn between not wanting to spill the secret she'd been holding on to for decades and knowing she had to tell the women what was going on. "Fine. I'll tell you. But you're not going to like what it is I have to say."

"Try us," said Gwyn quietly. "We're all listening."

"Yeah, spill," agreed Hazel. "We've waited long enough."

"Okay, okay." The ghost took a deep breath and floated to the corner of the room. "One day, years and years ago, Kat invited me over to help her with a spell that she was working on. Of course I came. I would have come for any of you if you'd needed my help. While I was here, I noticed all of Kat's nice things. Her magnificent paintings. Her expensive jewelry. Her tapestries, her silverware, her furniture, her rugs. Everything was so nice. And here Kat was, all alone. Her parents weren't around. She wasn't married. So I asked her, 'Katherine, how do you afford all of these nice things?'"

The women listed with bated breath, each of them lost in thought.

"Of course Kat didn't want to answer. It was because she was ashamed at the answer and she couldn't bring herself to tell me. So she told me a lie. She told me she'd been willed everything in her family's estate. But I was a very powerful witch. I knew a lie when I heard one. And that was a lie. So I followed her around that day, and there was one room she guarded carefully. Her spell room. The room on the third floor.

"That day, when it was time for her to make us lunch, I told her I was going to use the restroom, but instead I snuck up to see what she was hiding in her spell room. That was when I found out what Kat's secret was."

"What was it?" breathed Gwyn.

"Yeah, tell us!" said Phyllis.

"Katherine had found a spell that conjured money. It was a slow spell. It didn't make money quickly, but it did produce money. And in her third-floor spell room, she had a pile of it, with new bills being created constantly. That was how she'd paid for everything she owned."

"But the house, it was her parents'!" said Char.

Sorceress Halliwell nodded. "Yes, the house was her parents' house, but she'd replaced their modest furnishings with the antiques and exquisite designs you see in here today. Now, of course, I confronted Kat. But she already knew how I felt about conjuring money. Not only do I find it unethical, but it's also highly illegal. I warned her that if she didn't undo the spells and return everything she'd purchased with magical money, I'd be forced to turn her into the authorities. But she didn't want to hear it.

"I'm afraid before I could leave, we got into a fight and she unleashed a spell on me so strong and so vicious that I didn't even see it coming or have a chance to protect myself." Sorceress Halliwell looked like she might cry. "Never for a moment had I considered that someone I loved like a daughter would do something so evil to me."

"Oh, Kat," breathed Gwyn. "How could you!"

Jaws went slack around the room.

"Of course, after she'd done the spell and I'd become a ghost and my soul became tethered to this house, she immediately regretted what she'd done. She tried to reverse it. In fact, she tried for years. But nothing she did ever worked."

Char's face fell. "I can't believe this."

"I can't believe it either," whispered Gwyn. "And that's why we can't sell any of Kat's possessions? Because they've all been gained by magical means?"

Sorceress Halliwell nodded sadly. "I'm afraid so."

Loni lowered her brows. "Is that why you moved all

of the things we'd packed back to where they'd come from?"

"Yes. I couldn't let you sell her things."

"But the house?" asked Phyllis. "We could sell the house?"

She sighed. "Yes, I suppose you could. Kat didn't want you to sell it because I was tied to it. She wanted you to find a way to release me from this curse."

"Of course we'd never sell it until we've figured out a way to help you," promised Gwyn. "Oh, girls. What are we going to do now?"

Char's head fell into her hands. "Now? Now we take some time to think."

Gwyn shook her head. "Ugh. When will this ride stop spinning?"

28

The next morning the girls woke early. Char and Phyllis picked up a heavily costumed Loni on their way to the poker competition, while Gwyn drove a busload of seniors over, including Hazel. They found the auditorium to be a bustling center of activity. Mayor Greg Adams and a retired city councilman, Sam Jeffries, ran the registration table; some of the women from Char's church group had volunteered to run a refreshment station; and Minnie Cooper, who worked for the *Aspen Falls Observer*, was strolling around with a camera, looking for photo opportunities. The air of excitement was palpable. Char could only hope that they'd get a chance to put Hazel directly in front of Martin Sinclair.

Char looked down at Hazel, whose eyes seemed to sparkle. "Looks like fun to you, Hazel?"

"More fun than I've had in years. I can't wait!"

The first round of competition was easy for Hazel. So easy, in fact, that she'd racked up quite a tidy sum of chips, and by the time they'd moved on to round two, Char could tell that Hazel's mind was less on getting the intel they needed out of Martin and more on her newfound wealth.

"Hazel. You know what our mission is today, right?" asked Char, pulling Hazel aside from the crowd after the rest of the girls went to get one of Ida Washington's snickerdoodles and a glass of punch.

Hazel's eyes were big and vacant. She nodded like she knew exactly what Char was talking about, but Char could tell that all Hazel was seeing at that moment was dollar signs.

"Hazel," said Char, touching Hazel's arm. "You with me?"

"Huh?" asked Hazel, as if snapping out of her reverie momentarily.

"You know what we're here to do, right?"

"Oh, yeah. Uh, I'm supposed to read Martin's mind. I gotta be sitting at a table with him first, though," said Hazel.

"Yes, I know. I hadn't realized there were going to be quite so many entrants," said Char, scanning the crowded room. "The signup list I saw at the grocery store must have just been a partial list. But I checked, and Martin did make it to the next round. Hopefully you'll eventually end up in a game against him."

"Yeah, I can't wait to beat the smarmy face off that guy!" said Hazel, stomping her cane down onto the ground.

"Don't you mean *wipe* the *smile* off that guy's face?" said Char with a lopsided grin.

Hazel's eyes widened as if she'd just been busted. "Sure. Sure. That's what I meant."

"Hazel Prescott!" called a deep voice from behind them. "Just the woman I wanted to speak to!"

The two women turned around to see Detective Mark Whitman strolling their way.

"Detective!" said Char, trying to control a gasp. She glanced down at Hazel, who looked like she'd gotten caught in a hunter's sights. "What are you doing here?"

"Working as usual," he sighed. Then he turned his attention to Hazel. "I stopped at the Village and they said that you were here, so I thought I'd come see for myself."

"Yep. Here I am!" agreed Hazel. "See ya!" she added before trying to quickly shuffle away.

He reached a hand out to stop her. "Wait, wait! Do you have a minute?"

Char wrung her hands nervously. "Actually, Detective, Hazel just made it to the next round, and that will be starting in just a short time."

"Well, it will just take a second. Hazel?"

Hazel stopped moving and looked back at Char pleadingly.

"What's this about, Detective?"

"Oh, well, I'm working on the George Petroski case and trying to put together a timeline of the day he died. One of the suspicious things we discovered was that he was wearing some type of diaper under his clothes."

Hazel swallowed hard. "A diaper?"

"Well, it was a bedsheet. But it had been fashioned into a diaper. I've seen the sheets the Village uses on their beds and it definitely came from the Village, but the funny thing was, George's bedroom wasn't missing the top sheet, which tells me it came from someone else's room."

"Someone else's room?" asked Char, her turn to swallow hard.

Detective Whitman nodded. "Yes. Now, I've had a chance to visit with many of the residents. Two of them actually mentioned saying the last time they saw George alive, he was with you, Hazel."

Hazel's face went ashen. "Me? Who told you I was with him?"

Detective Whitman flipped backwards through his notes. "Umm, it was a married couple. Ernie and Mary Von Ebsen. They said they were walking in the courtyard behind the Village after breakfast and they saw you and George sitting on the park bench together. Do you recall sitting with George the morning that he died?"

Hazel pretended to think about it and then answered, "Mmm. Yep. I seem to recall sitting next to him on a park bench."

Detective Whitman smiled affably and jotted something down in his notepad. "Okay. Do you know what happened to him after that?"

Hazel shook her head, wide-eyed. "Nope. I don't recall."

Detective Whitman lowered his brows at that answer. "You don't recall?" He seemed a little taken aback.

Since Gwyn wasn't readily around, Char felt the need to step in. "Detective, Hazel sometimes has issues with her memory." Then she lowered her voice and leaned into him. "She's not all with it, if you know what I mean."

"I see. Well, do you know what *you* did after sitting with George on the park bench?"

"What *I* did?" asked Hazel, stalling.

"Yes."

"Umm..." She looked at Char out of the corner of her eyes.

"Well, Hazel, that was the day that you were sick, wasn't it?" Char looked at Detective Whitman with the biggest, saddest puppy dog eyes she could muster. "Poor thing was just burning up. Why, Nurse Brenda was keeping an eye on her that day. I think she'd just gone out for a breath of fresh air when she bumped into George sitting on the park bench. They said a few words and then Hazel came right back inside and curled up on her bed for a nap. I stopped by sometime after that with a little witch's remedy for that darn old cold." Char wiggled her fingers as if to emphasize the fact that she meant a magic remedy.

"I see. Is that an accurate statement, Hazel?"

Hazel swallowed hard and her head bobbed up and down slowly.

"Is that a yes?" he prodded.

Her head continued to bob slowly. "Yes, sounds like it."

Detective Whitman's head tipped to the side.

"Detective Whitman!" said Phyllis, coming up from behind them. "What are you doing here? Gambling for charity?"

The detective turned around. "Oh, Phyllis. Good to see you," he said. "No, I'm actually working the Petroski case. I came to ask Hazel a few questions. I was told she might have been the last one to see George alive."

Char's mouth went dry. *The last one to see George alive?* He hadn't phrased it like that, and the notion that he was investigating Hazel worried her. They had to get this case solved and pronto.

"You know, Detective, the scuttlebutt around the Village is that Noreen Petroski had something to do with George's death," said Gwyn.

It was obvious to Char that Gwyn was only saying that to take the focus off her mother. Whether she really thought Noreen was involved at this point didn't matter. It was about protecting Hazel. Char nodded.

"Yeah, we went to visit Noreen. You know, to offer our condolences. She seemed rather unaffected by George's untimely passing. Plus we found it rather shady that she'd moved George's things out of his apartment so quickly."

"Yes, I've spoken with Noreen also." He nodded. "But she's got an iron-clad alibi on the day that George died. I'm fairly confident it wasn't her."

"B-but she said that she didn't go have breakfast with her sister until seven thirty. Don't you think it's very likely that George was poisoned before then?" said Gwyn, her wobbly voice betraying her.

"We're still working on the timeline," he said. "But her sister stayed the night with her. I've spoken to many of the neighbors. Not only were both of their cars in the driveway all morning, but several people actually saw her and her sister leaving for breakfast. In addition, she was out of town when the body was found in the morgue. There's no way she could have managed that."

Gwyn's eyes widened. "B-but, she seemed very sketchy when we asked her why she'd moved George's stuff out of his room so quickly."

"Well, yes," he agreed, nodding his head. "That's because Martin Sinclair was a friend of hers. When he found out that George had passed, he called her and asked her to move things along. I guess he'd been trying to get a room there for quite some time, but never got in soon enough."

"I knew it!" barked Hazel, stomping her cane down gleefully.

"You knew what, Hazel?" asked Detective Whitman, looking at her curiously.

"What?" she asked, holding a hand up to her ear.

"You knew what?" he repeated more loudly this time.

"No, what?"

"No," he said shaking his head. "Not you *know* what, you *knew*—"

Suddenly a noise chimed in the room, followed by an announcer's voice. "Round two. Players and audience, please take your seats!"

Hazel's eyes widened. "Oh, money talks. Gotta go!" she said before bolting away to her assigned table.

As expected, Hazel won the next two rounds, to end up in the finals with none other than Martin Sinclair. From behind her enormous stack of chips, she stared at the man from across the table. Martin stared back at her through beady, coal-like eyes. He had his own stack of chips that rivaled hers, but Hazel knew she could take him. She couldn't wait to grind him to a pulp like she'd done to the rest of the players in the tournament. Then he'd know who was boss.

As the dealer began to deal, Char's waving from the sidelines drew Hazel's attention off of Martin and the game for a moment. Hazel wanted to cringe with embarrassment as the girls all jerked their heads towards Martin, making silly, dramatic faces and even going so far as to point. She certainly needed to teach the quartet a thing or two about poker faces.

Pay attention, Mom, make sure to find out what he's thinking! thought Gwyn.

Haze! Focus! You can do this! thought Phyllis.

Come on, Hazel, we need to figure this out. You need this just as much as we do. Detective Whitman's on to us! thought Char.

I wonder if Detective Whitman's really an FBI agent posing as a cop. They do that to infiltrate people's weaknesses so they can do sneak attacks on unsuspecting citizens, thought Loni. *I wonder if anyone here can tell who I really am.*

Hazel's mind went back to the game at hand. She stared at Martin as he lifted the leading edges of the two cards in front of him and peeked at what he'd been dealt.

Hazel focused her energy on his mind, but nothing came to her straight away. She frowned. Hearing the girls' thoughts was like stealing money from a safe with no lock, so it seemed a bit odd to Hazel that she couldn't read anything in Martin's mind yet. But she wasn't about to give up. She peeked at her cards. She had a pair of nines. *Not bad.* Hazel placed her bet.

Martin took a few moments to think about it. Then, lifting his brow, he raised her bet.

Keeping her face as even as a perfectly balanced teeter-totter, Hazel called.

The dealer laid down three cards face-up on the table. A three, a nine, and a jack. Hazel wanted to smile. She had three of a kind, with two cards to go. But she kept cool. She focused on his mind, but it was still like she was coming up against an impenetrable brick wall.

Feeling pretty confident with her hand thus far, Hazel raised the bet, sliding her chips forward.

She stared at Martin. It was obvious that he was lost in thought, yet the thoughts weren't appearing in her mind! What was going on?

He pushed his chips forward, and the dealer flipped over a fourth card. An eight of hearts.

Through her telepathy, she could hear the girls rooting for her and encouraging her to get the intel they needed as she rustled with her chips. Taking a handful off the top of the stack, she placed her bet.

Martin didn't even hesitate in placing his bet after hers.

Hazel found herself feeling frustrated. What could he

possibly have with a three, an eight, a nine, and a jack? She felt a bit of a panic setting in. Could he possibly be holding two jacks? She felt it was unlikely but held her breath until the dealer laid down the fifth and final card. Another jack! What would be the chances he had the two jacks now? *Slim*, she thought. The suits were all over the place. There was no way he had a flush. No possible way he could make a straight either.

For her part, Hazel was now sitting on a full house. She could let out a little sigh of relief and bet. She had to trust in herself, and she didn't want that smug SOB walking away with a single chip. She pushed her entire stack of chips into the pot.

Gasps rose up out of the crowd.

Mom! thought Gwyn. *What are you doing?*

Winning, thought Hazel with an inward snicker.

She glanced over at Martin, who was stacking his chips to match Hazel's bet. When he called, Hazel threw down her pair of nines. "Take that Sinclair." She had three nines and two jacks. A full house.

Martin then threw down his pair of cards. And Hazel couldn't believe it! The man had been sitting on a pair of jacks! He had four of a kind!

Gasps lit up the room again as the dealer began to stack Martin's winnings.

Hazel looked down at the empty place where her chips had once been. Somehow he'd cheated! She was sure of it!

Martin looked unabashedly smug. He reached a hand across the table. "Good game."

Hazel pretended to spit on his hand. "Good game my ass. You cheated!"

Martin looked taken aback. "I did no such thing!"

"You did!" She pointed her finger at him. "There's something suspicious about you. Don't think I don't see it."

Martin began to stack his chips into a little basket. Without looking up, he said haughtily. "Oh hey—you know, about those four tires, don't worry about it. I think we're even now."

Gwyn, Char, Loni, and Phyllis got to Hazel just in time to hold her back. "Why I oughtta…," she began, struggling to break free of their grasp so she could bean Martin over the head with her cane.

"See you at home, sweet stuff," he said with a little wink.

29

It was late in the afternoon by the time the poker competition wound down, so by the time that Gwyn managed to settle Hazel down and get the bus back to the Village loaded up, Gwyn was exhausted.

Gwyn, Loni, Char, and Phyllis all chatted outside the bus when a two-tone brown Ford pulled into a parking stall in front of the auditorium. Gwyn didn't have a chance to get nervous before Sergeant Harrison Bradshaw climbed out of the cab and jogged over to Gwyn and the girls.

"Harrison!" said Gwyn in surprise.

"Sarge," croaked Phyllis. "You're late. Party's over."

He grinned, his warm smile crackling the corners of his eyes. "I wasn't coming to play," he said. "I wanted to catch up with Gwyn. The front desk girl at the Village said you were down here."

A blush crept across Gwyn's neck. "You were looking for me?"

"It's Friday," he said. "You weren't at coffee this morning, and I still don't have your number. I just wanted to make sure that we were on for our date tonight."

Gwyn's eyes widened. "It's Friday?" she breathed, looking over at the girls. How had the week slipped by so fast? "I'm so sorry! Time got away from me this week. I didn't even realize what day it was!"

A glimmer of disappointment seemed to shoot across Sergeant Bradshaw's face. "Oh."

Gwyn held a hand out, touching his forearm. "But I'm still in for tonight!" she added.

His smile returned. "Perfect. How's Hazel feeling? Is she up to it?"

Char leaned against the bus. "If she's not, we'll babysit, don't worry. Nothing will stop Gwynnie from going out with you tonight. You have our word."

He squeezed her hand. "Good. I'm looking forward to it."

"I am too," said Gwyn softly.

He pointed at her before walking away. "Six?"

Gwyn looked down at the thin watch on her wrist. "Can we make it six thirty? I have to take all the seniors back to the Village, and I wouldn't mind getting in a shower before our date."

"Six thirty it is! Tell Hazel to bring her appetite!" he said with a wink.

Gwyn smiled at him. *Oh, he's such a sweet man. Where has he been all my life?* she wondered. "Okay, I will."

Char kicked Gwyn's shin. "Tell him to pick you up at

Kat's house. We'll help you get ready. It'll be like old times, when one of us went on a date."

"Oh, Harrison!" Gwyn called out, just before he'd reached his truck.

He turned around to face her.

"Pick me up at Katherine Lynde's place. Do you mind?"

"No, not at all. Kat's house. Six thirty. See you soon."

Gwyn had no sooner returned the bus to the Village than Char, Phyllis, and Loni pulled up in Char's car. "Come on in, girls. I just have to pack up what Mom and I'll need to get ready."

The five of them breezed into the Village shoulder to shoulder like the geriatric Rat Pack. Gwyn nodded at Arabella Struthers and then at Brenda Kayton, who was just locking up her office for the night. Brenda gave them a disgruntled grimace and slunk past them down the hallway.

Inside Gwyn and Hazel's apartment, they finally had an opportunity to corner Hazel about her efforts at the poker match.

Phyllis curled her lip after a several-minute-long interrogation. "So you didn't find *anything* out?"

Hazel scooted back further into her favorite armchair. "I don't know what went wrong. I could hear you bozos thinking without even trying. But that guy was locked up like Fort Knox!"

"That's so weird!" said Gwyn. "That rarely happens to Mom."

Hazel made a face. "It's happened before. But Gwynnie's right. It's a rarity."

"What does it mean?" asked Char.

Hazel crossed her arms across her bosom. "I have my suspicions, but I don't want to say until I know for sure. Let's just say, it's not looking good for Marty Sinclair. I think he's our killer."

Phyllis rubbed the balls of her hands against her temples. "Ugh, if only we had some kind of proof. Detective Whitman's never going to believe us if we don't have proof."

"Tying him to the Viagra would be a good start," said Gwyn.

Char nodded in agreement. "It would be a great start. But how do we do it? Nurse Brenda's not talking."

Phyllis sighed. "Char's right. You saw her when she was leaving. She looked at us like we killed her puppy."

"If only we could get our hands on her records," said Gwyn. "She said she keeps it all written down."

Phyllis's eyes widened. "I'll bet you she keeps that notepad in her office."

Char looked excited. "Phil! You're brilliant! She just left for the day, too. Let's run down there and see if she left it behind!"

Hazel clapped her hands together before putting them on either arm of her chair and trying to force her tired old bones to stand again. "Hot damn, we're gonna get that bastard," she said excitedly.

Char and Loni jumped to their feet to pull Hazel up, and the five of them left to do yet a little more breaking and entering. Gwyn magically manifested a key out of a small pocket knife she'd found left behind on the bus. Once inside Brenda's office, Loni drew the shades. From the outside, the room looked dark to anyone that walked by.

Char, Phyllis, and Gwyn all began the mad hunt for the notepad while Loni kept watch on the door and Hazel sat in Brenda's desk chair. Giving herself a little push with her cane, she spun around in circles while everyone else focused on the task at hand.

On her knees in front of Brenda's desk, Char shook her head. "I'm not seeing it inside any of her drawers. Anyone else having any luck?"

Gwyn shook her head. "I don't see it in the file cabinet."

"It's not in any of her pockets or bags," said Phyllis, checking the pockets of everything hanging on the coat hanger on the wall.

Hazel suddenly stopped swiveling and thwacked her cane on the top of Brenda's desk. "Is that it?"

Char poked her head up and stared at the end of Hazel's cane which now rested on a little notepad.

Gwyn turned around. Her eyes traveled the length of Hazel's cane to see the notepad too. "You didn't think to look *on top of* the desk, Char?"

Char smiled uneasily. "Heh, heh, heh. Who would have thought? Hiding in plain sight." She flipped open the notepad and found that each resident had their own page in the notepad. Brenda had chronicled each and every prescription she'd ever picked up from the Aspen Falls Pharmacy, who had gotten it, and the date.

Phyllis stared at the pad over Char's shoulder. "Holy cow bells," she gasped, "it's like we've struck gold!"

"Better than gold," said Gwyn. "This just might be the difference between life in prison and freedom!"

Char ran her finger down the first page, scanning for the words Viagra.

Hazel reached a hand up and snatched the notepad away from Char. "Gimme that. At the rate you're reading, I'll be dead before you've gotten to the new guy," she muttered. "He's our killer." She flipped to the last page in the notepad that had Brenda's writing on it. At the top, it read Martin Sinclair. There was only one entry in the journal and it was from the day before. "Jublia!" spat Hazel.

Char ripped the pad from Hazel's grubby hands. "Jublia!" she echoed. "The man got a prescription for Jublia?"

"Isn't that for toenail fungus?" asked Phyllis, wrinkling her nose.

Gwyn had to look with her own eyes. "That's it? No Viagra?"

From the doorway, Loni cocked her head to the side. "I think if I were a man, I'd much rather have toenail fungus than erectile dysfunction."

"Can we focus here?" snapped Hazel. "If Marty didn't get the Viagra that Brenda picked up from the pharmacy yesterday, then who did?"

Char continued flipping through the notepad, taking her time scanning each line to make sure she didn't miss it. Then she got to a page where she didn't have to scan. The word Viagra was written on each and every line. "Oh, girls. We found the Viagra kingpin! Look!" She handed the book to Phyllis.

"Duke Olson!" she breathed.

Gwyn sucked in her breath. "Duke! He was the one that took George's spot on the bus."

The five women exchanged a look. It was as if they all suddenly realized they'd pinned down George's killer.

"We've got him," said Phyllis, flicking the notepad.

"Except I don't know that Detective Whitman will be able to use this notepad as evidence, since it was obtained via breaking and entering. Maybe if we put together a timeline and present it to the detective, he'll have no choice but to subpoena Duke's prescription records?" suggested Gwyn logically.

Char scratched her forehead. "Timeline, huh?"

Gwyn nodded. "Alright, let's lay it out. We know George was still alive around seven thirty, because Mom said he snuck into our apartment while I was in the shower." Gwyn looked at Hazel for confirmation of that fact.

Hazel closed her eyes and nodded.

"Okay, so he had to be poisoned between the time he woke up that morning and seven thirty. We need to place him and Duke together prior to seven thirty," said Gwyn.

Char nodded. "I bet they had breakfast together."

"Is there any way to check?" Phyllis asked Gwyn.

"Does the Village keep records of who has breakfast every morning?"

Gwyn shook her head sadly. "Not that I'm aware of. But Miss Georgia might remember. We could ask her."

Loni flipped off the light and yanked the door open. "Then what are we standing around here for?"

Less than two minutes later the five women stood in front of the sneeze-guard-covered salad bar in the dining room while Miss Georgia busily stocked the salad dressing area with giant vats of creamy liquids.

"Miss Georgia, you don't keep track of who eats breakfast each morning, do you?" asked Gwyn.

Miss Georgia looked perturbed at the interruption from her task at hand. "Miss Prescott, in exactly twenty-two minutes there will be a line a mile long at that door, and you want to talk about breakfast with me?"

"I know. I'm so sorry to bother you. We're trying to help Detective Whitman figure out how George Petroski died," said Gwyn. It wasn't a total lie. They were trying to help him; he just didn't know it yet. "We're working on a timeline of who George talked to and saw that day. It's very important that we figure out what time George had breakfast and who he sat with. Do you recall anything about that morning?"

Miss Georgia sighed. She sat the vat of dressing down on the edge of the stainless-steel bar and wiped the ring with a plastic-gloved finger. "George didn't come down for breakfast that morning," she said.

"You're sure?" pressed Char.

She nodded. "Sure as I am that you're going to make

me late getting the food on this salad bar." She shook her head and popped the lid back onto the vat of salad dressing. "There was a big to-do about him missing that field trip, remember? It occurred to me then that he hadn't been down to breakfast either. But I already mentioned all of this to the detective when he asked."

"We're just following up," said Gwyn.

"Does he usually come for breakfast?" asked Phyllis.

Miss Georgia nodded. "All the men do. Like clockwork. They don't skip meals like some of the ladies do. I suppose there's no sense in worrying about your figure at their age."

"Miss Georgia," began Gwyn, "did Duke Olson come to breakfast that morning?"

Miss Georgia nodded. "Yes, ma'am, he did. I saw him. He sat right over there next to Carol Hamburg and the Von Ebsens." She pointed at a table for four next to the piano.

"Do you know what time he came down for breakfast?" asked Phyllis.

"I do. He was the first one in line when I opened the doors that morning, just like he always is. It was six thirty sharp."

"And do you know when he left?"

Miss Georgia shrugged. "As far as I can remember, he stayed on through the morning, playing cards with the men until it was time to load that bus up for the field trip. Then he disappeared."

"You didn't see him get up and leave anytime between the time he came and the time the bus left?"

"Well, you'd have to ask Ms. Hamburg or the VonEbsens. They were all at the table with him. I was working. I just know he was standing in the doorway when I opened up, and I saw him leave with the rest of the field trip–goers. Now, if you'll excuse me, I'm trying to finish up so I don't have an angry mob on my hands when they find out I don't have any blue cheese dressing."

"Thank you, Miss Georgia," said Gwyn. They walked away a bit heavy-hearted. They'd expected to learn that Duke had had breakfast with George, so to find out that Duke had seemingly been there while George was poisoned put a bit of a wrench in their timeline.

"I think it's time we go straight to the horse's mouth," said Char. "Don't you?"

Duke Olson answered the door in stockinged feet and wrinkled trousers. He said he'd been napping, and he looked surprised to see the five faces staring back at him.

"Come on in," he said, shuffling backwards. "Excuse the mess. Housekeeper's day off."

"Don't worry about that, Mr. Olson," said Gwyn. "Sorry to bother you."

He smiled warmly, lighting up his chocolate brown eyes. "Oh, no bother at all. It's not every day five ladies, er, people come to visit," he said, giving the costumed Loni a once-over. It was hard to tell what she was behind the Phantom of the Opera mask she wore. He gestured towards his modest furnishings. "Have a seat."

Hazel hobbled over to his recliner and plopped herself down. "Don't mind if I do." She scooted her butt back into the seat. "This recliner come furnished in your apartment?"

He nodded. "Why, yes it did. All the furniture did. Didn't yours come furnished?"

"We didn't get a recliner," said Hazel glumly. "All we got was a dumb old armchair. You wanna switch apartments?"

"Mom!" said Gwyn. She smiled at Duke. "I'm so sorry, Mr. Olson, we don't want to switch apartments."

"I'd switch with ya," he said earnestly. "That's the best wing. You're the closest to the dining hall, closest to the back parking lot, and I hear those rooms have a great view of the courtyard."

Hazel peered around, apparently mulling over her offer to switch rooms.

Gwyn shook her head. "We're fine where we are."

"So what can I help you with?" he asked pleasantly.

"I was just wondering about something that happened earlier this week," began Gwyn. "The day of the field trip to the paintball range."

Duke hung his head. "You're wondering why I went on that bus, aren't you?"

Phyllis nodded. "Yes, as a matter of fact, we are. It's kind of suspicious that you took George's place on the bus and then later he was found dead."

Duke sighed. "That's all anybody wants to know," he

admitted. "Even the detective from town came over and questioned me about that. I promise you, I regret doing it."

"You regret what?" asked Hazel. "Killing George?"

Duke's eyes widened. "I didn't kill George. I can assure you! It was a harmless prank. That's all it was."

"Giving Geoge Viagra knowing he had angina wasn't a harmless prank, Mr. Olson. It killed him!" snapped Gwyn.

Duke looked appalled. "Giving George Viagra? Who said I gave George Viagra? I didn't do that, I swear!"

"Then what was the harmless prank you played on him?" asked Phyllis, narrowing her eyes.

"I took his spot on the field trip!" Duke splayed his hands out in front of himself. "I knew he was going on that trip. It was all he could talk about for days before. I'll admit, I was mad at him because he beat me at poker the night before, and things got a little heated. So when he didn't show up to breakfast or cards that morning and they came and announced the bus was leaving, I assumed he'd overslept and I hopped on the bus. I thought if they had their head count the bus would take off and I could catch a cab back to the Village before anyone realized I wasn't supposed to be there. It was a silly, childish thing to do, I admit. But it happened so fast, and before I knew what I was doing, I was already back in my room. I had no idea that the reason George hadn't come to breakfast or gotten on the bus was because he was dead!"

"But you sell Viagra," said Char quietly. "It makes sense that you're the one that did it."

Duke's eyes widened. "Who told you I sold Viagra?"

Gwyn cringed. They weren't supposed to know that.

Phyllis waved a hand in an attempt to cover up Char's blunder. "Oh, golly. Who told us? I'm not really sure. *Everyone* knows. I mean, come on, who *doesn't* know?"

"They do?"

Phyllis nodded definitively. "Mm-hm."

"Yeah, but even if you didn't feed George the Viagra, you probably know who did, don't you?" said Hazel in an accusatory tone.

Duke shook his head. "Listen, I don't know anything. Sure, a lot of people come to me to grab a few pills here and there, and I make a few bucks doing it. It's poker money, that's all it is. But I don't keep track, and I certainly wouldn't know if one of them used the pills to kill George."

Hazel stood up. "Good enough for me. Let's go, girls."

30

The ride to Kat's was a flurry of conversation. Hazel swore up and down that Duke Olson had been telling the truth. She'd also sworn up and down that she thought Duke Olson had sold Martin Sinclair some Viagra, but the rest of the women weren't convinced that Martin Sinclair was the murderer.

"It just doesn't add up, Hazel," said Char from the driver's seat as they pulled into Kat's driveway. "Martin didn't move into the Village until *after* George's death. How would he have gotten George to take the pills?"

Hazel lifted her shoulders. "Look, I'm not a toxicologist. All I know is there's something sketchy about a guy who lives with a cat."

"What's sketchy about that?" asked Loni.

"You never hear people say that a cat's a man's best friend, do you? No, they say a dog's a man's best friend. You don't wanna know what they say about men who have a cat for a best friend."

"Mom, you're being silly. You just don't like Martin because he parked his scooter in front of our doorway and beat you at poker. That doesn't mean you can blame him for killing someone."

Hazel shook her head and wagged her finger. "You all just watch and see. Marty Sinclair isn't who he presents himself to be. Mark my words."

Gwyn nodded and pretended to write in the air. "Got it, Mom. Words marked! Now, can we get in the house? I have to shower, and then you girls have to make me gorgeous!"

"I thought Bradshaw was coming at six thirty," said Hazel, looking down at her watch. "I'm pretty sure we don't have time for a miracle."

While Gwyn was in the shower, Char busied herself in Kat's kitchen, whipping up an evening meal for the girls.

"You making any more Hazel fries?" asked Hazel, lifting her brows as she peered over the counter.

"Maybe," said Char slyly. "You wanna skip being the third wheel on Gwynnie's date and find out?"

Hazel slumped back in her seat. "Are you kidding? I haven't been out to eat at a real restaurant since Bill Clinton got frisky with that intern, Monica Lowenstein."

"Lewinsky," corrected Char.

"God bless you," said Hazel. "Gwynnie's too cheap to take me to fancy places."

"She takes you to Habernackle's all the time," protested Phyllis.

"I said *fancy* places, didn't I? Habernackle's is like a glorified McDonald's, except McDonald's sells french fries all day long."

"Reign and Linda make you french fries anytime you ask, Hazel," said Phyllis, a bit testy at Hazel insulting her family's restaurant.

"Eh, you gotta do backflips and promise your first-born to get 'em." Hazel held up a finger. "Not that that would stop me from ordering them, mind you. Gwynnie's old enough to go it alone now."

Out of nowhere, Sorceress Halliwell made a sudden reappearance in the middle of Kat's kitchen. Char put a hand on her hip. "Sorceress Halliwell, good to see you! Care to join us for supper?"

The ghost smiled sweetly. "Oh, I'll be here," she promised. "You just won't see me."

"That's not creepy," said Loni out of the side of her mouth.

"The perks of being a ghost," laughed the apparition. "So, how did the poker tournament go?" She looked down at Hazel.

Hazel looked at her hands on the kitchen counter.

"Hazel ran into a little stiff, er, competition," said Phyllis.

"Stiff competition?"

"An older gentleman who wasn't so easily beaten," added Char.

"It was rigged, I tell ya!" snapped Hazel.

Sorceress Halliwell looked surprised. "You mean you *didn't* win?"

"She won every round except the last one," said Loni. "Her powers didn't work against that guy."

"Ahhh." The Sorceress nodded. Then she smiled at Hazel. "Well, good! Then I don't have to ask you to donate the money to charity. It's better this way."

"Better my ass," snarled Hazel. "That money was going to go to a good cause!"

"Oh, it was?"

"Yeah, me! I'm a good cause!"

The Sorceress shook her head, emitting a soft laugh. "Well, girls, I'll let you cook and get on with your night…"

"Wait!" said Phyllis. "I've been thinking about something."

"Yes?"

"You said that Kat was conjuring money and you found a pile of it up in her spell room. I've been up there several times and I've never seen any money lying around."

Char nodded. "Yeah, whatever happened to Kat's money?"

Sorceress Halliwell looked around uncomfortably. "Her money?"

Hazel nodded. "Yeah, you know, her greenbacks, her dough, her cabbage, her scratch, her—"

Sorceress Halliwell held a hand out to stop Hazel. "I get the picture. You want to know what happened to her cash. I know. It's just that…"

"You don't want to tell us, do you?" said Char.

"Not really."

Loni tipped her head sideways. "Why not?"

"Because it's hidden somewhere and she thinks we're going to spend it," said Char. "Or use it to pay the tax bill."

"Well, why wouldn't I think that? Hazel was going to keep her prize winnings if she'd won any."

"Yeah, but that's different. That's Hazel," objected Char.

"Phyllis didn't seem to object," said Sorceress Halliwell.

Phyllis lifted her brows. "Hey, I was only joking."

"Sure you were, Phil," said Loni.

"I was! I wouldn't spend Kat's money without a good reason."

The Sorceress shook her head sadly. "That's just it. There isn't a good reason to spend ill-gotten money."

Phyllis rolled her eyes and shrugged. "Whatever."

"It's in this house, isn't it?" said Char, unable to peel her eyes off Sorceress Halliwell. "Right now."

Sorceress Halliwell mashed her lips together.

"It is!" shouted Loni, pointing at the ghost. "Where is it?"

Char looked around. Now everything she saw in Kat's kitchen was like a hiding place. An X marks the spot on a blank map. Her eyes widened. "You girls okay with Kraft Mac 'n' Cheese for supper?"

31

Sergeant Harrison Bradshaw rolled up in his freshly washed truck at six thirty on the dot.

Seeing him pull up from the window, Hazel glanced down at her watch. "Big surprise. Captain Hot Pants is here. I can set my watch by this guy."

"He's military," said Char. "I think they pride themselves on being regimented."

Hazel rolled her eyes. "Ahh, he's sure to be kicks in the bedroom."

Gwyn glared at her mother as she shoved the tube of lipstick she'd just finished applying into her pocketbook. "Mother, if you say a single crass thing on this date, so help me, I'll send you to live in a convent for the rest of your days."

"Well, that'll certainly be a welcome change from these criminals," said Hazel, cocking her head towards the rest of the women.

"Hey, it's your fault we've had to become criminals,"

snapped Phyllis. "If it weren't for you, we'd still be sweet and innocent old ladies."

Loni shook her head. "Doubtful. I'm pretty sure Caleb McGreggor took your innocence back in college."

Phyllis swatted at Loni. "Do you mind?"

They watched as Harrison took the porch steps two at a time to knock on the screen door.

Gwyn fought to keep the anxiety that welled up inside at bay. "He's only a man, he's only a man," she mumbled under her breath. Her pep talk didn't seem to help, but she opened the door to him anyway. "Hello, Harrison."

"Good evening, Gwyn," he said. His hand slid up her arm and latched onto the back of her crooked elbow. He pulled her in closer to plant a little kiss on her cheek. "You look stunning," he whispered in her ear.

Gwyn had to admit that she looked better than usual. She'd pulled the only little black dress she owned from her closet earlier in the week, when they'd set their date, and hung it in the bathroom so the steam would let out the wrinkles. The dress was long enough to cover what Gwyn considered to be her worst feature, her knees, and the neckline cut just low enough to show off a hint of her décolletage. The girls had swept back one side of Gwyn's hair and pinned it up, revealing her long neck, and she'd added a pair of pear-cut crystal drop earrings to match. She'd found them in Kat's personal jewelry collection and figured that Sorceress Halliwell couldn't get too upset as she wasn't planning to use the earrings outside of the single date. She felt like a million bucks.

"Thank you, you look marvelous yourself," she whispered back.

He tugged on his black suit coat and grinned. "Thanks. Hazel, you look beautiful," he said loudly to Hazel, who shuffled towards them wearing the dress that Gwyn had forced on her. It was a three-quarter-sleeve grey crepe number that she'd worn to Gwyn's oldest daughter's wedding several handfuls of years ago. Hazel had thrown quite the tantrum when she'd learned she couldn't wear the skirt and blouse she'd worn all day, but in the end, gwyn had put her foot down and threatened Hazel's ability to go at all if she didn't wear it. Thankfully, it had still fit.

"Yeah, yeah, yeah, my panties are staying on all night, thank you, and so are my daughter's. Now let's go," she muttered, leading him out the door.

Gwyn's face flushed red. "Maybe Mom should just stay home," she whispered to Harrison. She was afraid Hazel would behave badly all night and ruin any chances she had with Harrison.

He shook his head and stifled a grin. "Not at all. I welcome her straightforwardness. See, we've gotten it out of the way. Panties stay on all night. Now there's no wondering. Will Hazel's panties come off? Won't they? See how easy that was for me? No games."

That elicited a giggle from Gwyn. She squeezed his hand. "Right, thank you, Harrison." Then she turned to look at the girls, giving them a little wiggle of her fingers. "Bye, girls. Don't wait up!"

Harrison pulled his truck up and parallel-parked in front of a rustic-looking restaurant with two big whiskey barrels out front beneath a corrugated tin awning.

"Here we are!" he announced, shutting off the engine.

Hazel peered out the window. "I wore a fancy dress to eat at a horse barn?"

"It's not a horse barn, Mom," sighed Gwyn, burying her head in her hands in the backseat. "It's called the Whiskey Grille."

"It looks like a horse barn. They serve horses in there?"

"No, Hazel, they serve the best steaks in town. You like steak?"

"I do," she said. "Damn dentures don't. They like french fries. They got any french fries in there?"

"The best in all the Appalachian Mountains!"

"Alright. But I don't want any horse. That might make me puke."

Harrison leapt out of the truck and rushed around to the other side to open the door for Hazel and help her down to the curb. Then he turned to the backseat of the truck and helped Gwyn out next. "Sorry you had to sit in the back, Gwyn."

Gwyn shook her head as she hooked her arm into the crooked elbow Harrison had offered her. She was used to it. Hazel had a hard time getting in and out of vehicles.

Gwyn had to sit in the back a lot. "No problem. Thanks for bringing Mom along. I'll apologize in advance for anything else inappropriate she says."

Harrison patted her hand. "I'm retired military. I've heard my fair share of inappropriate in my life. I don't think there's anything Hazel could say that would shock me."

"Challenge accepted," said Hazel from several steps up ahead.

Gwyn leaned into Harrison and whispered, "She's hard of hearing, but she can read minds."

"Well, then, I'll be sure to keep my thoughts as pure as Hazel's mouth," he said with a laugh.

Inside they were seated at the best table in the house. Not too drafty, not too close to the kitchen, secluded, but not enough that Hazel couldn't see people coming and going. When they finally sat down at a table Hazel was happy with, she was worn to a frazzle. "Why don't they make all the seats good seats?"

"They're all good seats, Mom. You're just picky," said Gwyn.

"There's nothing wrong with being particular," said Hazel, opening up her menu. "Especially when it comes to men, that's what I always say."

Harrison pointed at Hazel's menu. "They make a really good beef tenderloin here, Hazel. Very little chewing required."

"Uh-huh," said Hazel, adjusting her glasses so she could read the menu better. "Do they have wine on tap here?"

Gwyn touched Hazel's arm lightly. "Mom, no wine for you."

Hazel slammed her menu down. "Dammit, Gwynnie, hush. I'm on a date. You're embarrassing me."

Gwyn held her breath to keep from exploding. She was usually a pretty even-keeled woman, but this was too much. What had she been thinking, agreeing to bring Hazel along on the date? The girls would have happily watched her for a few hours. She glanced up at Harrison and gave him a little head shake as an instruction not to allow Hazel to order wine.

The waiter came back and Harrison expertly avoided Hazel's wine order, instead asking her if she wanted extra fries with her beef tenderloin. Of course Hazel gladly accepted the extra fries and then set her sights on the table's bread basket while Gwyn and Harrison finally got an opportunity to visit.

"So, Gwyn, how are you and your mother enjoying Aspen Falls?"

Gwyn sighed happily. "Oh, it's so nice to be amongst friends again. Scottsdale was lovely, don't get me wrong, but Aspen Falls is like returning home to family."

"You know, I don't know much about you. Do you have family? Children?"

Gwyn took a sip of her water. "Mm. Two daughters. Grown. They're both married with their own families now. You?"

Harrison seemed to wince. "I had two daughters. Elena and Harper. Harper passed away last year. Elena lives in town."

"Oh, Harrison!" breathed Gwyn, laying her hand on his arm. "I'm so sorry to hear that!"

"Thank you. It's been a tough year. I lost my wife at the same time," he admitted.

Gwyn's eyes widened. She'd wondered what had happened to Mrs. Bradshaw. "How horrible for you!"

He forced a grin and then took a sip of his water. "This is the first time I've been out like this since then. The guys at coffee every morning are a welcome distraction from my lonely house. Elena checks on me now and again. You're lucky you've got your mother and all your girlfriends to keep you occupied."

Lately, Gwyn hadn't looked at her mother like that. Some days were better than others, but many days, especially in the last few years as Hazel's filter had begun to disappear, she'd become exhausting and more like a cross that Gwyn was forced to bear. So she was happy to have Harrison point out just how lucky she really was. She looked at Hazel fondly then. "Yes, I am lucky," she whispered.

"How are you enjoying living at the Village?" he asked, turning the subject.

Gwyn's eyes popped open a little wider. "Oh, it's lovely. The residents are kind. I get along well with the staff. The room is better than my room in Scottsdale, so that's a bonus. Of course it's a bit upsetting that my next-door neighbor was killed recently."

It was Harrison's turn to lay a hand on Gwyn's arm. "George Petroski was your next-door neighbor?" He shook his head. "I can imagine how upsetting that must be for you. Poor guy. I'd met him a few times. He didn't deserve to go."

"No, he didn't."

"And they know for sure how it happened?" asked Harrison.

"Oh, you don't know?"

He splayed his hands out. "I mean, I've only heard rumors. I'm not exactly sure what really happened."

"Well, we believe someone slipped him some Viagra. That combined with the nitroglycerin he was taking for his angina caused him to suffer a heart attack."

Harrison looked surprised. "Huh. I had no idea George had heart problems. I mean, I'd heard rumblings about them finding Viagra in his system, but that alone doesn't kill a man. Otherwise there would be a lot more dead men walking around right now." He smiled.

"You didn't know George had heart problems?"

He shook his head. "Nope."

Gwyn looked surprised. "Oh, I thought everyone knew about that." She had to think about it then. Where had she heard about his angina in the first place?

"No. I had no idea. When I heard he had Viagra in his system, I didn't think anything of it because he's such a ladies' man. You know, he sort of had trouble keeping things where they ought to be."

"Where they ought to be?" asked Gwyn, unsure of what he meant.

"Just say it. The man had trouble keeping it in his pants," said Hazel from across the table.

For a second Gwyn had almost forgotten Hazel was even at the table, she'd been so quiet.

Harrison pointed at her. "See, straightforwardness. That's the quality of a good woman."

Hazel ticked her finger back and forth at him. "Unh-uh-uh. Panties are staying on, smooth talker."

32

"Thank you for a lovely evening, Harrison," said Gwyn later that evening on Kat's front porch. Harrison had walked her and Hazel to the porch, and Hazel had grudgingly gone inside at Gwyn's prompting.

"Did you have enough fun that you might like to do it again?" he asked, his mouth curled into a grin.

Gwyn felt heat rushing into her cheeks. He wanted to do it again! She smiled and nodded. "Absolutely. Maybe next time I'll find a sitter for Mom."

"What?! That's not f—" screamed a muffled voice from inside the house, followed by a loud ruckus.

Gwyn leaned forward and peered through Kat's picture window. The curtains swayed, but no one was visible.

"Hazel was a hoot, Gwyn. She's welcome to come along on another date."

"We'll see. Dinner was delicious."

"It was," he agreed, patting his stomach. "I'm probably going to regret eating as much as I did."

Gwyn giggled. "You're telling me. Mom ate every single french fry on her plate. I'm going to be listening to her complain about heartburn for the rest of the night."

Harrison winced. "Sorry, I probably shouldn't have offered extra fries."

"It's okay, she doesn't get to do that often. I'm glad she had a good time too."

They looked at each other then. Gwyn was sure he was feeling the sexual tension between them just as much as she was.

After an unusually extended bout of silence, he finally cleared his throat. "Well, I better let you go," he said, his eyes intently focused on hers. "Goodnight, Gwyn."

"Goodnight, Harrison."

He leaned forward to lay a goodnight kiss on Gwyn's cheek. Gwyn closed her eyes and tilted her head just a bit to accept the chaste touch of Harrison's lips against her skin. But he changed course midway in and went for it, instead brushing his lips gently over hers.

Gwyn's mind turned to mush when she felt Harrison's soft, pillowy lips on her own. She was thankful when his strong arms encircled her, so she could melt into them. Her feet didn't seem to be working at the moment anyway.

A thumping sound followed by a hoot and a holler and then clapping and whistles pulled her from her bliss.

She pulled back slightly and her blue eyes fluttered open at the same time that Harrison's eyes did. They both turned to look at the window, where they saw Phil, Char, and Loni cheering like mad.

Hazel was in the window too. Her face carried a scowl, and she had a finger pointed in Harrison's directions. "Hands off my daughter, Captain Hot Pants!"

"What a kiss!" sighed Char as Gwyn fell against the inside of the door.

"Yeah, hubba hubba," agreed Loni, shaking a hand in front of herself.

Phyllis fluttered her fingers at Harrison as he pulled his truck out of Kat's driveway. "You're one lucky woman, Gwynnie. I hope you know that. That man is fine."

"Oh, girls, he's such a doll!" breathed Gwyn.

"He's a sexist!" shouted Hazel.

"Mother! Harrison is not a sexist!"

"He is too. He ordered my food for me. I can order my own damn food."

"He was just trying to be gentlemanly. I thought it was sweet."

Hazel shrugged. "Eh. Sweet. The wine would have been sweet. But I wouldn't know. I wasn't given any."

"Mom, I was the one that said no wine, not Harrison. You can't take it out on him. The man bought you dinner. Can't you at least be a little nicer about that?"

Hazel picked at her dentures. "The beef was a little chewy."

"It was perfect! Plus he got you a double order of fries."

Hazel put a hand to her heart. "I know, and I've got the reflux to prove it. I just spat up a little in my mouth."

"Haze, maybe you should go lie down, then," suggested Phyllis.

Hazel shrugged. "I'd rather lay in my bed. When are we going home?"

Gwyn closed her eyes and tried to regain some patience. "Shortly, Mom," she finally said. "Why don't you do like Phyllis said and go lie down? You could see what Kat's got on TV. She's got that great recliner you like so much."

Hazel didn't say anything, which meant she was considering how nice it might be to get to lie in a recliner with the remote control.

"Come on, Hazel, I'll help you," said Char, rushing over to take Hazel by the elbow.

Hazel swatted at her before waving her arms around her head like she was being swarmed by bees. "I don't need an escort to make it to the living room, for heaven's sake."

Char held her hands up and took a step away from Hazel. "Fine, suit yourself." Then she turned to the girls. "How about a cup of coffee before you go, Gwynnie? And then you can tell us all about your date?"

Gwyn nodded and let out a breath. "Coffee sounds heavenly."

Ten minutes later, Gwyn, Loni, Char, and Phyllis sat around Kat's kitchen table, listening to the sound of a spring thunderstorm outside and chatting about Gwyn's date.

"Did he ask you out again?" asked Phyllis, sipping her coffee.

Gwyn nodded. "Mm-hm. I mean, not a specific date, but he asked if I'd want to go out with him again."

Char clapped her hands together. "This is so exciting! Maybe Vic and I can double-date with you."

Phyllis stared at Char.

Char looked confused. "What?"

"I want to double-date too."

"Well, then, get a date."

"You're the one who knows all the eligible bachelors in town. I'm waiting for my hookup."

Char rolled her eyes. "I'll see what I can do."

"Thank you."

"What about me?" said Loni.

Phyllis raised a brow. "What about you?"

"I don't have a date either."

"*You* want a date?" Phyllis let out a little chortled laugh.

"Sort of," said Loni with a frown. "I've never been on a real date."

"That's because you lock yourself up and you wear those hideous costumes. Dress like a woman for once and admit that there's no FBI sitting outside your house and I'll hook you up with someone," said Char.

"So you're going to hook Loni up with someone before me?" gasped Phyllis.

"I didn't say that."

"You said if she dresses like a woman and admits there's no FBI, then you'll hook her up."

Char held a hand up to her mouth and leaned in closer to Phyllis. "Like that's ever going to happen?"

"Hey!" said Loni. "Secrets don't make friends."

"Neither do your weird costumes!" snapped Phyllis.

Loni slumped back in her seat.

Gwyn stirred some sugar into her coffee and then looked up. "You know, Harrison and I got to talking about George Petroski at dinner."

"Oh yeah? Does he know who killed George?" asked Char, swinging her eyes off Phyllis and Loni and onto Gwyn.

Gwyn shook her head. "Oh no. Of course not. He also didn't know that George had angina."

"Brenda said that she didn't think many people knew," said Char. "Remember? She was surprised that we knew about it."

"Yeah," said Gwyn slowly, "but where did *we* hear it from? I can't remember."

"It was one of the women at the Village who told us," said Phyllis. "Carol or Alice, maybe."

Gwyn nodded. "Oh yeah, that's right. You know, Harrison also mentioned that he wasn't surprised to hear that George had Viagra in his system because George was quite the get-around."

"Obviously. He slept with Hazel, didn't he?" said Loni.

"Hey!" shouted Hazel from the other room. "I may

not be able to hear you, but telepathy works through walls!"

"What if George was sleeping with other women at the Village?" said Gwyn.

"That wouldn't surprise me at all," said Char. "He was a single man, there are lots of single women there."

"But that wouldn't be a motive to kill him," said Phyllis.

Gwyn nodded. This was true. "No, but if he was sleeping with someone, maybe we can find out more information about George. Maybe he had enemies or something that we don't know about."

Char shrugged and took a sip of her coffee. Then she looked up. "It's worth exploring further. First thing tomorrow morning, we'll see if we can't investigate that idea a little further."

33

The sound of dishes and silverware clanking filled the empty spaces of the Village's dining hall the next morning. The hearty smell of bacon, eggs, and coffee was strong as Char, Phyllis, Loni, Hazel, and Gwyn all sat down to breakfast together just a table away from Carol Hamburg, Alice Buerman, and Ellie Wallace's table.

Loni hid her face with a green-and-blue Mardi Gras mask, pairing it with a black fringed flapper dress that on another woman might have hung just below her knees, but because of Loni's height, it hung down to the middle of her calves.

Phyllis leaned in. "Should we cut right to the chase, or should we eat first and then ask?"

Char glanced back at the women. They were all chatting casually over their breakfasts, not paying any mind to anyone else. "Let's eat first. I'm starving. We'll investigate once I've had my oatmeal."

Thirty minutes later, five satiated women leaned back in their chairs.

"*Now* can we ask?" said Phyllis. She gave a glance over to Carol, Alice, and Ellie's table. They'd already broken out a deck of cards.

Gwyn nodded. "I think it's now or never. Let's just hope this pans out." Gwyn scooted her chair back and then four other chairs followed suit. She looked back at the girls. "Maybe we shouldn't all go. It might be too much. How about just two of us go? The rest stay here."

Phyllis nodded. "I agree. We don't want to look intimidating or they might not share what they know. I'll stay here with Hazel and Loni."

"Why do I have to stay?" asked Loni.

"Because you look ridiculous. They're never going to take you seriously. You look like a New Orleans showgirl."

Char patted Loni's hand. "Phil's right, sweetie. But don't worry, Gwynnie and I will fill you in on everything they say." Char looked up at Gwyn. "Ready?"

Gwyn nodded, and the two of them stood up and walked over to the other women's table.

"Hi, girls," said Gwyn with a big smile. "How was breakfast?"

"Same as always," said Carol, dealing out the cards.

"How was yours?" asked Ellie. "Did Hazel get her french fries today?"

Gwyn smiled. "Not today. She ate too many last night for dinner. The blood in her arteries needs to thin out a little before we add any more fries."

Ellie giggled. "Poor Hazel."

"Speaking of arteries," said Char, "were you girls the ones to tell us that George Petroski had heart problems and was taking nitroglycerin for his angina?"

Alice lifted a shoulder. "Maybe. I've told a couple people this week."

"But you knew about that, right?" questioned Gwyn.

Carol nodded. "Yeah, we heard a long time ago."

"How long is a long time ago?" asked Gwyn.

Alice shrugged. "I don't know. I've known for a couple of months at least. Why?"

Gwyn waved off Alice's question. "Oh, no reason. We were just curious."

Char lifted a brow. "I assume George told you that himself?"

Alice shook her head. "Oh no. I'm sure I heard it from one of the girls."

"Oh?" said Char. "You wouldn't happen to remember who that was, would you?"

Alice looked over at Ellie and Carol. "Do you girls remember where we heard that? It's been a while. I'm not even sure anymore."

Done dealing, Carol straightened her cards and arranged them in her hand. "I'm pretty sure Mary Von Ebsen told us."

Elise nodded. "Yes, Mary told us. I think she said that George told Ernie."

Carol leaned over a little and said in a shushed voice, "We weren't supposed to tell. I think it was supposed to be a secret, but you know… George is dead and all, so he won't mind that we told."

"Riiight," drawled Char.

"You girls had breakfast down here the morning that George died, didn't you?" asked Gwyn.

Carol nodded and dropped a card onto the center of the pile. "Yep. George never come down for breakfast."

"You're sure?" asked Char.

"Yeah, I'm sure."

"Who did you have breakfast with that morning?"

Carol thought about it for a second. "Duke Olson and the Von Ebsens."

"Did Duke Olson leave at all during breakfast? You know, to use the restroom or something?" suggested Char.

Carol shook her head. "No. I don't think he did. I'm pretty sure he was there the whole time. He did get up and leave when it was time for the activity bus to leave."

"How about the Von Ebsens?" suggested Gwyn. "Did either of them get up to leave during breakfast?"

That made Carol stop and think. "Hmm. I don't think so…" Then she put a finger up. "No, wait. Mary did. She said the hot sauce that Duke used on his eggs turned her stomach. She went to use the restroom in her apartment. I offered to go with her, but she said she'd be fine."

"Carol, do you know what time you all met for breakfast?"

Carol nodded. "Yes, I do. I woke up starving that morning and came to breakfast earlier than usual. That was why I didn't eat with Alice and Ellie like I usually do. I came here right away when they opened. It was six thirty."

"Any idea what time Mary might have gone to her apartment?" asked Char.

Carol gave a little shrug. "I don't know. Not too long after we'd gotten our food and sat down. Maybe around six forty-five or seven."

"What's going on with you two?" Alice finally asked.

Char and Gwyn smiled.

"Oh, golly," sighed Gwyn. "We were talking about George the other day, and we just couldn't remember how we'd heard about George's angina."

Char nodded. "You know, Phil said that we heard in town, and Gwyn thought we'd heard it from the front desk gal… we were just trying to settle a bet."

"Well, then, why are you asking about Mary?"

"Oh, no reason. We were just making conversation, that's all," Gwyn assured the ladies. "Well, I suppose I better get back to Mom. You ladies enjoy the rest of your Saturday!"

Before they'd even walked away, the three women were absorbed in their card game.

Char and Gwyn didn't even bother to sit back down at their table. Instead, Char leaned down and whispered, "Gwynnie's room. Now."

"So, according to Carol, at some point, Mary got up and left during breakfast, right around the time that George was poisoned," finished Char.

"You aren't seriously trying to tell us that you think Mary Von Ebsen killed George, are you?" asked Phyllis.

Char could only shrug. She really wasn't sure if that was what she was insinuating or not. "I just find it very suspicious that Mary was the one who told the girls about George's angina when no one else supposedly knew. And she got up and excused herself during the time that George was poisoned."

"Not to mention, we did find Viagra in her apartment!" added Gwyn.

Phyllis's eyes widened. "That's true, she did have Viagra!"

No one spoke as they all stared at each other for a long moment.

Finally, Char tipped her head to the side. "Hey, Phil. Were there two nightstands in the Von Ebsens' bedroom? One on each side?"

Phyllis thought about it for a second. "Yeah. Why?"

"Whose nightstand did you find that Viagra in? Mary's or Ernie's?"

Phil shrugged. "Whoever sleeps on the left side of the bed. I didn't see a name tag."

"No books or picture frames or anything that might suggest whose side of the bed it was?"

Phyllis shook her head. "I mean, I didn't search the drawers or anything, but nothing readily stood out to me."

Gwyn sucked in a breath and smiled. "Oh, Char! Are you thinking what I'm thinking?"

Char grinned devilishly. "Why, yes, Gwyndolin

Prescott, I think I am."

The five women strode into the dining hall then. It was prime card-playing time. Groups of men and women clustered around the room at different tables, playing games of pitch, cribbage, gin rummy, or poker. Carol, Alice, and Ellie had welcomed Mary Von Ebsen to their table, and Ernie Von Ebsen sat across the room, playing cards with Duke Olson and Martin Sinclair.

"Can we really do this?" asked Gwyn, glancing around the room.

"We have to," Char whispered back. "We've got to get to the bottom of this before Detective Whitman puts two and two together and finds out it equals Hazel and company." She led the way to the empty table where they had eaten breakfast earlier.

"Back so soon?" asked Carol as she dealt out a fresh hand of cards to the table.

"Yes, we thought we might actually join in on the fun and play a game of cards ourselves," said Char with a wide smile.

"Well, we just finished a game. Would you all like to join us?" asked Alice.

Char couldn't help but smile. "Yes, we'd *love* to play!"

Phyllis didn't miss a beat before pulling up a table. Carol and Alice scooted their chairs over to allow room to put the two tables together and within seconds, there were nine chairs seated around the table.

"So what game should we play?" asked Ellie.

"Oh, I've got it," said Char. "Have you ladies ever played the game Bullshit?"

Ellie giggled.

Carol nodded. "Oh yes, we've played that game lots of times. We've got such a big group, we'll use two decks. Mary, pass me that second deck."

Mary slid over another deck, and Carol emptied the box and began to shuffle.

Phyllis grinned wickedly then. "How about we add another facet to the game to get to know each other a little better while we're playing?"

"That would be fabulous," said Ellie. "How do we do that?"

"Well, you know how the game usually works? Game-play moves around the table and each of us lays down a card or cards, but we have to call it. Like two sevens or three eights?"

Ellie nodded.

"And then anyone at the table has a chance to call bullshit if they think we're lying about the cards we played."

Ellie nodded again.

"Well, how about when it's our turn, if no one calls bullshit, we each get to ask a question to another player, and we can call bullshit on their answer? And if they're lying, then they have to pick up all the cards on the table."

"It sounds fun," said Ellie.

"But how will we know if they're lying?" asked Alice

as Carol began to deal the cards.

Phyllis and Char glanced over at Hazel.

"Hazel's pretty good about sniffing out a liar. I think we'll know," said Char.

Alice shrugged. "I'm in. Mary, Carol?"

Mary smiled. "Sure, why not?"

Carol looked up as she finished dealing. "I'm in, too. Are we ready?"

"I think you should go first, Phil, so you can kind of show everyone how this will work," suggested Char.

Phyllis nodded and pulled two cards out of her hand and put them facedown on the table. "Two aces," she said. When no one called bullshit, Phyllis looked at Carol. "How many times have you been married?"

Carol gave the table an easy smile. "Twice, but the first one didn't count. I had it annulled. I was much too young and stupid to have gotten married to that one."

Carol's friends grinned. It was likely they'd heard that story before.

Phyllis pursed her lips and nodded her head. "Yeah, I think I buy that. Your turn, Ellie."

Ellie pulled two cards out of her hand and played them facedown on top of Phyllis's card. "Two twos."

Phyllis looked both ways down the table, waiting for someone to speak up. "No one called bullshit. You get to ask a question, Ellie."

She grinned mischievously. "Okay, Hazel, would you rather be smart or beautiful?"

"Why can't I be both?" asked Hazel.

Several of the women laughed.

Ellie giggled. "You can only pick one."

"Oh, fine. I'd rather be smart."

From across the table, Gwyn shook her head. "Bullshit! Mom, I know you. You'd way rather be beautiful. Pick up the cards!"

Hazel's jaw dropped. "That's not fair. You don't read minds!"

Gwyn made a face. "Yes, but I live with you and I know you. You value beauty way more than you care to admit!"

Ellie shrugged as she laughed and handed Hazel the cards from the center of the table. "Too bad, Hazel. Rules are rules. Okay, Alice, your turn."

Alice pulled three cards from her hand and placed them down in the center of the table. "Three threes."

"Bullshit!" called several people from around the table.

Alice laughed before reaching forward and picking her cards back up again. "Darn it!"

"Okay, Gwyn, it's your turn," said Phil.

Gwyn nodded. She laid down two cards. "Two fours."

No one called bullshit. "Now you get to ask a question," directed Phil.

"I know, I know. I was just trying to think of a question to ask." She swished her lips to the side and then looked at Mary. "Mary, which side of the bed do you sleep on?"

Mary laughed. "That's a funny question." She paused for a second, likely debating whether she should tell the truth or lie. "Left."

All eyes flipped to Hazel.

Hazel nodded. She was telling the truth.

When no one called Mary out, she clapped her hands. "Yay!"

Char and her friends all exchanged excited looks too. They almost had her.

"Your turn, Mary," said Gwyn.

Mary plucked two cards out of her hand and played them. "Two fives." Her eyes swiveled around the table. No one said a word. "Yay. Okay, ummm, Gwyn. Is it fun still living with your mother?"

Gwyn grinned. Her blue eyes flashed towards Hazel. "Yes, it's fun. Every day is an adventure."

Mary looked at Hazel. "Well, was she telling the truth?"

Hazel smiled and nodded. "What can I say? I'm a riot."

The table laughed.

"Is it my turn?" asked Char.

Heads around the table bobbed.

She put a card on the table. "One six." There was an extended pause. Char wasn't sure she could ask the question that she wanted to, but she also knew she had to do it. She turned to Mary. "Mary, have you ever cheated on Ernie?"

"Char," breathed Alice Buerman, holding her chest.

The blood seemed to drain from Mary's face as her eyes flicked up to scan Hazel's expression. "What kind of a question is that? Of course I've never cheated on Ernie!"

Char tried to laugh it off, as her eyes flickered to meet Hazel's who lifted one eyebrow. It was a silent gesture of protest. Mary was lying. "I'm sorry, Mary. That was just meant to be funny."

Mary wasn't laughing now. Her face was still ashen, and her hands trembled slightly. Of course, Alice, Carol, and Ellie would assume her shaking would be from anger or embarrassment, certainly not guilt.

It was Hazel's turn then. She played a single card as well. "One seven."

The sound of commotion stirred up in the entry to the dining hall. Detective Whitman breezed in, looking intent on finding someone. Spying the women, he walked over to their table.

"Hello, ladies," he said with only a small, curt nod.

"Detective," said Char, lifting a brow uncomfortably.

"If you don't mind, I'm going to need to steal Hazel Prescott from your game." His voice was firm and authoritative.

"Steal Mom? What for, Detective?"

"I'd actually like to take her into the station. I have a few questions I need to ask her."

Char's eyes swung to Hazel. It was do or die. "But, Detective, we're almost done with our game and it's Hazel's turn. Can't she just finish her turn?"

He paused for a second and looked at Hazel. "Just one second."

Hazel nodded and then looked at Mary Von Ebsen. "Mary, did you kill George Petroski?"

34

Gasps crackled around the room.

"What did you just say?" said Detective Whitman, leaning down closer to Hazel.

Hazel held a hand up. "You said I could finish my turn. Mary has to answer my question before I go anywhere. Mary, did you kill George Petroski?"

Detective Whitman looked at Mary Von Ebsen then, his mouth agape.

Everyone's eyes swung towards Mary. Her face had gone even paler, if that was possible. She looked like a ghost of her former self.

The men playing cards at another table all stood up then and circled the women's table.

"What's going on?" asked Martin Sinclair.

"We're playing a game called Bullshit," said Phyllis. "To get to know one another better, and Hazel just asked Mary if she killed George Petroski."

Ernie Von Ebsen's eyes widened when he heard that.

"Well, that's just ridiculous! How dare you ask my wife such a distasteful question!"

Hazel shrugged but didn't respond.

"Well, we already found out that Mary cheated on you, Ernie," said Char.

"What?!" screeched Mary.

Char nodded. "Isn't that right, Hazel?"

Hazel grinned. "Damn right. She said she didn't, but I'm the best lie detector there is. And that woman's a liar!"

Mary sucked in her breath and stood up. "How dare you, Hazel Prescott! I am not a liar!"

Ernie shook his head. "What is all this about? Why in the world would you have asked my wife if she cheated on me?"

Phyllis stood up. "I can answer that Ernie. We asked because we believe your wife was having an affair with George Petroski."

Ernie's eyes widened. He opened his mouth to speak, but Phyllis continued.

"In addition, we found out that your dear sweet wife, Mary, is hiding a bottle of Viagra in your room."

Char closed her eyes and hoped that no one would ask how they knew that little tidbit of information.

"Viagra? B-but I don't use Viagra!" stuttered Ernie. Confusion had rattled his mind.

Phyllis wagged a finger at him. "Exactly! So why would Mary have Viagra in your room, then?"

Gwyn nodded. "We also discovered through our investigation that Duke Olson is the Village's Viagra kingpin!" She looked over at him uneasily. "I'm sorry to out you, Mr. Olson, but I can't let the practice continue. It's much too dangerous to the residents."

All eyes turned to Duke. His face was red. He hung his head. "It wasn't supposed to be a very big deal," he promised. "Just so the guys could have a little fun and I could earn a bit of spending money."

"Mr. Olson, have you ever sold Mrs. Von Ebsen some Viagra?" asked Gwyn.

Duke's mouth hung open as his eyes swiveled to look at Mary.

She shot him a look that clearly read, *If you tell, so help me God…*

"I…"

"Don't think of lying either," said Gwyn. "My mother is a mind reader."

Duke winced and then nodded. "She said Ernie needed it. I'm really sorry," he whispered. "I didn't mean for anyone to get hurt."

Ernie looked at his wife then. "B-but Mary, you know I don't need that!"

Mary frowned. "I know you don't need it right now, sweetheart. But when I learned that Duke was selling it, I thought maybe I'd just get some for the future. You know, in case you ever needed it."

Ernie swallowed hard and looked up at Gwyn. "Ms. Prescott, just because my wife had Viagra certainly doesn't mean she used it to kill George Petroski!" The conviction in his voice had waned considerably.

Mary smiled at her husband. "Thank you, Ernie. I

just wanted to spice things up a little! I can't believe you are all being so melodramatic about this! It's not against the law to possess Viagra, is it?"

Char held up a finger. "There was something else, though, Mary. George didn't come down for breakfast the morning that he died."

"So?"

"Well, the girls and I put together a little timeline about some of the things we knew about George's morning, and we deduced that he was given the Viagra sometime before seven thirty that morning."

Mary rolled her eyes. "I was at breakfast with Carol, Duke, and Ernie from six thirty until Duke left to get on the bus to the paintball field."

"Were you at breakfast the whole morning?" asked Char.

"Of course I was!" snapped Mary.

Carol cleared her throat then. "Umm, Mary, remember, you did step away for about fifteen to twenty minutes when you said that the hot sauce Duke had used on his eggs made you sick. You went to your apartment. Remember?"

Mary grimaced. Her eyes swung down to the table and she fiddled with her cards. "Well, it made my stomach turn. I hate the smell of hot sauce. You know that, Ernie."

Ernie nodded. "Yes, Mary doesn't like that smell, she never has."

"See! This is all just a big misunderstanding!" she shouted, her brows knit together.

"Oh," said Phyllis, holding her own finger out. "There's one more thing. Carol, Alice, and Ellie told us that George was suffering from angina and that the combination of the nitroglycerin he was taking and the Viagra is what led to his heart attack."

"So?"

"Well, we discovered that very few people knew about George's angina before he died. But you knew," said Phyllis. "Because George told you."

Mary shook her head. "No, he told Ernie. That's how I knew. Right, Ernie?" Her eyes swung up to look at her husband pleadingly.

Ernie glanced over at Detective Whitman. "I don't remember George ever telling me that," he admitted.

"That's because George didn't tell you. He told his girlfriend—Mary," said Phyllis.

"Girlfriend?!" gasped Mary.

Gwyn nodded. "When Char asked you if you'd ever cheated on Ernie, your answer was no."

"That's because I've *never* cheated on my husband. I wouldn't! I love Ernie!"

Hazel lifted a brow. "I know a lie when I hear one. That was most definitely a lie. She might love her husband, but she most certainly cheated on him."

Mary made a face. "Like you're all just supposed to believe this old woman is a mind reader because she's eccentric? How about you believe *me*! I didn't cheat on Ernie!"

Martin Sinclair stepped forward then. "Mary, were you having an affair with George Petroski?"

"*No*! Of course I wasn't!"

Martin nodded and pointed at Mary. "As I suspected. That woman is lying."

Detective Whitman, who had been absorbing this new, fast exchange of information quietly and with his mouth hanging open, looked at Martin curiously. "And why do you say that, Mr. Sinclair?"

"Well, few people know this yet as I'm a new resident here at the Village, but I'm a wizard. And as Ms. Prescott does, I also read minds," he revealed.

Hazel's eyes widened. She slammed her cane down onto the floor with a flourish. "Ha! I knew it! That's how you won at poker! You cheat!"

"Mary Von Ebsen is most definitely not being honest about what's going on here," he added. "She was in fact having an affair with George Petroski. And she did kill him!"

Mary shook her head wildly as she looked at Detective Whitman. "Detective, this is ridiculous! They can't prove anything! They can't! There's not a single shred of evidence to back up any of these claims!"

Martin lifted a single brow. "I bet if we go through George Petroski's things, we'll find plenty of your fingerprints and DNA all over. In fact, Noreen Petroski is a personal friend of mine. I know for a fact that she has all of George's things packed carefully away in a storage unit. I'm sure Detective Whitman would be happy to test George's things for any evidence of an affair between the two of you."

"Bu—"

Hazel cleared her throat then. "So, Mary. I'm going to ask you *one more time*. Did you *kill* George Petroski?"

Mary's eyes swung from Hazel to Martin to Detective Whitman and then landed on her husband. Ernie looked defeated and broken. Tears began to fill Mary's eyes.

"You don't understand. He was going to tell you," she whispered. "About the affair. I couldn't let him do it!"

"You didn't have to kill him, Mary. George was a good man," said Ernie, his own eyes now filled with tears.

Mary nodded. "I know he was, but he was going to ruin our marriage."

Ernie grimaced. "So you decided to ruin our marriage instead?"

"But, Ernie...," said Mary, making a move towards her husband.

But Detective Whitman was faster on the draw. "Mary Von Ebsen, you're under arrest for the murder of George Petroski. You have the right to remain silent..."

35

"Oh, girls, what a wild ride!" breathed Gwyn as she fell into one of Kat's parlor chairs.

Taking a seat on the sofa next to Phyllis and Loni, Char nodded. "Thank God we managed to get all that straightened out."

"You're telling me!" said Phil. She looked at Hazel. "How about you, Hazel? Do you feel better knowing Mary's going to get what's coming to her?"

Hazel wrinkled her nose as she sat in her favorite reclining chair. "Eh, I don't feel any different. I knew it would all work out."

"How could you be so sure?" asked Char.

Hazel shrugged. "I'm just psychic, I guess."

Phyllis laughed and swatted the air. "Hazel, you're not psychic. I'm psychic." She stopped talking and made a face. "In fact, I have a funny feeling that everything else is going to work out okay, too."

"What do you mean?" asked Char.

Phyllis looked around. "I don't know, I just have this feeling like we're going to figure out how to keep Kat's house."

"Do you think we're going to find the money Kat hid?" asked Gwyn. "Because even if we do, I don't think that we should use it for our tax problem."

Phyllis shook her head. "You know, I really don't know what it is. I just feel like we're supposed to do something now."

Loni nodded. "I bet we find the money. Maybe we should start looking."

Gwyn looked around. "But I would have no idea where to even start looking for it. This place is crawling with good hiding spots."

Char scooted forward to the edge of her seat. "If we want to find the money, we have to think like Kat."

The room fell silent as everyone tried to put themselves in Kat's shoes. Where would she hide her money? They all looked around, each of them deep in thought.

Finally, Phyllis sucked in her breath, just as Gwyn, Char, and Loni all jumped to their feet. "The garden!" they announced in unison. Kat's favorite place in the whole wide world.

"I'll find some shovels," said Char.

"I'll help you with that," agreed Loni. The two of them headed towards the garage.

Gwyn looked over at Phyllis. "Phyllis, how's your intuition feel about the garden?"

Phyllis shrugged. "So far, I'm feeling pretty good

about it. How about we go out there and see if we can't rustle us up a little green?"

Gwyn and Phyllis pulled Hazel to her feet, and the three of them met Loni and Char in the garden.

Kat's rose garden was large and surrounded on all four sides by a white picket fence. At the center of each of the four sides was an arched white trellis covered in pink and purple clematis and lavender wisteria. The center of the garden featured a stone fountain and a black cauldron where Kat had performed her very last spell before her untimely death.

"Where do we dig?" asked Char, leaning on a spade.

The women surveyed the garden, considering their choices. Had Kat buried the money beneath her rose bushes? Or perhaps she'd buried it beneath one of the four arbors? Then their eyes fell on her cauldron. She'd used it last to conjure a special rose growth potion. But was the money buried beneath it?

"I feel like Kat buried the money and then built the garden on top of it. If so, I'd think it would be in the center of the garden," said Gwyn, pointing to the stone fountain.

Char made a face. "There's no way we're moving that thing."

"Not with our muscles, no." Gwyn wiggled her fingers as she looked at Loni.

Loni lifted her brows. "There's no way I'm lifting a stone fountain! I'm an old woman! That's too heavy for me!"

"Oh, come on, Lon," begged Phyllis. "You have to give it a try."

"Ugh, fine," she sighed, her shoulders slumping. Then she widened her stance and held her arms back. "Stand back." She closed her eyes and focused her energy on the fountain. Holding her hands out in front of her, she wiggled her fingers.

For its part, the fountain moved ever so slightly, barely rocking on its base. Loni was right. It was just too heavy for her to move alone. She grunted and stopped trying. "It's no use. I can't do it by myself."

Gwyn took Loni's hand. "You don't have to do it alone. You have us. We make a great team!"

All the women joined hands then, and Loni began to chant.

"Heave, ho, the fountain must go,
Heave, ho, the fountain must go."

Soon everyone had joined in on the chant. When all the voices blended together, the stone fountain began to move. It rocked on its base until finally, it loosened itself from its place in the ground. It lifted a few feet into the air and the women used their minds to transport it safely to an empty spot in the garden, several feet away. When it was safely back down on the ground, the women cheered.

"Yay! Great job, Loni! Good job, everyone!" said Gwyn happily.

Loni gave a little bow. "My pleasure."

The group of them strode over to the recessed spot in

the ground where the fountain had probably sat unmoved for decades.

Phyllis pouted out her bottom lip. "I don't see anything."

"Well, of course not. She buried it!" said Char, handing Phyllis a shovel. "It's time to get to get dirty."

The women spent the next thirty minutes digging through the dirt. Of course, Hazel couldn't be persuaded to get them glasses of lemonade, let alone dig or move dirt.

And then, Char's shovel made a *dink* sound as it hit something hard. "Oh my goodness," she breathed. "I think I found something!" She dropped her shovel back down to the ground again. They heard the sound again, a distinct *dink!*

Gwyn, Phyllis, and Loni helped Char excavate the area, piling the dirt into a wheelbarrow until finally, they'd uncovered what appeared to be a treasure chest.

"Oh, girls," screeched Gwyn. "This is so exciting!"

Phyllis and Char reached down and pulled the box out of the ground, dusting off the layers of dirt. Phyllis gave it a good shake.

"Let's bring it into the house," begged Gwyn. "Sorceress Halliwell should get to be a part of this."

Char nodded. "Gwynnie's right. It's only fair."

They carried the box into the house and put it on Kat's kitchen table. Bits of dirt spilled around the box and onto the floor. The women stared at the box.

"Sorceress Halliwell," called out Char. "We found it!"

"Come out, come out, wherever you are!" sang Phyllis.

Gwyn cupped her hands around her mouth. "Sorceress! We found Kat's buried treasure! It was in her garden."

A gust of wind blew up around the women's shoulders, setting their hair gently aflight. "Hello again," said Sorceress Halliwell, appearing in the air above them. "You rang?"

Char held two hands out towards the box excitedly. "We found Kat's treasure! It was buried in her garden!"

Sorceress Halliwell looked stunned. "You found it? How did you know it was in the garden?"

"Because we know Kat," said Loni, tapping a finger against her temple. "And we know how she thinks."

Sorceress Halliwell's hands went to her hair then. "I didn't want you to find it."

"We aren't going to use it for personal gain," said Gwyn. "We promise. Something inside just moved us to find it."

"Something magical," said Phyllis, rubbing the goose bumps from her arms.

"We haven't opened it yet," said Char. "We thought you should be here when we did."

Sorceress Halliwell gave Char a thankful smile. "I appreciate that."

"Well," said Loni, "what are we waiting for? Let's open it!"

Char and Phyllis each took a side of the lid, and together they slowly lifted it. Inside was a black plastic bag wrapped around something. Char reached in and pulled the bag loose, turning it over to pour out the contents. Once she did, bundles of perfectly crisp bills tumbled into the treasure chest. Bundle after bundle.

Hazel's eyes widened. "Holy Toledo," she breathed. "I've never seen so much money!"

"That's a lot of money," agreed Phyllis, nodding her head, her eyes just as wide. She looked up at Sorceress Halliwell. "We can't touch it, though, huh?"

Sorceress Halliwell shook her head. "No. It's an illusion. It's counterfeit. It will make you prisoner to it as it did me and Kat."

Char nodded her head. "You know, Sorceress, Kat hung on to this money for all of these years. She held on to all of her prized possessions too. And it all came from the same source. Magic. Maybe that's been the problem all this time. Maybe that's the reason your soul cannot be untethered from this house. The wrong hasn't been righted yet."

"I don't understand," said Gwyn, looking at Char curiously. "What do you mean?"

"I mean, maybe the reason the unbinding spell we did didn't work was because we were still in possession of what had bound Sorceress Halliwell to Kat's house in the first place. The money! The material things the money purchased! What if we gave it all back?"

"Gave it all back?!" breathed Phyllis. "You can't be serious?"

"I am serious. We could give it all back to the spirits.

What if we returned everything? Maybe *then* we could release Sorceress Halliwell from her prison."

Gwyn smiled. "Char, that's a really great idea!"

Phyllis curled her lip. "Yeah, but what if it doesn't work? What if we return all the money and all the stuff and in the end, the unbinding spell *still* doesn't work?"

"Well, then, maybe we'll never be able to do it. But what will we be out?" asked Char.

"The money!" said Phyllis. "And all Kat's cool stuff! Then there's no way we can have a garage sale or an eBay sale! We might even lose the house!"

Char shrugged. "It's a chance I think we have to be willing to take!"

Gwyn nodded. "I agree with Char. We have to take that chance. What do you think, Loni? Are you in?"

Loni swallowed hard. Gwyn knew the thought of them giving up all of Kat's worldly possessions was a hard pill for Loni to swallow. The pack rat in her wanted to keep it all forever. "I understand why we have to do it, but it makes me sad to give away all of Kat's things because it's kind of like we have to say goodbye to Kat all over again."

"Yeah," whispered Gwyn. Loni had a point. Saying goodbye to Kat had been hard enough the first time.

"What about you, Phyllis?" said Char quietly.

Phyllis looked up at Sorceress Halliwell. "I mean, I sure don't want to," she began. "But I understand. We have to do what's right. And that's making everything good again. We have to fix this for our friend and our mentor. So I'm in. We give it all back."

Char looked up at Sorceress Halliwell. "Well? What do you think? Do you think it will work?"

Sorceress Halliwell smiled as tears shone in her eyes. "I think no matter what, you girls doing this for me—giving back all of Kat's things and her money—means that I taught you right, and that means more to me than anything else in this world. So I appreciate it, whether it works or not. I appreciate all of you."

Char clapped her hands together. "Now we just need to figure out how we're going to do it."

"I'll grab the spell book from upstairs," said Phyllis taking off like a shot.

"I'll get the candles," said Loni.

"I'll move the rug," said Char.

"And I'll get the water," said Gwyn with an ear-to-ear smile.

Candles flickered around the darkened room. Burning incense filled the witches' nostrils. Low music played on a CD player in a corner, and a treasure chest of money lay in the middle of the casting circle in Kat's parlor.

"Spirits, spirits, hear our plea,
The error of our ways we see.
Ill-gotten gains are full of spite,
Take them back and make it right.
We give thee tokens of our truth,

Take what Kat stole in her youth."

The air picked up slightly. Sorceress Halliwell's eyes flicked up to meet Gwyn's. The spirits were listening!

"Again," whispered Gwyn.

"Spirits, spirits, hear our plea,
The error of our ways we see.
Ill-gotten gains are full of spite,
Take them back and make it right.
We give thee tokens of our truth,
Take what Kat stole in her youth."

Again and again they recited their chant until the wind whipped so hard up around their shoulders that a twister formed within the casting circle. Item by item, it sucked Kat's prized possessions into the ring, where they were pulled into the vortex.

The witches watched as Kat's cross-stitched linens were sucked down the stairs and added to the collection, then the Wedgewood dishes, the beautiful tapestries and paintings, and the dining room's mahogany table and chairs. Kat's prized salt and pepper shaker collection went too.

The twister juggled so many heavy pieces of furniture like it was nothing and then, just as easily as it had seemed to form, the twister plunged everything down to the eye of the tornado and shoved it into the treasure chest with all the money. And in a brilliant burst of light, the box belched out a terrific, cracking lightning noise, and the lid slammed shut! And just like that, everything was gone!

Gwyn blinked and looked down. She was still sitting on a chair, but it wasn't the one that had been there minutes before. This chair was upholstered in a faded mustard-gold velvet. The arms were worn and the seat springy. Hazel sat on a matching chair, and Phyllis, Loni, and Char all sat on a matching sofa. A simple wooden coffee table sat between them, and there were plain lamps and other pieces of furniture around the room, but nothing like Kat had had before. Everything looked dated and old, not like the well-taken-care-of furniture that Kat had had.

"It worked," said Char with a half smile.

"Yeah," agreed Phyllis glumly.

"I liked her old stuff better," said Loni, curling her lip.

Hazel didn't have to speak. The expression on her face was enough. She agreed with Loni.

"Hey, girls. Cheer up. Life's not about material things," said Gwyn, trying to bring them back up again. "It's about setting Sorceress Halliwell free. We're halfway there!"

"Gwyn's right," said Char. She rubbed her hands together. "Let's get that spell started. I'm dying to know if it's going to work!"

They took a few minutes to set everything up for the spell. Sorceress Halliwell hovered above them as they worked. Every once in a while, Gwyn looked up at her and gave her a reassuring smile. She felt it in her heart. They were going to be able to do this! When everything was settled. Char held the lit unbinding candle in her hands along with the scissors.

Gwyn began to chant.

"Power of good, power of light,
Break this binding with all your might.
Allow Sorceress Halliwell to move about,
She should be free, there is no doubt.
We cut the cord, we cut the bind,
Set her free, spirit, heart, and mind."

Char carefully cut through the binding as the candle burned, being careful not to light her pants on fire as she tilted the candle sideways.

Gwyn continued the chant.

"We call on you to set her free,
We call on you, so mote it be."

The rest of the witches joined in and the chant became louder, more sure of itself. Gwyn stood up, and after Char had cut the last bit of the twins, Gwyn took the scissors from her.

"We call on you to set her free,
We call on you, so mote it be."

The second the chant was finished, the air once again began to move. As had happened before, Sorceress Halliwell's ghost rose higher into the air. She threw her arms back, her chest beaming towards the ceiling.

Gwyn strode to the doorway confidently and began to cut the air as she'd done before. She cut and cut at the invisible ties that had held Sorceress Halliwell prisoner for all those years. Air from outside began to pour into the room, more and more with every smooth slice of the scissors. The witches continued their chant all the while. The flame on the unbinding candle inside the casting circle began to grow, reaching higher and higher, threatening to touch Sorceress Halliwell's feet.

Finally, Gwyn made her last cut along the wall in the room.

The wild vortex of air was back! All eyes were on the candle. Would it tip over? Would they have to put out the flame this time?

They repeated the chant one more time.

"We call on you to set her free,
We call on you, so mote it be."

They watched carefully as the candle held its ground this time. Sorceress Halliwell's spirit was sucked up into the vortex and then just as quickly as she'd been sucked up, she was spat out the top! Her ghost flew out of the casting circle towards the exterior wall of the house. And just like that, she was thrown right through the wall and into Kat's front yard. The air dropped immediately and the unbinding candle extinguished itself. Only silence echoed through Kat's house in the seconds that followed.

The girls looked out the window as Sorceress Halliwell stood up on the front lawn outside Kat's house. She dusted herself off and looked around. It had been years since she'd been outside in the fresh air. Feeling all eyes on her, she looked up.

Gwyn sucked in her breath. She couldn't believe that they'd done it. She was the first to stand up and race outside. The rest of the women were quick to follow her.

"You did it!" breathed Sorceress Halliwell. "You actually did it!"

Phyllis put an arm over Char and Loni's shoulders. "You bet your ass we did it!"

"Gotta admit, I'm a little impressed with us," said Char, putting an arm around Gwyn's waist.

Gwyn linked arms with Hazel, leaning her head on the top of her mother's. "I'm impressed too. This is amazing!" She felt tears threatening to fall.

"Now what?" Char asked Sorceress Halliwell.

Sorceress Halliwell spun around to face the street—the unknown. "I don't know," she whispered. "It's kind of scary being let out like this. I'm not even sure who I am anymore."

"You're an amazing sorceress, that's who you are," said Char.

She smiled tightly. "That's who I *was*. I'm not human anymore. I'm a ghost. What do ghosts do all day?"

"Haunt things, mostly," said Loni.

Hazel held up a hand. "Stay away from the Aspen

Falls Retirement Village. That's all I've got to say about that. If I want to see you, I'll come visit Kat's house."

Sorceress Halliwell laughed. Then she took in all of the women. "I appreciate everything you did for me. You gave up all of Kat's things to save me. How can I ever repay you?"

Char put a hand on her hip. "You taught us to be good witches. This is how *we* repay *you*."

Sorceress Halliwell grinned sadly. Then she looked at the road again. "Well, I think it's time that I go. I think I'll go on a journey of self-discovery. I need to find out who I am again."

"Will you ever come back?" asked Loni.

"Maybe. Only time will tell."

"We'll miss you!" said Gwyn.

"We will," agreed Phyllis.

"Oh, girls, you're all like the daughters I never had. I'll miss you forever!" She waved at them with one hand and blew ghost kisses with the others. "Goodbye!"

"Goodbye!"

36

"What a beautiful morning for coffee!" said Gwyn as she helped Hazel up the sidewalk in front of Habernackle's.

"Are you kidding me? It's cold out here. Did you bring my sweater?" asked Hazel.

Gwyn rolled her eyes. "You mean the sweater I tried to convince you to put on before we left the Village?"

"Yeah, that one."

"No, Mom. You refused to put it on, so I didn't bring it."

"Well, you should have brought it. It's nippy out here."

Gwyn sighed. "Come on, the girls are waiting for us. It'll be warm inside."

Gwyn pulled open the door and the bell above it chimed.

From across the room, Harrison Bradshaw looked up from the coffee he was having with his buddies and smiled at Gwyn. Immediately he stood up, mumbled something to his friends, and then headed towards her.

Gwyn spotted Char waving. She gave Hazel a gentle push towards their table. "Oh, look, there's Char, Mom."

"I see her, I see her. Geez, Gwynnie, you don't have to push," she mumbled before hobbling through the crowd.

But Gwyn didn't follow this time. Instead, she turned and waited for Harrison. "Good morning," she said, not feeling the usual nerves welling up inside of her stomach.

"Well, hello, beautiful," he said sunnily, giving her a quick kiss on the lips.

Gwyn still felt the familiar butterflies, but now, she felt much more confident talking to Harrison in front of their friends. "Did you hear the news?"

"That you and the girls solved George Petroski's murder? Are you kidding me? It's all anyone can talk about!"

Gwyn's eyes widened. "It is?!"

He nodded emphatically. "I'll admit to gloating a bit that *my new girlfriend* was the one to solve the case." He chuckled lightly.

"Your new..." Gwyn swallowed hard. Had she just heard him right?

He put a hand to the base of his throat. "Oh man. Right. Was that too presumptuous? I haven't dated anyone in years. I'm not really sure how all of those boyfriend/girlfriend stuff works anymore." His face turned a light shade of red. "In fact," he whispered, "after being married for so many years, I feel a bit silly calling you my girlfriend. It's almost like I'm a teenager again!"

Gwyn giggled. "Yes, I feel the same."

He looked at her seriously then. "So…too soon?"

Gwyn shook her head, her heart in her eyes. "No, not too soon," she whispered as a doorbell chimed behind her.

Harrison threw his long arms around her neck then, nuzzling his face in her hair. "Great." When he let go, he looked at her. "So, back to what I was saying. I've been bragging that my new girlfriend helped solve the Petroski murder. Pretty impressive!"

"Impressive indeed," said a voice behind them.

Gwyn spun around to see none other than Noreen Petroski entering Habernackle's. Gwyn's eyes widened. She glanced over to her table to see if Char and the girls had seen the woman come in. They had, their eyes were huge as they stared at Gwyn, Harrison, and Noreen.

She ticked a finger at Gwyn. "I need to have a word with you, but first, I'm picking up a to-go order."

Gwyn looked around and then pointed at herself. "You need to have a word with me?"

"You and your little friends," she spat, pointing at the girls across the room.

Gwyn's mouth went dry. "About what?"

Noreen rolled her eyes and began to walk away. "You'll know soon enough."

Harrison squeezed Gwyn's hand. "Looks like you got on the wrong side of Noreen Petroski. Maybe I should go sit with you?"

Gwyn squeezed his hand back. "No need, Harrison. I think the girls and I can handle Noreen. But thank you. That's sweet of you."

"Well, we'll talk more later. I'm anxious to get our next date on the calendar. I was thinking maybe next time, I could cook for you and Hazel."

Gwyn smiled. "Maybe I'll just let you cook for me. I think Mom's got her own plans next time."

Harrison's smile grew even larger. "More for us, then." He pulled her in for one more quick peck and then let her go. "See you soon."

"Bye, Harrison."

Gwyn didn't have time to dawdle over her feelings for Harrison. She scuttled back over to tell the girls that Noreen was on her way over.

"What was that about?!" breathed Char as Gwyn pulled up a chair.

"Noreen said she has something she wants to talk to us about!" said Gwyn as she pulled up her chair.

"Talk to *us* about?!" said Phyllis. "Oh hell, what did we do now?"

Char shrugged.

Gwyn lifted a brow. "Loni? Is that you?" she asked a woman in a dog costume sitting next to Hazel.

"Shh," she hissed. "I'm supposed to be Phil's dog, Sparky."

"Really? You think anyone's buying that?"

"Oh, let her be," said Char, swatting at Gwyn's hand. "We got her out of the house and to breakfast. Baby steps! Maybe someday she'll even have breakfast with us *without* the costume!"

Gwyn looked at her menu. "Have we ordered yet?"

Char shook her head sadly. "While we were waiting for you, we all agreed it'll just be five cups of coffee today. We're all on a budget now that we have none of Kat's things to sell to pay the tax bill."

Gwyn slumped down in her seat. "Oh, yeah, that's right. I figured that would be the topic of conversation today. How in the world are we going to swing it, girls? Cutting out a bowl of oatmeal and a sticky roll every day isn't going to produce an extra twenty-five hundred dollars."

"I know," agreed Char. "We're going to have to get creative. What were you saying about broomstick-riding lessons?"

Phyllis patted Char's hand. "Oh, girls, don't look, but Noreen Petroski is on her way over here right now!"

"I wonder what she wants," said Gwyn.

"I don't know, but we're about to find out," whispered Char before looking up to greet Noreen. "Well, if it isn't Noreen Petroski. Hi, Noreen, how are you doing?"

"Oh, I'm doing just fine. Just fine indeed," said Noreen, cocking her leopard-printed hip out to one side.

"What can we help you with?" asked Gwyn, feeling a little uneasiness settling into her stomach.

"Detective Whitman came to see me yesterday, after that little reveal you pulled in the Village's dining room."

Gwyn looked down at her hands. Had they made Noreen upset about the public way in which they'd exposed George's killer? She would have thought Noreen would be happy to have been off the hook of suspicion.

"Did he?" sang Char.

"Mm-hmm," nodded Noreen. "He went over the whole thing. You know, I always thought George had a thing for Mary Von Ebsen. Of course I could never prove it. George and I used to double-date with Mary and Ernie before our divorce. Something about the way Mary looked at my... er, George, never sat right with me."

Gwyn gave her a tight smile. "I'm so sorry, Noreen."

The woman shrugged. "Eh, what's done is done. But you certainly shouldn't be sorry. You have nothing to be sorry for!"

"We don't?" asked Gwyn before receiving a prompt kick under the table from Char.

"No! Of course not! You caught George's killer! I owe you a debt of gratitude," she said. "Because of the five of you, my name was cleared all over town. Everyone realized that I wasn't the one that killed George."

Phyllis smiled a fake smile. "Well, gee, Noreen. That's great. We're really happy for you."

Noreen nodded. "*And* because of that, I actually got an offer on my house this morning. I just got done signing the papers at the realtor's office. It was a cash offer. Full listing price too!"

"Well, good for you!" breathed Gwyn, thankful that Noreen hadn't wanted to chew them out for something she thought they'd done.

"Yeah, good for me!" agreed Noreen. "George's estate can be settled and his life insurance paid out since I'm no longer a suspect in his murder case, which means I should be getting that money very soon. I get to move to my tropical island now! And leave all of this… this… mountains and snow and all that behind!"

Char patted Noreen's hand. "We're really happy for you, Noreen. We're sorry we had to come harass you the other day. Maybe you'll understand now that we were only trying to get the facts."

Noreen smiled. "No, I completely understand, and I'm incredibly appreciative of what you did for me. So appreciative, in fact, that I'd like to offer you a little reward for helping me sell my house so fast. Without you clearing my name, it might have been months before I got an offer on the house. And then it might have been a fraction of what I was asking. I feel like you really helped me out, and I'd like to help you out."

"Help us out?" breathed Gwyn, stunned at what she was hearing. "Oh, we couldn't possibly…" Her sentence ended when she was kicked under the table by Phyllis.

Phyllis plastered a smile on her face. "Oh, how sweet of you, Noreen! What a kind gesture! We accept your help!"

She nodded and set her cheetah purse down on the table, pulling out a checkbook and a pen. "Now, I don't know what a situation like this would call for, but"—she pulled the cap of her pen off with her teeth—"I was thinking ten thousand. How does that sound?"

Eyes around the table widened to the size of quarters. "T-ten *thousand*?" mumbled Char.

"Dollars?" clarified Hazel.

"Yeah. Not enough?" she said with a bit of an inquisitive look. She swished her mouth to the side. "Okay, you got me. Let's just do it for an even fifteen. How does that sound?"

Char's puffy white head bounced up and down. "F-fifteen sounds just right to us. Right, girls?"

Heads bobbed around the table, including Loni's dog head.

"Fifteen sounds perfect," said Phyllis.

"Oh yes, very generous," added Gwyn.

Noreen smiled and scrawled out a check for fifteen thousand dollars. "I'll just leave the *To* part blank." She tore the check out of her checkbook and handed it to Gwyn.

Gwyn looked down at it. She suddenly felt a weight lifted off her shoulders, as if the ride had finally ended and she could get off and go home and relax for a change. "Thank you, Noreen. You have no idea how nice this is."

"Oh no, I know it's nice. But I figured one good turn deserves another!" She shoved her checkbook and pen back in her bag and turned around to face the door. "Well, off I go. I need to get breakfast home to my sister. We're packing up the rest of her stuff, and then off we go to catch our flight to Fiji! Ta-ta for now!"

"Bye, Noreen!" said the women at the table in unison.

"Thank you, Noreen. Fly safe!" added Char.

When she'd gone, all eyes turned to the center of the table. "Can you believe that?!" breathed Gwyn.

Char shook her head. "Barely. I think I'm still in shock."

"Well, like she said, one good turn deserves another!" said Phyllis.

"Now we have enough money to pay the taxes on Kat's house for years to come!" said Gwyn. She waved the check in the air. "Maybe we can even buy Kat some nice furniture with *real* money."

"Maybe!" said Phyllis. "But first, I think we should splurge on a big, hearty breakfast! What do you say, girls? Splurge day?"

Hazel nodded. "I want Hazel fries and *two* sticky rolls today."

Phyllis pointed at her. "You want it, you got it, sister!"

"I'll have a steak and eggs and hash browns," said Gwyn.

"Oooh, go, Gwynnie!" said Phyllis. Phil pointed at Loni. "What are you having, Fido?"

"I'll have what Gwynnie's having, *and* a sticky roll," said Loni, her voice muffled by her costume.

"Ooh, I want a sticky roll too. Linda's rolls are the best," said Gwyn. "Add that to my order too."

"What the hell, let's make it three orders of steak, eggs, hash browns, and sticky rolls," said Phyllis. She looked at Char and lifted a brow. "What are we having, Char? Cream of wheat and a Geritol?"

Char giggled. "Oh, I can live once in a while, you know. I'll have what you're having."

Phyllis's jaw dropped. "Awesome! Good for you, Char."

Linda showed up then. "Sorry it took me so long, ladies. We're kind of swamped today, and my help didn't show up. What can I get…" She stopped jotting things down on her pad and looked up at the girls. "Wait. Lemme guess. The usual, right?"

Phyllis shook her head. "Nope, not today, Linda, dear. Today we want four orders of steak, eggs, hash browns, and sticky rolls, and one order of Hazel fries and two sticky rolls, please."

Linda's jaw dropped. "You're kidding me, right?"

Phyllis smiled at the girls. "Nope. I told you one day we'd surprise you!"

HAZEL FRIES RECIPE

Ingredients

3 Russet potatoes cut into fries

2 Tbsp of olive oil

8 cloves of garlic, minced

1 1/2 tsp dried thyme leaves

1/2 cup grated Parmesan cheese

2 Tbsp parsley minced

salt and pepper to taste

(Extra parsley, thyme, and Parmesan for garnish)

Instructions

1. Preheat oven to 375 degrees. Preheat the baking sheet. Remove from oven once preheated and spray with cooking spray.

2. Combine olive oil, garlic, thyme, Parmesan, parsley, and salt and pepper in small bowl.

3. Place potatoes in a large bowl and add parmesan combination. Toss well to coat potatoes.

4. Place potatoes in a single layer on the greased, preheated baking sheet.

5. Bake until golden brown and crisp, approximately 30 minutes, turning halfway through.

6. You can use your broiler if you'd like to get them extra crispy!

7. Garnish with the extra parsley, thyme, and Parmesan cheese.

ALSO BY M.Z. ANDREWS

Ready for more Coffee Coven?

That Old Witch!: The Coffee Coven's Cozy Capers - Book 1

Hazel Raises the Stakes: A Coffee Coven's Cozy Capers Mini

Want to get an email when the next books are released? Click here to join my newsletter! I promise not to spam you, I send newsletters only when I have a new release or something important to share.

And, if you like this series, you can read more about Aspen Falls in my Witch Squad Cozy Mystery series, also set in the cozy, Pennsylvania town. Find out more about Phyllis and Char's families.

Reading order:

The Witch Squad: A Witch Squad Cozy Mystery - Book 1

Son of a Witch: A Witch Squad Cozy Mystery - Book 2

Witch Degrees of Separation: A Witch Squad Cozy Mystery - Book 3

Witch Pie: A Witch Squad Thanksgiving Holiday Special - Book 4

A Very Mercy Christmas: A Witch Squad Christmas Holiday Special - Book 5

Where Witches Lie: A Witch Squad Cozy Mystery - Book 6

Witch School Dropout: A Witch Squad Cozy Mystery - Book 7

Witch, Please! - A Witch Squad Cozy Mystery Short Story

Other Books by M.Z. Andrews

Deal or Snow Deal: The Mystic Snow Globe Mystery Series - Prequel

Snow Cold Case: The Mystic Snow Globe Mystery Series - Book 1

Behind the Black Veil: The Witch Island Series - Book 1

ABOUT M.Z. ANDREWS

I am a lifelong writer of words. I have a wonderful husband, whom I adore, and we have four daughters and two sons. Three of our children are grown and three still live at home. Our family resides in the midwest United States.

Aside from writing, I'm especially fond of gardening and canning salsa and other things from our homegrown produce. I adore Pinterest, and our family loves fall and KC Chiefs football games.

If you enjoyed the book, the best compliment is to leave a review - even if it's as simple as a few words - I tremendously value your feedback!

Also, please consider joining my newsletter. I don't send one out often - only when there's a new book coming out or a promotion of some type that I think you might enjoy.

For more information:

www.mzandrews.com

mzandrews@mzandrews.com

Made in the USA
Columbia, SC
27 February 2018